A
TIMELESS
Romance
ANTHOLOGY

California
DREAMIN'
COLLECTION

A TIMELESS Romance ANTHOLOGY

California DREAMIN' COLLECTION

Six Contemporary Romance Novellas

HEATHER B. MOORE
KAYLEE BALDWIN
ANNETTE LYON
JENNIFER MOORE
SHANNON GUYMON
SARAH M. EDEN

Mirror Press

Interior Design by Rachael Anderson
Edited by Annette Lyon, Cassidy Wadsworth and Jennie Stevens

Cover design by Mirror Press, LLC

Published by Mirror Press, LLC
TimelessRomanceAnthologies.blogspot.com

ISBN-10: 1-941145-77-9
ISBN-13: 978-1-941145-77-7

TABLE OF CONTENTS

MORE TIMELESS ROMANCE ANTHOLOGIES

Winter Collection
Spring Vacation Collection
Summer Wedding Collection
Autumn Collection
European Collection
Love Letter Collection
Old West Collection
Summer in New York Collection
Silver Bells Collection
All Regency Collection
Annette Lyon Collection
All Hallows' Eve Collection
Sarah M. Eden British Isles Collection
Mail Order Bride Collection
Road Trip Collection
Blind Date Collection

Too Good to Be True

Heather B. Moore

OTHER WORKS BY HEATHER B. MOORE

Esther the Queen
Finding Sheba
Lost King
Slave Queen
The Aliso Creek Series
Heart of the Ocean
The Newport Ladies Book Club Series
The Fortune Café
The Boardwalk Antiques Shop
The Mariposa Hotel
Eve: In the Beginning

One

Gwen changed the lens on her Canon EOS, then lifted the camera and adjusted the settings until the bride and groom came into sharp focus. In the background, the oranges and pinks of the fading sunset were a perfect blend of everything romance.

"Stand closer," Gwen said, "and look into each other's eyes." *Click.*

A gorgeous beach wedding shot, if Gwen could say so for herself. One that might rival the wedding shoot from the week before.

The couple started kissing, apparently the "looking into each other's eyes" too tempting to resist. Gwen shot a half a dozen more pictures, directing the couple into various poses, then lowered her camera and smiled over at the waiting family members.

The mother of the bride held up her champagne glass toward Gwen. "You should try some, sweetie. You've worked yourself to the bone today."

Gwen laughed and waved away the offer. Photography was hardly work—at least, the actual shoots were a pleasure. A dream, really. Everything else in life—before and after the sessions—those were the hard parts. Shooting weddings was great as long as she didn't let herself think too much of her own wedding six months ago. She swallowed back a swell of emotion and crossed to the beach chair holding her camera case and bag.

The setting had been vastly different. Nothing so informal as a beach, but a small church in Oregon. It had the potential to be every bit as romantic and nostalgic as any dream wedding with the elegant flower arrangements her mother had ordered and the bridesmaids' pale-blue organza dresses, not to mention Gwen's custom-designed gown.

But for three days leading up to the wedding, she'd had a knot in her stomach. It started with the arrival of Paul's ex-girlfriend—who was supposedly close friends with his younger sister and who his sister insisted had to be a bridesmaid with her. Gwen had seen Hollywood movies where the bridesmaid steals the groom, but those were fiction, right? Wrong.

It took two miserable months of marriage to Paul before Gwen allowed herself to believe the signs. He was still in love with his ex. So when Gwen's sister, Leisa, came up with the idea of offering photography sessions with her catering company, Gwen drove down the coast to San Diego without looking back.

"Thank you so much!" someone said, and Gwen turned, and was almost tipped over by a hug from the enthusiastic bride.

The groom showed his thanks more formally, holding out his hand with a smile.

Gwen's heart pinged as she shook it. His blond hair and

easy smile reminded her a little of Paul—but she wasn't about to go there anymore. "I'll put the proofs into DropBox by Tuesday or Wednesday, so when you get back from your honeymoon, you can decide which ones you want."

The bride gushed another thanks, then was caught up in saying farewell to the rest of the party.

As the wedding guests sent off the bride and groom, Gwen took a moment to breathe and enjoy the scenery. This stretch of beach was Gwen's favorite, and she brought most of her wedding clients here who wanted a beach setting. To the right, the shoreline seemed to stretch endlessly, and to the left, majestic cliffs soared, topped by multi-million-dollar homes.

What it would be like to live in a house overlooking the ocean, Gwen would never know. She was lucky to afford a tiny apartment near her sister's neighborhood. Living with her sister wasn't an option—Gwen loved her sister to death, but where Leisa was the perfect businesswoman, Gwen was a dreamer. She got things done, but in her own way.

A breeze kicked up, pushing against Gwen's messy bun. It hadn't been so messy when she'd arrived, but the beach was nearly always breezy, so Gwen had made a habit to keep her hair back while working.

"Do you have plans for later?" a male voice asked, and Gwen cringed before turning. The bride's brother—Taylor or Thomas or Tyson—had been hitting on her all afternoon. And it only got worse because he'd been refilling his wine glass over and over.

"I've got a full evening of work ahead, sorry," Gwen said, bending down and removing the lens then securing the camera into the case as if to prove her point.

"Oh, too bad," he drawled, and Gwen suspected it was more from drinking than from the fact that he was apparently from Texas—something he'd mentioned more than once. "What about tomorrow? I've got a late flight, but my day is free. I'd love to see your town."

Oh boy. Gwen straightened. "I've got work tomorrow too, and I have plans with my boyfriend." She hoped he didn't notice the slight flush of her face—something that always happened when she lied.

"Yeah," Taylor-Thomas-Tyson said, taking a step back. "I get it." He raised a half-empty wineglass and said, "All my best to you."

Gwen pasted on a smile and pretended that he wasn't being sarcastic. "Have a good trip home." *And stay there.* She returned to packing, and by the time she looked up again, Taylor-Thomas-Tyson was gone and only a couple of guests lingered.

Breathing out, Gwen smiled to herself. She could do hard things. Like turning down flirtatious men, starting over in California, and becoming closer to her sister.

And forgetting Paul's blue eyes.

Two

When Jack came jogging back down the stretch of sand, the wedding party he'd passed at the beginning of his run looked to be leaving. The chairs had been loaded into a pickup, and the flower-entwined arch taken down. Running in the afternoon wasn't Jack's first choice, but his schedule had been crazy lately. With the acquisition of one of his holding companies by a Japanese investor, his conference calls tended to happen in the middle of the night. He often took a nap in the afternoon, then was wired by sunset and needed to burn off the energy. Running also helped with the stress of unexpectedly taking over his father's company the year before. Right out of grad school, Jack was suddenly the CEO his father's venture capitalist firm.

He'd decided to sell QTech to the Japanese investor when a major competitor out of China had risen six months ago. The Chinese software company had a better, faster product, so it was either dump a ton of capital into revamping his own product line or let it go then integrate the QTech employees into SureBoard, one of his father's newer acquisitions, which made computer components out of Arizona. SureBoard received rave reviews in *PC Magazine*, and as a result, purchase orders nearly doubled. The QTech employees would be happy at SureBoard.

Jack's life might look good on paper. He'd even been featured in the local San Diego magazine a few months ago as one of the wealthiest bachelors of the state. But reality was that his life was a mess. Money did strange things to people, and once someone found out who he was, he could literally see their eyes change—from mildly curious to calculating.

For that reason alone, he'd sold off two of his father's homes and let his sister manage several other properties. Silvia was about the smartest woman he knew, so it hadn't been a difficult decision. That left Jack the firm, and he knew if he wanted to do it right, he had to spend a lot of time on catch-up.

About a hundred yards from the beach wedding, Jack slowed to a walk. The wedding truck had left, as had the guests, and only one woman was left. She had a huge camera bag over her shoulder and was trudging through the sand, carrying a beach chair and another large bag. She looked ready to tip over, so Jack jogged over.

"Can I help carry some of your stuff?"

She turned to look at him. "I'm all right. My car's not far."

Jack felt his heart skip. Her green eyes were brilliant against her tanned face, and her wind-whipped hair curved around her neck, making her look like part of a surfing commercial. She hitched the camera bag up, but the second bag slid off her shoulder and landed in the sand.

"Really, let me help," Jack said. "I promise I'm not a creep. I live here, well, up on that ridge."

The woman looked to where he was pointing and frowned. Then she laughed as if she didn't believe him. "Ha. Ha. Very funny. I think I'm all right. Thanks, though."

"I didn't mean to be funny," Jack said. "Why are you laughing?" He'd tried to be a gentleman but this woman wasn't having any of it. So why didn't he just continue his run? What did it matter to him if she had to make two trips to her car?

She shifted the second bag onto her shoulder, then picked up the beach chair again. "No one lives in those houses. They belong to Europeans and Asians who come once a year—maybe at Christmas?—I don't know."

She eyed him up and down, and for some reason, it made his face heat up. Was she mocking him? Checking him out?

"But you . . ." she said, looking directly into his eyes. "You're like, normal."

"Well, I'm flattered to be called normal."

She narrowed her gaze. "I've seen you somewhere."

Of course she had. He'd had this conversation before. She'd rattle off a few names, and then it would dawn on her that she'd seen him on the news. And maybe her pretty green eyes would turn a hard emerald.

"Oh." Her face flushed.

Now Jack was intrigued. "What's wrong?"

"Do you run along this beach a lot?"

"Yeah," Jack said, growing curious. "Like I said, I live on the ridge."

The woman looked away, and then her eyes were back on him. "I think I've see you out running a few times. I shoot a lot of weddings on this stretch."

She was blushing, and Jack hid a smile. "Are you a wedding photographer?"

She lifted a shoulder. "Mostly. I also do graduations, retirement parties . . . Right now weddings are at a premium, being summer and all."

"Yeah, I've seen quite a few lately," he said. "I guess the traditional church thing isn't too popular anymore."

"No." Her voice went tight, as if Jack had said something that bothered her.

She hefted the chair a notch higher and headed toward the parking lot again.

It took only a second to decide what to do next. He caught up and took the chair from her, then held out his other hand. She sighed and handed over her bulky bag—not heavy, but still awkward for carrying in the sand.

"I'm Jack Mead."

"Gwen Kilpack."

Jack waited for recognition to dawn on her about his name, but there was nothing. "How long have you been a photographer?"

"Since I was about ten," Gwen said.

He smiled. "And professionally?"

"I've been doing it for a couple of years, although my family still sees it as more of a hobby." She stopped by an older model Honda Accord. Unlocking the doors manually, she said, "I've never cared about 'making it.' I just want a good life, you know? I mean, simple things are better . . ."

Jack waited for her to finish, but she turned away and opened the trunk, then loaded her camera bag into it. He set the beach chair and other bag inside the trunk with the other one.

She looked up at him. "Thanks for your help, and sorry about the philosophical run-down."

"No worries," Jack said. She climbed into her car, and he couldn't think of anything that would delay her.

He stood in the parking lot long after she'd pulled out and turned onto the main road. Simple. His life was anything but. Every email, every conference call, every letter had to be diplomatically crafted. His personal life grew less and less private as newspapers and magazines ran feature articles about his inheritance of his father's firm.

Clearly, he and Gwen lived on different planets.

Jack turned back to the beach and walked toward the path that climbed to the back of his house. The sun was well beneath the horizon now, and the first stars had appeared in the deep-purple sky.

It was way too late to find simplicity in his life—*simple* died along with his father.

Three

Gwen pulled up to La Jolla beach. Only three days had passed since her last wedding here. Three days of thinking about that guy—Jack Mead.

When she'd driven out of the parking lot, there had been a few bikes chained to a rack and a well-worn minivan sporting a couple of car seats. Gwen suspected that neither the bikes nor the minivan belonged to Jack, which meant he might very well live in one of those huge houses on the ridge. In which case, she'd completely insulted him.

She'd earned two notches that day—turning down a drunk guy and insulting a rich guy all in the same evening.

This morning's shoot was for an older couple who were renewing their vows. Forty years of marriage. It was amazing really. She wondered what their secret was.

Since it was early yet, Gwen set off toward the water to set up where the sun would be in the perfect position for the ceremony. The ceremony was supposed to start about 9:30

am, which really meant 10:00. A few joggers were out, a couple of them with their dogs. Gwen waited for one particularly obnoxious dog to lose interest in her before she set up her chair and piled her stuff on it.

The breeze coming off the ocean tugged at Gwen's dress. It was one of the three that she saved to wear at weddings—nice but not too dressy. She walked the shoreline with her camera, taking a few photos, then analyzing the background and the angle of the shots on the screen. She didn't want the guys from her sister's catering company to set up the chairs and portable arch any random place.

When she found a great place for the ceremony, far enough from the ocean's edge, yet away from the parking lot so that there'd be plenty of privacy for the wedding, Gwen fetched the beach chair and bags and relocated them. Now all she had to do was wait.

After kicking off her sandals, she walked barefoot toward the water, snapping a couple more pictures of a yacht out on the water.

Someone called her name, and she turned, assuming that the set-up crew had shown up so this early. But it wasn't Jeff or Chris.

"Gwen?" the guy said, striding toward her. "That's your name, right?"

It was him. Jack Mead. He wasn't wearing a shirt, and his tanned chest glistened with perspiration in the morning sun. And he was out of breath.

"Yeah, good memory."

He smiled, and Gwen smiled back, although nerves thrummed through her. "Out running again?" she asked, stating the obvious.

"I am—glad it's not as hot as the other day."

But *he* was definitely as hot.

"Got another wedding shoot?" he asked.

"Yeah." Apparently she was lame at making conversation. He stood only a few feet from her now. She was suddenly insanely curious if he had a girlfriend or was married. This guy was way too good-looking to be single.

"So what do you do for a living?" she asked.

He looked out over the ocean. "I'm in business. Took over my dad's company about a year ago after he died." The sudden transformation on his face was remarkable, from relaxed to tense in a split second.

Gwen lifted her camera and snapped a picture of it. He looked at her with surprise, and she felt mortified. "Sorry," she said. "Habit. I can delete it."

"No, it's okay." Jack moved to her side.

Gwen angled the camera so he could see the picture, then zoomed in and said, "Look. You have a worry crease between your eyebrows."

Jack leaned closer, and Gwen caught his scent—sand, sweat, and spice. "I do," he said in a thoughtful voice.

"Does your job stress you out?" Gwen looked up into his eyes; they weren't quite brown, but not quite green, either.

"Does my job stress me out?" he repeated. His mouth lifted into a half-smile. "That's one way of putting it." He scrubbed his hands through his dark hair, and Gwen glanced away so she wouldn't be caught staring at the flex of the muscles in his arms.

Would it be a bad thing to take another picture of him?

"I hear that running is good for stress," she said, when he didn't offer anything more.

"Running is my only sanity," he said quietly, staring at the ocean.

"Sorry about your dad."

He glanced at her and gave a short nod. "Thanks. I never thought I'd live here again. But life has a way of changing plans."

Gwen had never heard truer words. "I hear you. This time last year, I was happily engaged and had my own photography studio in Oregon." She clamped her mouth shut, her face growing hot. She'd sworn to keep her past completely in the past, especially around strangers.

Jack was silent for a few moments, and just when Gwen was about to tell him she had to get going, he said, "What happened?"

Gwen fiddled with her camera settings. "His ex-girlfriend came to the rehearsal dinner. He seemed really happy to see her, but I ignored the signs, and two months later, Paul annulled the marriage."

"Ouch," Jack said. "Must make it hard to shoot weddings."

Gwen smiled, even though she was starting to feel sorry for herself again. "I just try to do my job—it's not like I'm bitter—but yeah, I'm constantly surrounded by love and marriage."

A seagull screeched past them and landed a few feet away. The water sparkled behind the bird, making it look like it was surrounded by tiny pricks of light. Gwen lifted her camera and took a shot.

"Do you ever go anywhere without your camera?" Jack asked.

"Sure," Gwen said. "But I always regret it."

Jack laughed; it was a good sound.

"So where are you from?" she asked.

"I grew up mostly in California, but I went to school back east and haven't been home for a while."

"Your dad's company is here, then?"

"The corporate offices are in San Francisco. But I had to consolidate a few things, and I couldn't part with the beach house down here."

Gwen nodded, as if she understood perfectly, but her mind was racing. To own some of the most expensive real estate in California, Jack's dad must have run a major company.

"So you really do live on the ridge."

He grinned. "Like I said." He touched her shoulder and steered her to look at the ridge looking over the ocean. "The white one with all the windows."

"Wow." Gwen really couldn't say anything else. When her brain started to work again, she asked, "Have you ever rented it out for weddings? I mean, it would be a spectacular venue."

"No," Jack said with a laugh. "It's my *home*."

"Yeah, but—" Gwen rubbed her forehead. "Ignore me. Sometimes being a photographer distorts my perception of reality."

Jack's hand had dropped from her shoulder, but she still felt the warmth from his touch. "I can take you on a tour of it sometime," he said, "and then you'll see why it would be a horrible wedding venue."

Gwen looked up at him, surprised at the bold invitation. She involuntarily took a step back. Maybe he was one of those rich guys with a dark side, and—

"Look," he said, raising his hand. "I am completely normal, despite what others might say."

Had he read her mind? "I'm thinking that *normal* in your world may be different from normal in mine." Gwen gave him a smile to let him know she was teasing . . . although she wasn't.

"Then maybe we should go to dinner or something first, so we can see if that's true."

There it was. He'd asked her out. Gwen exhaled, not feeling as unsettled as she'd expected. Sure, she was intrigued by Jack, not because he owned the mansion on the ridge—well, maybe she was curious about his life—but because he *did* seem normal, and pretty amazing. His eyes weren't bad either.

Four

On his walk back home, Jack realized he had no idea why he pointed out his house to Gwen and then asked her out. As he had with every other woman who discovered who he was, he'd seen the information click in her expression.

But instead of smoozing him, she'd suggested that his house could be a backdrop for a wedding. Which was kind of funny. His mother would absolutely die if Jack ever let the public into one of their homes.

As the wife of a business tycoon, his mother had quickly learned that the more private she kept her life, the better. She even used a pen name for the children's books she published. Now, walking away from Gwen with her number in his phone, Jack knew that she and his mom would get along great.

Why that thought had suddenly appeared in his head baffled him.

But the fact was, he'd just asked a woman out for the first time since his father's death. It had been way too long, yet standing on the beach in the early-morning light, with Gwen's green eyes practically singeing his skin, he'd given in to the impulse. He was probably an idiot for doing so; he didn't have time to date or entertain any sort of significant relationship. And he wasn't looking for a one-night fling, either.

He climbed the snake path from the beach to the back of his house. Once inside, he grabbed a water bottle from the fridge and settled on a chair on the upper balcony, where he had a good view of the arriving wedding party.

Gwen was already at work placing groups of people together and taking pictures. She moved easily among the guests. *Graceful.* That was the perfect word to describe her. While Jack felt as if he were constantly barreling through thick doors of red tape, Gwen's job was to observe others and capture their many layers on camera.

Her picture of him frowning had been startling. In a photo that captured one split second, he'd seen the toll of past months of trying to keep it all together and somehow make his family proud.

His cell rang, but on seeing the caller ID, he hesitated before answering it. His sister could easily talk for an hour, and she was impossible to hang up on. But he had no good excuse not to answer. "Hey, Silv."

"Jack! It's a miracle," Silvia said. "You answered the phone!"

"I always answer if I can—"

"Which is almost never for your sister," she said with a laugh.

Jack smiled, despite the guilt trip she'd just sent him on.

"Look," Silvia went on. "Mom and I are flying in on

Friday to meet the organizers of her favorite charity. Can you meet Mom and me for dinner? We're staying at the La Valencia. Mom wants to fly back Saturday morning, so that doesn't give us much time."

"Why don't you stay here?" Jack suggested.

"You know Mom. She wants to get in and out without inconveniencing anyone. So how about dinner?"

He was about to say yes until he looked out over the beach again, remembering *Gwen*. Their date was Friday night.

"Jack?" Silvia's voice came through the line, her tone curious. "Don't tell me you're putting me on hold."

"No," Jack said, trying to think fast. If he gave so much of a hint about plans for a date, Silv's questions would be endless. And if his mother found out, she'd hire a detective agency to investigate Gwen. "I just have something I can't get out of that night. Can't you stay longer on Saturday? We could do brunch."

Even as he suggested it, he knew that a date one night with brunch the next morning would only pile on the stress. As it was, he didn't have enough time to do the final proposal review for the QTech sale. Then again, it might be nice to discuss some of the specifics of the proposal with his mom and sister.

"Jack," his sister was saying. "You've got to take breaks once in a while. I saw the QTech sale in the paper, so I know things must be crazy right now. If you're anything like Dad was, working to make big things happen, you'll need to be dragged outside to see that the sun is still rising and setting."

Jack scrubbed a hand through his hair, a reminder that he still needed a shower. After that he had to conference in with the board of directors. "I'll have you know, I just came back from a run—*and* I watched the sun rise."

And I spoke to a beautiful girl, who is shooting pictures a few hundred yards away.

"You've been running? I told you, you're exhausting yourself."

"No, running is great for relieving stress," he countered.

"Okay, you're right," Silvia said, her voice softening. "But Mom and I really miss you—we miss hanging out."

Had he really ever *hung out* with his mom and sister? Maybe as a teenager on family vacations. His father had usually holed up in the office of their vacation home while the rest of them went sight-seeing. "I miss you guys too," Jack finally said. "I wish I could make it work, but—"

"Fine. You're off the hook this time," Silvia conceded. "But once the deal with QTech is done, we'll put a weekend together."

Jack was nodding, although his sister couldn't see it. He was still looking down on the beach, where the minister had shown up, and wedding guests were settling into chairs. Gwen shook hands with the minister, and then she moved off to the side and snapped more candid shots of the seated wedding guests. Her green eyes returned to mind. What was she seeing right now through her viewfinder?

"Hello? Jack?" Silvia said.

"What do you think of beach weddings?" Jack asked before he thought through his question.

A pause. "Who is she?"

Finally, Jack snapped his attention back to the phone and his sister. "Who's who?"

"You have a woman on your mind."

Jack silently groaned. "There's just a beach wedding going on below the house right now."

His sister was silent for a moment, something much more dangerous than her nonstop talking.

Jack felt obliged to cover for her silence before too many ideas popped into her head. "I mean, Mom and Dad got married in a church. That used to be the traditional way, but traditions don't seem to hold anymore. The couple getting married right now has to be in their sixties."

"Maybe they're renewing their vows," Silvia said. "And for the record, I think beach weddings are romantic—as long as it's not too hot or windy."

"Yeah," Jack said absently as he watched the groom/husband take his place next to the minister. The bride/wife began her short walk down the aisle. Gwen was deftly capturing it all on camera.

"What's her name?"

"Gwen," he said automatically. Then he let out an audible groan.

"I was right!" Silvia sounded triumphant. "Who is she? What's her last name? What does she do?"

"Don't go detective on me, and *please* don't tell Mom," Jack said. "We're only going on one date."

Silvia sounded breathless. "Wow, Jack. I mean, wow. What does she look like? Where did you meet?"

"Slow down," Jack said. "This is exactly why I didn't want to tell you anything."

"You're going out on Friday, aren't you?"

His silence was his answer.

"Just tell me something about her—just *one* thing," she said, "and then I'll shut up."

"That's like promising not to breathe."

"Jack!"

"All right. She's a photographer." He could practically see Silvia putting the rest of the pieces together.

"A *wedding* photographer?"

"Look, I've got to go. I need to shower before the

board's call." He didn't trust himself on the phone with his sister for even a minute longer; he'd already said way too much.

Standing, he finished off his water bottle, then watched for a moment while the older couple exchanged vows. Only when the wedding guests were clapping, and Gwen was taking pictures of the kissing couple, did Jack turn away.

Five

Friday took forever to come, yet it arrived all too fast for Gwen. She had stayed busy, though, trying not to think about Jack Mead. On Friday afternoon when that proved nearly impossible, she downloaded his picture onto her computer and played with the hues and contrasts until she was happy with it. She spent longer than planned toying with the picture, then realized she had only half an hour to get ready to meet Jack at the hole-in-the-wall Mexican restaurant he'd suggested. She was sort of surprised at the choice, given his house, but then, Jack didn't seem like the typical rich guy. Not that Gwen knew a bunch of rich guys—she wasn't exactly a stunning catch.

She was average looking, a bit on the short side, and didn't stand out from women who spent a lot of time on their appearance. But tonight, Gwen fussed with her hair—she had it down and let the natural waves take over—then leaned close to the mirror and added another layer of mascara. She didn't wear much eye shadow but wasn't opposed to thick mascara and a bit of lip gloss.

Her phone buzzed, so she checked it. Leisa. The call likely meant that she'd be working tomorrow. She rarely had a Saturday off, and Gwen had looked forward to it. But she couldn't ignore her sister, who was also her boss.

"Hey," Gwen said, leaving her bathroom and walking down the short hallway of her apartment.

"You home?" Leisa asked.

"Just leaving, actually." She hoped she wouldn't have to elaborate; Leisa was always overeager to set Gwen up with some new single guy. "What's up?" She snagged her keys from the kitchen counter and opened the front door.

"David wants to take me out tonight, so I was wondering if you could come over and watch Ella."

While Gwen's niece was an adorable two-year old, she was also full of more energy than anyone should have a right to. She was glad she had a valid excuse, even if it meant confessing that she had a date.

Bracing herself as she headed to her car, Gwen said, "I have a date tonight. I'm leaving now."

"Ooooh." Leisa didn't sound in the least put off that Gwen couldn't babysit. "When did you meet him?"

"Ha-ha. Very funny. I'll give you the scoop *after* the date." Gwen climbed into her car and started the engine. "Hey, I've really got to go—"

"You are not hanging up on me, Gwenie," Leisa ordered. "Not until you at least tell me his name."

Gwen sighed. "All right. It's Jack Mead. But I really have to go. I'll call you tomorrow to tell you what a disaster it was for me to start dating again. Bye." She hung up before Leisa could drill her with a million and one questions.

What does he look like? How tall is he? Where does he

work? Where did you meet? Does this mean you're over Paul?

Gwen backed out of her parking space and pulled onto the adjoining street. Her phone buzzed again; Leisa calling. Gwen turned her phone to silent, feeling proud of herself for dating again. She wouldn't let her sister badger her. So far so good.

Her confidence diminished, however, as she pulled into the parking lot of the Mexican restaurant that Jack had suggested. The place was fairly run down, and only one other car—an older Audi—was in the lot. The restaurant didn't look too popular, which probably meant the food wasn't great.

So much for practically starving herself all day so she could justify eating a bunch of delicious Mexican food.

Gwen parked and walked across the lot, then pushed through the doors of the restaurant. The first thing that hit her was the wonderful smell of hot food. It was a like a comforting, warm balm that made her stomach grumble like crazy.

The second thing that hit her was Jack, standing in the waiting area, and how good-looking he was dressed and showered. He was leaning on the hostess counter, wearing a half-smile he watched her walk in. He had on worn jeans and a button-down shirt with the top button of the collar undone and his sleeves rolled up.

His hazel eyes met hers, and she flushed. Not exactly an unwelcome feeling, but then, she wasn't about to put her faith in another man any time soon. Yet walking into the heavenly smelling restaurant and seeing Jack in a more civilized setting than running on the beach, she no longer cared if the food was awful.

Enjoy yourself for once, she thought, echoing what Leisa had told her over and over.

"Hey, you made it." Jack's deep voice sent a wave of heat through her. Had his voice always been so deep, his eyes so watchful?

"So did you," Gwen said.

One side of his mouth lifted. "I did invite you, you know." He straightened from the hostess desk.

"That's true."

Would their conversation ever progress from inane words? But she realized that even if it didn't, she wouldn't mind. Just talking to him about nothing at all was enough. Tonight she would try to enjoy herself and not think about all of the broken promises in the past.

Jack flashed her another smile. "You look great."

"You look different," Gwen said, then wished she could take back her words. "I mean, you look great *but* different. It's just that you're dressed." She closed her eyes and exhaled. "That came out wrong."

Jack only laughed. "Come on, our table's ready." He grabbed her hand and led her through a room of tables all set with plates and utensils, but without a single customer at any of them.

He's holding my hand. What does that mean? Okay . . . Don't over-analyze it. Just relax.

"Do you come here a lot?" she asked, trying to calm her racing thoughts.

"Yeah. You'll love it."

Gwen still couldn't believe there was no one else here—on a Friday at 6:30 p.m. "Is it usually this slow?"

Jack stopped, released her hand and pulled out a chair for her. As she sat down, he said, "No, it's actually quite popular." He came around the table and sat opposite her then picked up one of the menus on the table. "I thought it would be nice if it was just us."

Gwen frowned. Did that mean he owned the place or something . . . ?

A woman who looked to be in her 50s came out of the kitchen and bustled toward them. She wore an orange and yellow dress and a white apron. She beamed at Jack. "When Mario said you were coming, I told him that it made my day."

Jack rose from his seat and kissed the woman on the cheek, then turned toward Gwen. "Gwen, this is Rosa. She's the best waitress in San Diego."

Rosa swatted Jack's arm. "You're too nice." Her warm, brown eyes settled on Gwen. "You're a lucky girl. I keep telling Jack that he needs to find a good girl." She leaned forward. "And you look like a good one. I can tell." Before Gwen could respond, Rosa turned to Jack and said, "The usual?"

"Yeah, that would be great."

Rosa's eyes went back to Gwen. "What will you have?"

Gwen hadn't even looked at the menu, so she ordered her standby. "Chicken enchiladas with mild sauce."

Rosa smiled. "Great choice." She moved away and disappeared through the kitchen doors.

"Wow," Gwen said, looking at Jack.

"She likes you." Jack grinned. "And that's pretty much a miracle."

"Do you bring in a lot of women she doesn't like?"

He lifted one shoulder. "I haven't brought any here for a while."

"And for those women you do bring here—do they continue to go out with you after Rosa meets them?"

Jack laughed. "I think you're on to something."

Gwen loved his laugh, his eyes crinkling slightly. If she'd brought her camera, she wouldn't have been able to resist taking a picture. "So tell me about yourself, besides the fact that you apparently rented out an entire restaurant, and that you know Rosa, the best waitress in San Diego, idolizes you."

Jack propped his elbows on the table, and Gwen had to deliberately look up from his tanned forearms. "How about you just ask your questions so I don't mistakenly give you boring biographical information."

Gwen studied him for a moment. "I don't think there could possibly be anything boring about you, Jack Mead."

He leaned slightly closer, his eyebrows raised. "Try me."

"All right, where did you go to college?"

"What makes you think I went to college?"

Gwen scoffed. "Because I know the type who did—*I* didn't go to college. I can spot people like you a mile away."

Jack grinned. "Boston University. I warned you—pretty boring."

"I'm not so sure about that," Gwen said, trying to drag out more information than he was giving. "Why Boston?"

"Do you have a second job as a journalist?"

"No," Gwen said, laughing. "Just a really nosy sister who's trained me well. And who gives me tons of advice on a daily basis."

"We should lock our sisters together in a room for twenty-four hours," Jack said.

The kitchen door swung open, and Rosa appeared, carrying a tray with two huge steaming plates of food and two tall glasses of Mexican soda. The smell alone about did Gwen in.

Rosa set Gwen's plate down first. "Careful, it's hot. Mario added extra beans and rice after I told him how thin you are."

Thin? Me? She'd never been called *thin* in her life.

"Here are your chimichangas, Jack. Enjoy." She gave him an exaggerated wink, which made Jack laugh.

"Thanks, Rosa," he said as she left.

Gwen dug in and savored the first bite, and the next, and then she was ready to get her first question answered. "Okay, so why Boston University? You grew up in California, right?"

Jack finished chewing and took a drink. "Honestly? To piss off my dad. But I ended up loving it out there, and going to Harvard for my graduate degree made him pretty happy."

Harvard? Gwen stared. "You are so not normal."

Jack shook his head. "Hey, you already said I'm normal. You can't take that back. I'm holding onto that one for life."

Okay. Gwen was charmed. But she wouldn't let herself fall for any guy so easily. "What did you study at Harvard?"

"Business," Jack said. "See? Boring."

Gwen laughed. "I'm sure you have interesting talents somewhere, just waiting to be discovered." She took another drink and leaned back. "Maybe you could borrow one of my cameras for an afternoon."

"I'd need a tutor," Jack said. "If using it is more complicated than the camera on a cell phone, the pictures will be out of focus."

"I may be able to tutor you," Gwen said, feeling fluttery all over.

The time passed quickly as they talked, and the sky outside faded to deep blue with the setting sun. At one point, Rosa turned on the miniature lamps at each table and brought another round of drinks.

"I am so full," Gwen said. "I won't be hungry until Sunday."

"That was my goal." He pushed back and stood. He pulled out his wallet and left a few bills on the table.

"Thanks for a great dinner," Gwen said, walking to the exit with Jack. The night was warm and breezy as they stepped outside.

"I would ask you to go dancing or to a movie, but I've got some early conference calls."

"It's okay. You don't need to make an excuse to get rid of me."

She meant it as a joke, but then his hand brushed hers, and he linked their fingers, sending bits of warmth across her skin. "I'm not trying to get rid of you." His voice was low.

Gwen's heart thudded like mad as they walked to her car. The Audi was still in the parking lot, it was definitely his.

"What did you think?" he asked as they stopped by the driver's side of her car.

"About what?" She didn't know why she continued to give Jack a hard time with every question.

"About tonight? About . . . me?" His voice sent another wave of warmth through her.

"I wished I would have brought my camera." It was the best compliment she could give.

"Is that a good thing?"

He was standing really close, and Gwen could only nod because her stomach was fluttering like crazy. Was he going to kiss her? Shake her hand? If he didn't kiss her, she might just have to kiss him. She was more than curious about this guy who turned out to be everything unexpected. Maybe kissing him would tell her if she should stay or run.

But she didn't have long to debate, because Jack leaned down and brushed his lips against hers, his hands resting on her hips. He drew back half an inch, as if waiting to see what she thought, as if asking another question.

Maybe Gwen had been bewitched, but she had no trouble twining her hands around his neck and drawing him closer. She kissed him back, and he pulled her tightly against him. His mouth was warm and urgent, and his body molded against hers until suddenly the kiss wasn't nearly enough.

That was when she drew away, breathless. Her skin flushed hot as she realized he was breathless as well.

"Jack . . ." She had no idea what to say, so her voice trailed off, with Jack's arms still around her.

He lowered his forehead to hers. "Next time bring your camera."

Six

Gwen woke to the sun piercing through her blinds. She sat up, amazed that she'd slept until almost noon. Then the memory of kissing Jack the night before returned, and she smiled, remembering how it had taken her forever to fall asleep because she'd replayed the kiss over and over.

She grabbed her phone, and the tingles started all over again when she saw that he'd texted her a couple of times.

Sleep well, read the first text, sent just before midnight. She'd been home for three hours by then, but had forgotten to turn her phone sound back on.

Good morning, read the second. Gwen checked the time. He'd sent it at 7:30 a.m.

She texted back. *Good morning. Just woke up.*

Seconds later the phone buzzed. *Haven't slept. Been on calls. About ready to call it a day/night/whatever.*

Sweet dreams, Gwen typed.

Counting on it, Jack replied. *Call you later.*

Heat zoomed through Gwen. *Counting on it*, she typed back.

She climbed out of bed and opened the blinds. The weather was at San Diego's best—clear, blue skies and a few high clouds. Walking into the kitchen to get something to eat, Gwen scrolled through her missed texts from last night, surprised at the number of them—all from her sister.

Call me!

You can't just hang up after telling me you're going out with Jack Mead!

Where on earth did you meet him?

Gwen frowned. Leisa was totally nuts. Good thing Gwen had turned off her phone. But then Leisa's next text stopped her: *I can't believe my sister is dating San Diego's businessman of the year & she won't even call me back! It's midnight! What are you doing? How did it go? I'm dying over here!*

Jack was San Diego's businessman of the year? That meant . . . For a moment, Gwen couldn't breathe. She hoped that Leisa was wrong. But something told her that she wasn't. The clues began falling into place, his beach house, renting out the restaurant, graduate school at Harvard . . .

She hurried over to the magazines on the lowest shelf of the bookcase in the living room. She kept issues of *San Diego Life* so she could peruse local trends and keep her photography fresh. She pulled out the last year of issues and sat on the floor, sorting through them. At the April issue, she stopped. There was Jack on the cover, looking debonair in a suit, grinning into the camera like he had the whole world at his fingertips.

Gwen leaned against the couch and groaned. She didn't need to read the article; she'd read it months ago. At the time, she'd written off the details of what seemed to be a playboy's life—traveling the world, making business deals where the dollars numbered in the millions, jetting from house to house, hobnobbing with the who's who.

She didn't know how long she sat on the floor, trying to comprehend it all, but eventually she reached for her phone and called her sister.

"It's about time!" Leisa practically shouted. "I was just about to come over there and break down the door, but I didn't know if he'd spent the night."

"Oh, please," Gwen said. "Give me some credit. My first date in months, and you think I'm letting him into my bedroom?"

"Well . . . How did it go? I have a million questions, so start at the very beginning, and don't leave one single thing out."

Gwen did, telling Leisa about the first day at the beach, when Jack carried her stuff to the car and how she'd laughed at his claim of living in one of the houses on the ridge. By the time she told Leisa about the restaurant, and kiss, and the texts from that morning, Leisa had decided that they were perfect for each other.

"That's the problem," Gwen said. "He *is* perfect. I'm so . . . not. I'm like the gum under his shoe."

"Stop it," Leisa said. "He's totally into you!"

"He's into a girl with no education, who wears one of three dresses on a rotating basis, spent years in therapy—and should probably go back—and wouldn't be able to form a coherent sentence around his friends." The more Gwen thought about it, the more she couldn't even imagine being a small part of Jack's life. In any capacity. Not even as a friend—and that made her the saddest.

"You're nuts, Gwenie," Leisa said. "There's a reason Mom and Dad adopted you. They fell in love with you, and you're the best sister I could ever have."

"I'm your *only* sister—but I'm still adopted, and I have a million issues." Gwen pulled her knees to her chest. "I just know I can't pull this off. I don't get why he asked me out, but for some reason he did. All I know is that I can't put my heart out there again. Besides, Jack Mead is definitely too good to be true. You know I don't do Too Good to Be True."

Leisa was quiet for a few moments. "Give him a chance."

"So the resulting heartbreak can be colossal instead of just shattering this time around?"

"How do you know he'll break your heart?"

"Because just looking at his picture makes my heart crack."

Seven

"**C**all me, Jack," Silvia's voice sounded on his voicemail. "I looked up Gwen, and there's something I think you should know."

Jack shook his head, hating the open-ended message and the fact that Silvia was already trying to jump into the middle of his relationship with Gwen when everything was still so new. Silvia must have called after he'd crashed following the conference calls.

With a sigh, he walked onto the balcony overlooking the ocean and called his sister. The sun was nearly touching the western horizon, and it was strange to think that an entire day had passed since his date with Gwen. Would it be too forward to ask her out again for tonight?

Silvia answered, and he wanted to chew her out then hang up, but instead he said, "I don't care what you've found. I like her. End of story."

"I hear you," Silvia said, talking fast. "But you know that

running Dad's corporations, you have to think of more than yourself. You have to think of the whole family."

Jack had heard it all before, whenever he'd dated women back east. It was always about the family image, about company image, about upholding some fantasy for the media. And he was tired of it.

He settled onto one of the balcony chairs and propped his feet on the small coffee table. "Shoot."

"She was a foster kid until about fifteen, and then she was adopted by one of her foster families. She barely graduated from high school—she had a 2.1 GPA." Silvia paused for effect, but Jack said nothing.

He'd met many different people in his life, most of them privileged. Gwen was right; someone who had lived on a different level did have a different persona. What had Gwen said? He went to college; she could sense it.

What would Gwen think of his sister?

"Did you hear me?" Silvia said, her voice calm, yet clearly with frustration behind it.

"I did."

"Jack, this doesn't make me happy either. But you need to know it now, before it's too late."

"Too late for what?" Jack said, even though he knew what she was getting at.

"Before you become attached to her," she said. "Her biological mom was in prison for years, and her bio dad is completely out of the picture. There's still an active missing person's report on him from fifteen years back. And, she's been married!"

At least he knew *that* already. "What's your point?" Jack blurted. "Gwen isn't her parents. The first guy she married was a jerk. But she's one of the most genuine women I've ever met. Why are you judging her when you've never met her?"

Silvia sighed. "She's a risk, that's all. I love you too much to see you hurt, for something to go wrong because of a woman you happened to think is pretty. Forget the business for a second. Just think of yourself and *your* future. Think of her, too. Take her to one event, and the media will be all over her. They'll crucify her, Jack."

He lowered his legs and leaned forward. "I get what you're saying, and I appreciate your concern. We've been on *one* date, and I know this will sound crazy, but I'm willing to take the risk."

He hung up, leaned back in his chair, and closed his eyes. He thought about everything he knew about Gwen, which wasn't a lot, but then he thought about who she was, how she reacted to things, and the way he felt around her.

It didn't take long for him to text her. *You hungry?*

He waited a few seconds for a reply, and smiled when his phone buzzed. He read the text, and his heart plummeted.

Sorry, Jack. I'm an idiot & can't date you. Really sorry.

Jack stared at the words for several moments. Was she joking? Had he imagined that they both had a great time last night? Hadn't she kissed him back? The woman his sister had just criticized as being unworthy had just rejected *him*.

Exhaling, Jack tried to decide what to do. He rose and paced the balcony. Should he text her back? Call her? What had happened in the past few hours to change her mind?

Had her ex come back?

Jack leaned against the balcony rail, looking down at the few people remaining on the beach. In the business world, backpedaling by a client meant that communication had broken down. So that's what Jack had to do—communicate to find out what was really going on.

He pulled out his phone and called Gwen. It clicked

right over to voicemail. So he texted. *You're not an idiot. If you want to call things off, I'll respect that. But can we at least talk in person? This texting thing is awkward.*

Four minutes and fifty seconds passed before she replied.

Ok. I'll meet you at the beach in an hour.

The next hour and nine minutes was pure torture as Jack waited near the parking lot of the nearly deserted beach. Silvia's investigative work hadn't turned him away from Gwen. If anything, it made him respect her more. When her Honda pulled up, relief pulsed through him.

She'd come. That was all that mattered. If nothing else, he'd at least get an explanation.

His heart thundered as he watched her climb out of her car. She wore a strappy beach dress and no shoes. He had to smile at that. He'd been out with women who took two hours to get ready for a date, but Gwen held no such pretentions.

She folded her arms as she walked toward him, her gaze everywhere but on him.

"Hey," he said as she stopped a few feet from him.

She peered at him. "Sorry about the text. It's just, you know, complicated."

"How complicated?" he asked. The breeze tugged at her messy bun, and tendrils of hair played about her face. He inched closer. "On a scale of one to ten, ten being completely impossible."

Her expression relaxed slightly, and she shot him an amused look. "Eleven?"

"Ouch. Am I that bad?"

"Not you. *Me.*"

"Oh, well, *that* makes complete sense," Jack said, moving closer again. He didn't like the space between them. He didn't like that she looked vulnerable and worried. "What's wrong with you?"

She turned away.

Jack walked around her, and lifted her chin so she'd look at him. He was surprised to see tears in her eyes. "What's wrong, Gwen? Tell me."

"I—" She shook her head. "You—you're Jack Mead."

"Yeah, I told you that before we went out."

"But *I* didn't know. I mean, I knew your name, but I didn't realize you were . . ."

Ah. Jack scrubbed his hand through his hair. "I know what you're saying, but your first impression of me was right. I *am* normal. And if there are some things in my life that aren't normal, then believe me, I wish they were."

"That doesn't really help," Gwen said. "Nothing about you is normal. I mean, you're even better looking than most men I know, and now I find out that you're Mr. Forbes or something."

Jack's breathing came easier than it had been since before the phone call with Silvia. At least Gwen was talking. And at least this wasn't about her ex. "I'm not Mr. Forbes, but that would be pretty cool if there were such a thing."

She loosened the tight knot of her arms, and she was looking at him now. Both good things. Jack stepped closer and brushed a hand along her arm. "Would it be easier if I *were* Mr. Forbes?"

She smiled and shook her head, and then she was leaning against him. He wrapped his arms around her, and she released a soft sigh, her head fitting perfectly against his neck. Holding her felt so natural. And standing there, in the twilight of the beach, with the lull of the ocean yards away, it was easy to forget anything that could come between them.

Eight

Gwen never wanted to step out of Jack's arms, but the breeze had shifted from warm to cool, and they couldn't stay at the beach forever. They'd been talking for an hour, and Jack had listened to everything she had to say.

She told Jack about growing up in foster homes, about failing out of high school, and then being rescued, quite literally, by her adoptive family. When she drew away from Jack and looked up into his eyes, she found compassion, not pity, which was a relief.

"I told you it was *me*, not you," she said. "But because you are you, *we* are impossible." It hurt to say the words, yet she knew they were right—even though Leisa had told her to give it a chance. Going through a farce of a marriage with Paul had set her back. She'd even gone into counseling again for the first couple of months after arriving at San Diego. She wanted to stay strong, and the only way she knew how to do that was by staying single.

Jack had drawn away too, and now his hands rested loosely at her hips. "I'm sorry about all the crap you went through as a kid. I don't know how you survived it all, but you came out of it amazing."

Gwen scoffed. "I'm not amazing. I'm *pretending*."

Jack brushed back the hair blowing against her cheek. "Then I look forward to getting to know the real Gwen."

She shook her head at the irony. "This is the real me, the girl crying on your shoulder and complaining about her crappy childhood." She stepped out of his arms and spread her hands. "I'd only bring chaos to your happy life and—"

"Wait," Jack said, grabbing her hand and tugging her closer. "You think I have a *happy* life?"

"Uh, yeah," Gwen said. "Just look at yourself in the mirror and read some of the articles about you. You're Prince Charming, Gandhi, and Bill Gates all rolled into one."

Jack laughed. "I think I liked Mr. Forbes better." He kept hold of her hand. "Come with me. I want to show you something."

Gwen followed, even though her heart warned her that she was getting in deeper. His strong, warm hand made her feel safe, calm. "Where are we going?"

"To show you a multi-million-dollar home that is about the loneliest spot on earth."

Gwen was stunned into silence. They walked down the beach until they reached a winding path that led up the hillside. About halfway up, they stopped at a gate, which Jack unlocked with a code. Then they continued up the hill until they reached the lower terrace. The bottom floor of the house above them was lit up, but the second floor was dark, the windows glinting in the moonlight.

The landscaping was exquisite, and the house was breathtaking. Gwen felt as if she'd stepped into a postcard of Florence.

"Amazing," she said. "It reeks of happiness."

Jack flashed an amused smile. "You'd be surprised." He opened the back door, and they walked into what looked like a palace. Marble floors, elegant furniture, gilded molding.

"Fancy. I take it you didn't decorate?" She rotated in a full circle to take it all in.

"I don't know who did," Jack said. "Someone hired by my mother, or her assistant, or maybe even by my sister." He walked to the middle of the main room. "But look around. There's nothing personal; it's like being in a museum."

Gwen walked over to him. "I can see that, but still . . ." She looked up at him, feeling a danger of standing so close to him. "You can't seriously be complaining about living here?"

"Not in the way you may think," he said. "Come here." He led her through a maze of hallways, then into an office filled with gorgeous dark wood and exotic plants. After opening the closet door, he pulled out a box.

Gwen watched him remove the lid and take out a couple of photo albums. He set them on the desk and leafed through them, turning page after page, as if looking for something.

"Hang on," she said, scooping up one of the albums. "Let's go through these properly, and then you can tell me all of your deep dark secrets." She walked back the way they'd come, Jack following. She stopped when she reached an elegant kitchen with white cupboards and white and gray granite counter tops. Setting down the photo album, she sat on one of the padded bar chairs.

Jack settled next to her and opened the album he carried. This time he turned the pages more slowly. "Notice anything missing?"

Gwen studied pictures of Jack as a young boy with a little girl, who was obviously his sister. Most of the pictures were with her, but some had other children in them as well. "No parents."

"I saw my dad a few times a year. For a long time, I thought our nanny was my real mom. I was sent to boarding school at eleven. My mom and I have established a relationship only since my dad died. It's like she misses having a man as part of her life, although I don't know how close my parents were. They were hardly ever together."

Gwen opened her album. It had pictures of Jack a bit older, maybe ten or eleven. He was smiling in most of the shots, but her photographer-trained eye didn't miss the loneliness in his gaze. Her heart tugged for the kid Jack used to be. And now . . . she looked at him and realized that he was still the same kid, still felt alone in the world.

"Never thought I'd feel sorry for a rich kid," Gwen said.

Jack smiled. "Tell me how you really feel."

"I just did," Gwen teased.

Jack reached for her hand and intertwined their fingers. "I know this may sound crazy, but I think we're good together."

"If opposites can be considered good for each other."

"I think there's an old saying about that."

Gwen exhaled. "You are seriously tempting, Jack. I mean, the only thing missing is the white horse."

"I've got a horse ranch in—"

Gwen started laughing, and it escalated until she couldn't stop. When she could finally breathe normally again, she said, "Of course you do."

"So, what do you say?" Jack asked, smiling at her laughter. "Can we start over? Pretend like you never sent that text?"

Gwen looked down at their linked hands. "I have a better idea. Let's just start from here."

"Even better," Jack said.

"But I want to hear the story behind each of these

pictures," Gwen said, pulling the album Jack had been leafing through closer to her.

"Deal, but I'm starving. Do you want pizza or something? I can order delivery."

Gwen raised a brow. "Don't you have a personal chef?"

"My mom does, but my sister and I like our own spaces," Jack said with a grin. "I could hire one for you if you want."

"No thanks," Gwen said, playfully hitting him on the shoulder. "I like my space too."

Jack took her arm and pulled her with him as he stood. "Hmm. Maybe we could share some of that space."

She ran her other hand up his arm and stopped at his shoulder. "What would your mom and sister think? They probably have a supermodel picked out for you."

He lowered his head and whispered against her lips. "Nope. Mr. Forbes is all yours." Then he did kiss her.

It was hard for Gwen to imagine any place she'd rather be than being kissed by Jack. She quickly realized that her memories from the night before were only half accurate. Kissing him was even better than she remembered. Her body pressed against his as the kiss deepened.

His hands moved up her back, warm and strong, and she curled her fingers into his hair. Jack backed her up against the counter and slowed his kissing, moving down her neck. She became intently aware that they were alone in a gorgeous house and how it would be all too easy to become more intimate.

"Jack," she whispered, placing her hands on his chest and pushing.

He lifted his head and met her gaze, his eyes searching hers. "Too fast?"

She nodded, then pulled him into an embrace. His arms

tightened about her. It wasn't as good as kissing, but her heart had only started to heal. "Thanks," she said.

"For what?"

"For listening to me, for not trying to fix me, for just . . . being you."

He released her, grasped one hand, threading their fingers together. "Thank you for giving us a chance."

She smiled. "So . . . pizza?"

He grinned and picked up his cell phone from the counter. "Pepperoni?"

Nine

Three weeks later

Gwen was waiting for the ball to drop. Which ball, she wasn't sure. Maybe it would be a former girlfriend coming back into Jack's life, or maybe Jack's mom would make him choose between his family and her, or maybe Gwen would contract a terminal illness.

She climbed out of her car, a full hour early for the afternoon's beach wedding. She came early because she needed time to think. To take aimless pictures. To let the ocean soothe her soul. Tonight she would be meeting Jack's mom and sister, who were apparently flying in to meet her.

And Gwen was petrified.

To make matters worse, they'd be dining at a nice restaurant, in public—not one rented out. Not that she expected Jack to do that again, but it meant that people would see the initial meeting between her and his family. And who knew what might happen after that? Of course, meeting at his house and having empty silence around them would have been much worse. The restaurant was clearly the better choice—it meant less pressure. At least, that's what Gwen hoped.

Leisa helped her pick out a dress: a strappy black thing that was basic yet elegant. And it had been on the clearance rack—a double bonus. As Gwen loaded up her camera bag and chair then headed toward the pulsing waves, she thought of all the things she and Jack had done over the past few weeks. She'd seen him almost every day, except for the weekend that he'd flown to Dallas on business.

If there was one thing she'd learned from being around Jack, it was that business deals never slept. Middle of the night, weekends, holidays, no time was off limits. Jack had sold off one of his companies to an investor in Japan, and when he told her for how much she'd practically fainted. Jack explained that the money would go toward former employees' compensation packages, and the rest would roll over into another company, Gwen found she could breathe better. It wasn't like he and his associates were exchanging suitcases of large amounts of cash. The money was all accounted for and all had to be reported, down to the last dollar.

Suffice it to say, Gwen thought Jack was fairly brilliant, which only made her stomach knot up tighter as she strode across the beach. He was everything she'd ever thought a successful business man would be, but he was also so much more. Her skin heated as she thought about the way he looked at her and touched her, about their deep conversations, about how they were slowly getting to know each other.

Gwen set down her beach chair and put her stuff on it, then picked up her camera and walked toward the incoming

HEATHER B. MOORE

tide. She stood for a long time, just gazing out over the water. What was it about the ocean that brought peace and made her realize that she was part of something bigger, part of an amazing tapestry of nature? People were different at the beach. They breathed easier, laughed more, and appreciated the smaller things. Gwen lifted her camera and snapped some pictures of a miniature crab scuttling along the wet sand, and then she found herself focusing toward the ridge of homes where Jack lived.

Someone was coming down the path behind Jack's house. She lowered her camera, her heart thumping. It was Jack; of course it was. When he reached the sand, he started jogging, and it took only a few moments for him to reach her.

"I thought I saw you out here," Jack said as he drew closer.

It was probably a good thing that Gwen didn't see him without his shirt too often. It was also a good thing they were on a public beach and that Gwen would be working soon. She gravitated toward him and wrapped her arms around his waist. His torso was warm with the sun. He rested his chin on top of her head.

"I can't wait for tonight," Jack said.

Her nerves were back. "I'm a wreck."

"It'll be fine," he said, running his hand along her arm. "They'll love you. They won't be able to help it."

Gwen nestled against him. "I'm going to hold on to that, because if I don't, I might not make it to the restaurant."

"That's why I'm picking you up," Jack said. "To make sure you *do*."

Gwen sighed. "I'm only doing this for you, you know." She drew away and looked into his hazel eyes.

"I know." Jack smiled, then cradled her face with his

hands and touched a kiss to her mouth. "Hopefully dinner will be really short, and then we can ditch them."

"Mmm, that would be nice." She stepped backward. "Don't move." She snapped a picture of him, the ocean as the background, his hair blown by the wind, no shirt. Perfect.

One side of his mouth lifted in amusement. "What are you doing with all these pictures you're taking of me?"

Gwen gave a nonchalant shrug. "You can't expect an artist to reveal her secrets."

Jack walked over and wrapped his arm about her. Then he took hold of the camera, aiming it at both of them. "Smile."

"No selfies," she said with mock horror. "Those are the worst."

"Too bad." He snapped some pictures before she could get the camera back.

As she scrolled through the images he'd taken, he wrapped his arms around her from behind and rested his chin on her shoulder. "I think we take good pictures together. Do you need an assistant for your shoots?"

"That would be an interesting slice of life story for the media," Gwen said, leaning back into his warm embrace as she deleted a half a dozen blurry pictures. "'Jack Mead starts up new business venture working as photographer assistant.'" Gwen felt him smile against her neck.

"I wouldn't mind," Jack said in a low voice.

Way too low and sexy.

"You're distracting me, Jack Mead," Gwen said, turning in his arms. "The wedding guests will be arriving soon, and I need to start acting like a professional."

Jack grinned and kissed her again, long and slow. "All right. I'll see you tonight. Can't wait."

"Me neither," Gwen said, although the nerves had

started to jumble inside her stomach again. She exhaled and stepped away from Jack. The hours were about to move way too fast.

Ten

ack couldn't ever remember being this nervous for a date. As he pulled up to Gwen's apartment complex, his heart thudded in anticipation. Having Gwen meet his mom and sister was more than an introductory meeting—Jack really wanted them to connect, because the more time he spent with Gwen, the more he realized he was falling in love with her.

Not only did he want his mom and sister to see Gwen for who she really was, but he also wanted Gwen to feel comfortable around them. He pulled up to Gwen's apartment complex and climbed out of his car, then knocked on Gwen's door.

When she answered, he sucked in his breath. He hadn't seen Gwen so dressed up before, and she looked beautiful. He couldn't decide which look he liked better—the casual one on the beach with windblown hair, or the fancy look with a black dress and heels. He decided he'd take both.

"Hey," Gwen said. "You're early."

Jack leaned against the doorframe, closing the space between them. "I can wait."

"I'm ready." She didn't move, but tipped her head up toward him. It was too tempting. He leaned down and kissed her. She slid into his arms as if she belonged there, and Jack's thudding heart told her that she did.

After a few moments of kissing her, Jack reluctantly drew back.

"Let me grab my purse," Gwen said.

When they reached the restaurant, they were still running early. No surprise, though, that his mom and sister were already seated at their reserved table. The restaurant was quiet and elegant, and although it was a bit too trendy for Jack's taste, it was one of his sister's favorites. Both women stood to greet them, and Jack made introductions, paying careful attention to the women's interactions. His mom seemed genuinely pleased to meet Gwen, but Silvia's smile didn't reach her eyes, which immediately put Jack on edge. More than once, they'd talked about Gwen. He didn't need his sister hung up on details that didn't matter.

After they ordered, Jack finally sent Silvia a text while Gwen was telling his mom about the most recent wedding she'd photographed. *What's wrong?*

Did you see the paparazzo outside the restaurant? Jack's pulse increased. *Maybe someone famous is coming tonight.*

Like you.

Jack decided to ignore that. *This restaurant is exclusive. He won't get in.*

Silvia frowned as she read his text.

Then he wrote, *What do you think of Gwen? Mom seems to like her.*

She's beautiful, but naïve and unpolished. I can tell she really likes you, and you're way past liking her.

Do I get official sister approval? He hadn't realize how much he valued his sister's opinion until she answered.

Yes. I just hope she puts up with you.

Jack looked up at Silvia and grinned. She smiled back, and suddenly everything was right. Gwen and his mother were still taking about her job, and then Silvia joined in, asking a few questions. The conversation turned to his mom's books, and Jack could only feel pleased. His mother didn't even talk about her work with her casual acquaintances, so this was definitely a good sign.

As it turned out, Gwen had bought some of his mom's books for a niece. By the time they'd finished dessert, Jack felt pretty confident that Gwen had won his mom and sister over, and they'd won her over.

He hadn't realized how much stock he'd put into the evening until they walked out of the restaurant after saying good-bye. Jack felt as if a huge weight had lifted off his shoulders.

He linked hands with Gwen as they waited for the valet to bring around his car. "So," he said, leaning close to her ear, "what did you think?"

"The food was delicious."

He slipped an arm about her waist. "About my mom and sister."

She looked up at him, her expression sober. "You're a lucky guy to have such a great family."

He wasn't expecting such a serious answer, and he suddenly realized how much meaning that one sentence had in it, coming from Gwen.

The valet pulled up, and Jack gave Gwen a quick kiss on the forehead before opening the door for her. The evening couldn't have gone better. He took Gwen home and was pulling into his driveway when his mom called.

"She's lovely, Jack," she said. "Such a sweet girl."

Jack couldn't help grinning as he climbed out of his car. "I was hoping you'd think so."

"And you are adorable around her," his mom continued. "It makes me miss your father and when we were first dating. Of course, life eventually gets in the way of romance, but your father always took care of me."

Jack was quiet for a moment as he unlocked the front door and went inside the house. He flipped on the lights, wishing his father were still alive and could meet Gwen. His phone beeped—Silvia.

"Mom, Silvia's calling. Can we talk later?"

He switched the call over as he settled onto the kitchen barstool, prepared to hear Silvia praise Gwen as much as their mom had.

"Are you on Twitter?" Silvia asked.

Her tone of voice made him straighten. "No, what's there?"

"Pictures of you and Gwen," Silvia said. "And a bunch of links, to a collection of articles that were simultaneously published about fifteen minutes ago."

Jack blew out a breath, his neck heating up. "How's that possible?"

"I don't know. Maybe they already had the articles written, but they just needed a picture to sensationalize it more."

At this, Jack froze. "Sensationalize? What's being sensationalized?"

Silvia went quiet for a moment. "Everything about Gwen. At least enough of it to hurt her—and you—and everyone."

Jack squeezed his eyes shut. "No."

"Listen to me," Silvia said. "You've only been dating Gwen for a few weeks and—"

"Stop," Jack said. "I need to talk to Gwen. I'm not going to let the media or any article run my personal life."

"Jack—"

He hung up, knowing he'd have to apologize later, knowing that his sister was only trying to help, to protect him. He opened the Twitter app on his phone and typed in a search for his name. A half-dozen specific news tweets showed up, some of them retweeted and favorited hundreds of times. He clicked on one of the article links. His blood went cold as he scanned the article.

Silvia was right; this could hurt Gwen. The pieces were downright nasty. They villainized her biological parents, one going so far as to call Gwen "trailer-trash." The sites all focused on celebrity gossip, and although Jack didn't consider himself a celebrity, the fact that he had more money than most of them apparently made his personal life news fodder.

Eleven

Gwen put her phone on silent and pulled the covers over her head, blocking out the morning light. Jack had called three times, texted more than that, and then the *Unknown Caller* started calling. Gwen had made the mistake of answering one of those, only to find out that the mini-media storm wouldn't die out any time soon.

Last night had been more than perfect, and Gwen had finally managed to relax around Jack's family. They were both amazing women, yet they made Gwen feel appreciated. And Jack had been his usual adorable and gentlemanly self.

But now, anxiety pulsed through Gwen. Because of her background, she and Jack's picture was on every gossip website, and now moving to the mainstream channels. She'd talked to Leisa just moments ago to confirm it. When Gwen had said, "Maybe we aren't meant to be together after all. The articles are all true, and it just puts our vast differences in black and white," Leisa had gone quiet.

That was answer enough for her. She knew Jack would call, knew what he'd have said if she answered. He'd tell her to ignore the media, that it didn't matter, that he still cared about her. But it was plain to Gwen that it would get old. Jack's family would get tired of the constant comparisons that would follow them around if she and Jack stayed together.

It wasn't fair to put Jack or his family through that. They'd suffered enough with the loss of their father, and Jack was incredibly busy taking over the company reins. Life was complicated enough without involving the rest of the world in her private relationship with Jack.

She scrolled through her missed phone calls and stopped at Jack's number. She clicked to the voicemail and listened to his voice.

"Call me as soon as you can," the first message said.

The next was more urgent and added an apology.

She reached the third one. "Gwen, I know how you must be feeling and what you might be thinking, but please, let's talk. Don't shut me out. I have to leave in a few minutes to make my flight, but Silvia is still in town and offered you a room at her hotel so that you can have some privacy from the media. I'll be back in a few days, but please call me anytime. Day or night. I'm worried about you."

Gwen exhaled. She didn't want to involve herself in Jack's life any more than she had to—especially if she was about to break things off. She listened to the next message, which was from a different number. Instead of hearing a reporter's voice, she was surprised to hear Silvia extending the same invitation Jack had.

Before she could change her mind, she called Silvia back. She answered on the second ring.

"I'm sorry, Silvia, but I can't take you up on your offer. I feel like I've already complicated things for your family."

Silvia shook her head. "Last night I was worried about what was said, but after talking to Jack, I realized that his feelings about you are more important than anything the media might pick on." She flashed a smile. "So, welcome to Mead Enterprises. Although I'm sorry you had to jump into the fire so quickly." She sounded like the media blowup wasn't a big deal.

That gave Gwen pause. "Look," she started. "I'm really sorry. If I'd have known this would happen, I wouldn't have let things go so far with Jack and—"

"Gwen," Silvia interrupted. "How do you feel about my brother?"

Her heart twisted at the question. Being honest would only make things more complicated. But then, Silvia already knew everything about her. And as Jack's sister, she deserved the truth. "I've fallen in love with him. I know it's fast and it sounds crazy, but he's the most important thing to me. That's why I think it's best that I go my way, and he goes his. My past will always be a part of me, and the media has proved that in the last few hours."

Silvia was quiet for several moments. Finally, she said, "I'd like to talk to you, face to face. Can I come over to your place?"

"All right," Gwen said.

Silvia showed up eighteen minutes later, and by the time Silvia reached the steps of Gwen's apartment, she'd opened the door.

Even after what must have been a long night for Silvia, she looked immaculate. Her ivory pantsuit was pressed and her makeup fresh. Gwen ushered her in, afraid that a photographer might be lurking somewhere.

As they sat on the couch, Silvia watched her closely. "Are you all right?"

"I think I'm in shock—it's a lot to take in," Gwen confessed. "I can't put you guys through this. I feel like such a jerk."

"You know, a few hours ago I might have agreed with you," Silvia said.

Gwen stared at her, a lump forming in her throat.

"I might have told you that it would be best for you to stop seeing Jack," Silvia continued. "But this morning, I drove Jack to the airport, and—" She broke off and looked away. A moment later, her gaze returned, and Gwen was surprised to see tears in her eyes.

"He really cares about you, Gwen," she said in a soft voice. "I've never seen my brother so worried about anyone else. Not even me or our mom." She reached for Gwen's hand and grasped it. "I'm serious. He . . . he probably wouldn't want me to say this, but I think he's in love with you too."

Gwen looked at her hand in Silvia's and blinked back tears. Was it possible that Jack really felt that deeply for her?

Sylvia went on. "And that's why I think you need to come with me to San Francisco to see him."

Gwen snapped her head up and stared at Silvia.

She only smiled. "His meetings will be over in a few hours, and you can surprise him." She squeezed Gwen's hand. "We'll get away from the media for a couple of days. You and I can do some retail bonding, and at night we can hang out with Jack."

"But—what would he think? I created a media firestorm, and your family is the top gossip everywhere. He probably wants to stay clear of me for a while."

"Honey, he'd love to see you," Silvia said. "Trust me."

Twelve

Less than an hour later, Gwen boarded a private jet with Silvia. Gwen couldn't believe she was actually flying this way—and going to see Jack. The flight was much too short and didn't give her a chance to calm her nerves. In fact, they were in even higher gear by the time she and Silvia were being driven through downtown San Francisco.

Silvia was growing on Gwen, not that she hadn't liked her, but Silvia was out-spoken yet savvy, and considerate to everyone she came in contact with.

"We aren't going to interrupt his meetings, are we?" Gwen asked as their chauffeured car glided through traffic.

Silvia checked the time on her phone. "Jack should be finished within the hour. I'll tell him that I came to meet with him in one of the other conference rooms." She looked up and smiled. "You'll be there, he'll see you, you'll apologize for ignoring him, and everything will be made right."

Gwen let out a stuttered breath. "Are you sure about this?"

Silvia narrowed her eyes. "Completely sure. Now quit worrying."

The car stopped in front of an elegant building with massive pillars and a stone edifice over the doors that read *Mead Enterprises*. Before Gwen knew it, she was inside, seven floors up, and seated in a conference room with plush leather chairs while Silvia typed out a text to Jack.

Moments later, Silvia's phone buzzed. "He says he'll be here in twenty minutes." She stood. "Call me later. We can meet for dinner. But I'll understand if you two want to be alone."

"Wait. You're leaving me here?"

"Don't worry," Silvia said. "It'll be a good surprise for Jack." She bustled to Gwen's side and gave her a brief hug. "Good-bye now."

Gwen stared after her as she left, then proceeded to wait the longest twenty minutes of her life. Even so, she jumped when the door opened and Jack stepped through.

She stood, clutching her hands together. He looked surprised, yet wary, and Gwen didn't blame him. She'd ignored all of his phone calls and texts.

He stayed in the doorway, his hand on the knob, as if he couldn't decide if he should enter or leave.

"I'm sorry I didn't answer your calls," Gwen said, her voice shaky. She took a deep breath. "I was steeling myself to break things off with you. The articles about my past really shook me up." Still, Jack said nothing, but he stepped into the room.

"Silvia thought it would be better to do this in person," Gwen continued.

At this, Jack turned and shut the door, then he faced

Gwen, his gaze hard, defensive. "So you're breaking up with me?"

Gwen placed her hands on the back of a nearby chair to steady herself. "No," she said. "I came to apologize, and . . . to tell you that I'm ready to face whatever the media wants to say about me."

His face softened, and he walked around to her side of the conference table. "It wasn't your fault—not the articles, not your past."

Tears threatened, and she looked down. "I know, but it's still hard to accept. And it's hard to embrace the good things sometimes. It's like . . . you're too good to be true."

"Gwen," Jack whispered.

She looked up, even though she knew her eyes had filled with tears. Jack's gaze was tender, warming her entire body.

He cradled her face. "Believe in the good. I'm here, you're here. We have to believe in each other. That's all that matters." His lowered his head, then hesitated.

When she tilted her face upward, he kissed her, softly at first, then deeper. His hands slid down her back and pulled her closer until she was completely breathless. When he drew away, he rested his forehead on hers. "So you're not breaking up with me?"

"Not if you can handle the heat."

He smiled and brushed another kiss on her lips. "I think I can handle the heat."

Gwen sighed and leaned into him, letting his arms hold her up and surround her with comfort. Jack was real. *This* was real. And she'd let herself finally believe.

ABOUT HEATHER B. MOORE

Heather B. Moore is a *USA Today* bestselling author. She writes historical thrillers under the pen name H.B. Moore; her latest is *Finding Sheba*. Under Heather B. Moore, she writes romance and women's fiction. She's one of the coauthors of The Newport Ladies Book Club series. Other works include *Heart of the Ocean, The Fortune Café,* the Aliso Creek series, and the Amazon bestselling Timeless Romance Anthology series.

For book updates, sign up for Heather's email list: HBMoore.com/contact
  Website: HBMoore.com
  Facebook: Fans of H.B. Moore
  Blog: MyWritersLair.blogspot.com
  Twitter: @HeatherBMoore

Gone Fishing

Kaylee Baldwin

OTHER WORKS BY KAYLEE BALDWIN

Meg's Melody
Silver Linings
Six Days of Christmas

One

Of course Brig Bryson couldn't have a normal office in a building. Not even one of those break-apart wooden stands at the entrance to the pier. Why Claire thought her dad might be normal for once was beyond her. The man who used to make mini-parachutes for her dolls then help her launch them off the roof of their house, or who insisted on giving her a standing ovation at every single choir event of her life—despite her begging that he stop—would not do something as expected as having a regular storefront.

No, he had to locate the main office of Double B's Deep Sea in a boat at the end of the dock.

Claire glanced down at her impractical, but gorgeous shoes. Four-inch peep-toe heels had seemed like a good idea when she'd thought about making a dramatic entrance, demanding he put this midlife crisis business behind him, and move back to Colorado so he could be involved in her life again. But now, standing at the edge of an uneven surface, she questioned more than just her choice in footwear.

She rarely made impulsive decisions like leaving work without notice or taking a spontaneous trip, but she'd been desperate. Then Jade, her older sister, told her that their dad had broken his arm on one of his excursions, and Claire knew it was time for this dream of his to sink.

Besides, no one but Dad had ever been able to stand up to Mom, and Claire was drowning in her mother's expectations. Rather, one expectation, namely Everett Pickford. Claire shuddered and pushed thoughts of her mom's latest over-achieving protégé to the farthest corner of her mind.

First to talk some sense into Dad. Then deal with Mom's arranged-marriage style of matchmaking.

The sun was setting over the Pacific, caught in a perfect moment of amethyst reflection over the water. People lounged in groups along the beach, while the locals cleaned their boats after the day's excursions. Independence Day was tomorrow, when Jade said tourism here exploded. Not the best time for a panicked, last-minute trip to San Diego, but when Everett pulled out a two-carat ring—emerald cut with Mom's signature pearls flanking the sides—Claire fled.

She inhaled the briny ocean air and stepped onto the dock. Her heels wobbled, one heel caught momentarily in the crack of a warped board, but Claire was a pro at navigating harsh terrain. Anything to add a few inches to her height.

Her bag clicked behind her on the slats with the gentle roll and hiss of the ocean. The dock was empty, except for Dad's boat at the end. *Double B* was stamped at one end of it in navy print against the white hull of the double-decker yacht lined with benches.

A man stood on its deck, elbow deep in something slimy looking. She crinkled her nose when the smell hit her. Fish. With the fading sunlight silhouetting him from behind, she couldn't make out the man's features, but wild hair framed his face, and tattoos lined his bare biceps and forearms. Everything about him screamed, *Don't mess with me.*

"I'm looking for Brig Bryson," Claire called, keeping her distance.

The man glanced up then stared at her for a long time before he nodded to the side. "He's in the office."

She took a deep breath, gathered every bit of adventurous spirit she'd ever had, and stepped closer. The sport fishing yacht was much bigger than the pontoon she'd imagined. She tamped down the feelings of pride that her dad owned this. For as long as she could remember, he'd talked of his dreams of having adventures at sea. Together, they read *Treasure Island*, *Robinson Crusoe*, and *The Swiss Family Robinson*. As a teenager, even after Mom and Dad were divorced, she sneaked library copies of romances at sea past her disapproving mother and used the light on her phone to read them under the dome of her blankets after Jade fell asleep.

Then Dad shocked everyone by quitting his mechanical engineering job of twenty years and moving to California to start up a deep-sea fishing tourist business. Claire had been in her third year of business school and couldn't have come with him even if he'd invited her, which he hadn't. Somewhere along the way, his dreams had become her own, and she always thought that if he ever went to sea, he'd take her with him. But Dad's only goodbye had been a hurried voice message with a promise to make her proud. After he left, the novels about reformed pirates, stowaways, and life or death on the high seas lost their appeal.

"Let me get the ramp for you," the man said as she reached the edge of the dock. Close up, he looked even more intimidating. He wore a full beard, and though she'd guessed him to be her dad's age, this close, she could tell he was probably only a few years older than she was—a far cry from Everett Pickford, that was for sure.

"It's okay," she said. "I've got it."

"It's too slippery. Take my hand, at least." He swiped his raw-fish palms across the front of his apron and held them out to her. Scars, both pencil thin and jagged, lined his knuckles and met up with the dark ink of loopy, unreadable cursive. Fish guts still glistened between his fingers and oozed out of his nails.

Claire grimaced. "Uh, no thanks. I've got it."

He folded his arms and stood right in front of the opening as if he hadn't heard her.

"I'm good," she repeated.

He offered her a lazy smile through his voluminous beard but didn't move. She huffed out a breath, resigned to the fact she would have to do this in front of him. Gingerly, and once again cursing both her shoes and the genetics that bestowed her with such short legs, she stepped one foot onto the boat. Easy.

She lifted her suitcase and her other foot at the same time. "See, I've got it—" Her bag got caught on the edge of the dock, throwing off her balance, and with an embarrassing squeal, she realized she was falling backward into the ocean she'd been straddling moments ago.

Two strong hands wrapped around her upper arms and yanked her into the boat. Her bag banged against her leg before she dropped it to the deck. She stood in front of him, lopsided, panting. One of her shoes—from her most expensive pair—had fallen off.

"I heard a splash," the man said, indicating her bare foot. He still held her, as though he doubted her ability to walk without assistance. "You okay?"

"Fine." Claire kicked off the other shoe, which lowered her forehead close to his collarbone. He let go and stepped back. Her arms felt sticky with substances she didn't even want to think about.

"Miguel Rodriguez," he said. "I own Double B's with Brig." He went back to the table with the fish and picked up a huge knife. For a moment, when he'd held her, she thought she'd been wrong about how scary he looked. But holding the knife like that? She shivered. Yep, this guy had gang member written all over him. More proof Dad had completely lost it and needed to come back home with her.

"Brig's back there?" she asked, avoiding eye contact.

"Down that hall. Door on the left," he said. She left her bag on the deck and started walking, but jumped when Miguel banged on the wall and yelled, "Brig, someone's here to see you!"

The door opened as she reached it, and behind it, she saw emotion wash over her dad's always expressive face. First shock, then excitement, before he pulled her into the tightest hug she'd had in over four years. Despite her lingering anger, she wrapped her arms around his chest and breathed in his familiar scent, now overlaid with salt and fish. Still, even after all this time, he used the same soap, something that made her eyes fill.

"Claire-bear!" His voice caught in his throat as he rocked her back and forth, still not letting her go.

"Hey, Dad."

He pulled back but kept a hand on her shoulder, as if he was afraid to let her go. Only then did she realize his arm was in a sling.

71

"Jade mentioned you got hurt."

"Just a small fracture." He waved his good arm as if it weren't worth talking about then pulled Claire into his office. "I had no idea you were coming."

"It was kind of a whim." Claire sat in the chair he'd motioned her towards, and he lowered himself across from her. His desk was in complete disarray, filled with papers and forms, pictures and pens. The edge of a laptop peaked out from under a tower of stuff. Claire's eyes caught on a picture hanging on the wall behind his desk. A photo taken almost ten years ago of Claire, Jade, and their dad, arms slung across each other's shoulders, standing in front of the first sail boat Claire had ever been on. The print used to sit on Dad's desk, first in his home office, then in his apartment after the divorce.

Dad's gaze followed hers, and he smiled at the picture. "One of my favorites. How long are you in town? Do you have time to go on a tour with us?"

His words snapped her out of her warm memories. She was here on a mission. "I'm only here for the night." She crossed her legs, trying to ignore the fact that her feet were bare.

"So quick? Well, at least we have a few hours together. I've missed my girl."

"Then why haven't you come home?" The moment the words left her mouth, Claire wished she could take them back. Especially since they'd come out sounding broken and needy. She was twenty-four, not a little girl anymore.

He sighed and ran a hand over his mouth. "I've wanted to come see you for years. But opening this business took more out of me than I thought it would. I work every single day of the year, and haven't had a break since we opened."

"You can't keep up this pace forever."

"Maybe not, but sometimes you do what you gotta do."

"But you *don't* have to do it. Can't you see that?"

"Claire," he began, but her phone rang before he could finish.

She pulled it from her purse. Mom. She closed her eyes and took a deep breath. Time to set emotion aside and salvage what she could of this meeting. She didn't know whether Dad would listen to reason, but he'd never said no to her when she needed him. And right then, she needed him more than ever.

"Dad, you need to give this up and move home. I know we always talked about coming out here and doing something like this, but you're an adult with adult responsibilities. You've lived this fantasy life for a few years now, and all it's done is hurt you—and us. Jade is even wilder since you left; she can't settle on a job for longer than a few weeks. Mom is trying to run our lives, and there isn't anyone to stop her. And now you're getting hurt. This time, it was only an arm, but next time, it could be your neck."

The words sounded good as they rolled from her mouth, but Dad only stared at her with a half-amused smile. Where was the look of shame? The dawning realization that Double B's had been an irresponsible, unrealistic midlife crisis, and not the actions of a father with responsibilities?

"You sound so much like your mom."

Claire recoiled. She wasn't anything like her mom, a woman who took pleasure in controlling her daughters' lives. Claire wasn't trying to control anyone; she just wanted her dad to see the error of his ways.

"Thank you for worrying about me. You've always had a sensitive heart." He stood, and she knew that in his mind, the matter was resolved.

Coming here had been one of the most spontaneous

things she'd ever done, and she couldn't go home without him. Not without a fight.

"Why don't we grab some dinner and I'll take you to your hotel?" Dad rifled through the mess on his desk until he found his billfold.

Her phone rang again, only this time Everett's picture flashed across the screen. Her stomach twisted at his fake, golden-boy smile. "Please, Dad," she said, not above begging. "Come home."

"What's going on?"

"It's Mom." She rubbed the ever-present ache at the bridge of her nose. "I don't know how to make her listen to me. You're the only one who can stand up to her."

He pulled her into a hug and kissed the top of her head. "Hold your ground, baby. Don't let her bully you into doing something you don't want to do."

"Easier said than done," she muttered.

Her mom employed a sort of psychological warfare that left no survivors. Claire needed her dad on her side for any chance of getting through the Everett debacle. She'd left out one thing from her earlier argument—the biggest reason she wanted him to come home, and the one that left her most vulnerable.

She held her breath then let the words out. "Dad, I miss you. I want you to come home."

Dad's gaze softened. "I've missed you too, Claire. Your being here means the world to me." Emotion choked his voice, and he cleared his throat. She waited for him to agree to leave the business to his partner and come home, but the promise never came.

"Where are you staying?" her dad asked instead as he led her outside. When they emerged, the fish guts were gone and the pebbled deck was hosed off.

"All the hotels I've tried so far were booked, so I don't have anything yet."

"Stay here. We've only got small rooms with cots, but nothing can beat the waves rocking you to sleep."

She nodded, thrilled at the idea of sleeping on the water despite her disappointment with how their conversation had gone. She'd never slept on a boat before, never been on one longer than it took to get a few pictures and touch a rope. It had been years—four, to be exact—since she'd read or watched or even talked about anything boat related, but it turned out that her old fascination hadn't died.

"Miguel, come meet my daughter!"

He came over and held out his hand. Claire hesitated only a moment before putting her hand into his larger one. It was warm but damp with his grip firm against her soft palm. The fish-gut apron was gone, and he wore an unbuttoned black shirt over his undershirt. His hair dripped water onto his collar, and he smelled fresh, like the ocean.

"Your daughter?" He raised his eyebrows. "I've met Jade. You must be Claire."

Her heart raced in her chest, so she only nodded before pulling her hand from his.

Miguel folded his arms, emphasizing the toned muscles in his arms and chest, as he turned to her dad. "There's fish frying in the galley. I'm going to run into town for a few hours. Need me to grab you anything?"

Her dad shook his head then watched as Miguel jumped over the side of the boat and onto the dock like it was nothing. He held his hand up in a wave and jogged away.

"He seems . . ." She searched her mind for a word other than *intimidating* or *criminal*, but came up blank.

"Rough?" her dad supplied with a smile.

"Yes," she said, relieved. "Why did you hire him?"

"I didn't. I *found* him." He smiled in the mysterious way he always did when he knew more than he'd tell her. Curiosity tugged at Claire, but she ignored it, not wanting to give him the satisfaction of knowing that his co-owner intrigued her.

Dad squeezed her into another side hug as if he couldn't bear to let go. "Now go grab your things and take them to room one while I check on the fish."

Claire shook her head, still not confident in her dad's sanity. She had only until tomorrow morning to convince him to come back to Colorado with her, and it would take more than begging to be successful.

She picked up her bag to take it to the room, but paused. Because there, sitting on the deck beside her suitcase, were both of her shoes. One dripping wet.

Two

iguel stretched his neck from one side to the other before flipping the sizzling egg in the frying pan. He hadn't slept well after spending hours in town to give Brig time alone with his daughter. But Miguel lasted only a couple of hours before winding up at the beach, where he played ukulele for the dolphins and a few tourists camping there.

Feet shuffled behind him then stopped abruptly. He turned, accidentally poking the egg yolk with his spatula.

Claire Bryson. Miguel had heard plenty about her over the years. Few things existed that Brig liked talking about more than his dreams of sailing and his daughters. Jade had been out a few times and seemed to have a free spirit like Brig. She stayed only long enough to have an adventure before moving on to the next great thing in her life. Claire was different. More reserved. Cautious.

He recognized the ridiculous shoes from the night

before, one of which he'd had to dive into the ocean to retrieve, but she also wore a muted pink skirt and a white, ironed shirt buttoned all the way to the top. Some people had school-marm fantasies, but this look crossed straight from fantasy to grandma. Except for those shoes, which he could only scowl at.

"You look very . . . corporate this morning," he said.

"And you look very homeless." She tucked some light-brown hair behind her ear and looked everywhere but at him or his chest. He wore no shirt, only his board shorts and flip flops—one of the perks of living on the ocean. "Have you seen my dad?"

"Had to go talk to the fishing and licensing office this morning."

"He's gone?"

Miguel nodded. "Told him I'd show you around."

She glanced at the clock over his head, obviously stressed. "My flight leaves at four."

"He'll be back long before that. We have a tour at two."

She still looked disappointed, but what had she expected? She showed up without telling anyone, and they already had business commitments. He lifted the ruined egg from the pan and added it to his plate.

"I've got some bacon and eggs here, if you're hungry. There's bread by the toaster."

He stepped toward her with the plate, and she stumbled back. Catching his reflection in the microwave door, he could see where she got the homeless thing from. His face hadn't seen a razor in weeks, and without a shirt, all of the tattoos from his old life were on display. He made her nervous, that much was for sure. It shouldn't have amused him that she looked ready to jump out of her skin every time they got close, but it did.

He held out her plate, but when she tried to tug it away, he held on to it, showing extra teeth with his grin. "I know I look wild, but I don't bite."

"That's what they all say—right before they bite you." She snatched the plate, amusement lighting up her eyes.

"*They*? So you've been bit before?"

"Many times. I may not work in the ocean, but I work with plenty of sharks."

He laughed, glad to see a small showing of spunk. Someone who wore bright-yellow heels on a boat had to have at least a little bit of spunk—or maybe she just lacked common sense. He ran a hand over his hair and beard. "I think I'm more lion than shark. Guess you'll have to risk it." He grabbed the filled plate and a loaf of bread for good measure. "There's not much room in here. I usually take my food outside. Want to grab some cups and the orange juice?"

He wasn't sure she'd follow, but a moment later, she came onto the deck, slipping with every step across the wet floor on those awful shoes.

He swallowed a mouthful of food then said, "So Brig says you work with your mom."

"He's told you about me?"

Nonstop. So much that Miguel was surprised he hadn't recognized her the moment she stepped onto the boat last night. He'd heard about how she graduated from college with a bachelor's degree in only three years, how magical her performance in *Oliver* had been in the high school play, how she was a genius with computers, as beautiful on the outside as she was on the inside, and a million other little details that amounted into the making of the perfect girl.

Brig worried over her more than anyone else. Worried that working with her mother at the design firm was draining her spirit, over how much the divorce had changed her, and how she'd stopped being a carefree romantic and had turned into a forced mold of her mom. Brig suspected that his ex was so afraid of Claire slipping away that she kept their daughter in a stranglehold.

After Brig took Miguel in, they'd spent many days and nights side by side, building this business, learning about each other, unloading their pasts and cares. Wary at first, Miguel had mostly listened, but over time, he'd come to learn something. Brig Bryson loved his daughters in the fierce sort of way Miguel had never experienced from anyone in his life.

"Did he tell me about you?" He raised his eyebrows. "I could probably recite from memory the poem you wrote in eighth grade better than you could."

She choked on her bacon, but when he stood to pat her back, she held up a hand. She drank some juice until her eyes watered, and when she finally spoke, her voice was raspy. "He did *not* tell you about that!"

"'On the sea, I wend my way, Past the fears of yesterday—'"

"Stop!" Her face was completely aflame now. "You seriously have that memorized?"

He grinned. "It's catchy. Brig and I even wrote music for it."

She groaned. "Don't you guys have a business to run?"

"There's a lot of down time."

"And there's egg in your beard," she said, folding her arms.

He ran his napkin around his mouth, and it came away dirty. One of the downsides to the beard. And it itched like crazy in the heat. "He loves you."

"I know that," she said, but it came out defensive.

He folded the napkin and set it on his plate. "So what brings you out here this week?"

She paused, then leaned forward. "Maybe you can help me, actually. I'm trying to convince Dad to sell Double B's Deep Sea and move back home."

Ice rushed through Miguel's veins. No.

Four years ago, Brig and the Double B saved his life, in more ways than one, and Miguel would be forever indebted to him. If Miguel thought that leaving all of this would make Brig happy, he'd help sell off this boat piece by piece. But this was Brig's dream. For as long as they could keep afloat, anyway.

"Why?" he asked.

"Because it's ridiculous!" Her voice rose, along with her tiny self. She stood there, her hands flying on either side of her as she spoke. "He's a grown man, living on a boat."

Miguel raised his brows. "So am I."

A choked sound came from the back of her throat. "Well. True. But he could get hurt! He already has."

"That didn't even happen on an excursion," Miguel said, standing now. "He was nicked by a car while riding his bike into town. Something you would know if you ever came to see him."

"Why does it always have to be me? Planes fly both ways."

"Running this business is a twenty-four hour job."

"Exactly! He's too old to work that hard."

"You make it sound like he's a decrepit old man. He's only in his fifties!" He paused and took a moment to try to cool down. The last thing he needed was to have Brig come back and catch him yelling at his beloved baby daughter. "This used to be your dream too."

Her mouth tightened. "You know nothing about me or my dreams."

Which was untrue, of course, thanks to Brig. They were

both quiet for a moment, catching their breath. Miguel realized that while they fought, he'd moved closer to her, and now they stood nearly toe to toe. When he stepped back, she blinked, her eyes wary again.

"Look, your dad has given me everything I have, and I would never help anyone take away something he has worked so hard for. Not even you."

Her breathing became harsh again, her eyes wild with whatever she was holding back. He didn't question why he wanted her to scream out whatever she was thinking, or how exhilarating fighting with her was.

"He's my dad," she said. "He belongs in Colorado, working as an engineer. Not here."

"If you really believe that, you don't know your father at all." He grabbed the plates from the table and headed for the galley. He paused. "I told Brig I'd take you around to a few places this morning. If you want to come and maybe see what he loves about this life so much, meet me out here in ten minutes." He could feel her glare staring holes in his bare back until he was out of sight.

Three

*T*hinks he knows my own father better than I do?

Claire tossed her shoes into the corner of her tiny room. She grabbed some flip flops and exchanged her nice skirt and blouse for a pair of shorts and a tank top, feeling free right away.

He doesn't even know how to use a razor. At least he showers, though.

When he'd bent close to grab the plates after their argument, she couldn't help but inhale the masculine scent of his soap. She shook her head. So what if he was clean? He still looked like a mangy dog, ready to attack.

She stepped onto the deck, pausing to watch Miguel check some ropes. "Ready?" she called.

He glanced up, but paused. "Wow."

Her heart kicked into overdrive. "Let's go," she said brusquely, trying to cover the unexpected effect he'd had on her.

"Legs look good on you, Corporate." He sauntered over, his gaze taking her in.

She rolled her eyes. "And you still have food in your beard."

"It's all a part of my charm." He'd thrown a shirt on, covering most of his tattoos, and had a pair of leather flip-flops on. "The ladies love it. Kisses for now, snack for later."

Claire grimaced, glad to be back on comfortable footing with him. "That's disgusting."

He grinned and stepped from the boat onto the dock. "Will you let me help you this time, or are you still afraid to touch me?"

"I wasn't afraid to touch you," she said, though part of her was lying. "You had fish guts all over you."

"I'm fish-gut free." He held his hands up and twisted them back and forth as proof. Before she could even hold out a hand to grab his, he'd jumped back onto the boat, wrapped his arms around her waist, and lifted her up to the dock. She let out a tiny squeal, which made him laugh, and then he popped up beside her. "I can't believe you did that!"

"I didn't want to have to jump in after you."

"You could have dropped me."

He looked at her, insulted. "I've caught fish heavier than you."

Well. She followed him over the dock and to the beach, where they walked for about fifteen minutes. She kept her distance, giving herself time to formulate a next step in her ill-thought out plan. The warm sand slid around in her flip-flops until she bent over to slip them off and hook them in her fingers like Miguel was doing.

They arrived at a pier, where it seemed as though a whole different world teemed with life. Massive ships with nets and people were pulled up alongside jutting docks. Men and women called out to one another in languages Claire had never heard before. They walked through the noise and masses of people until they came to an open-air shop with what looked like a warehouse in back and a long counter in front. Fish flew over the workers' heads from one person to another. The pungent scent nearly overwhelmed her.

"Welcome to the fish market," Miguel said over the crowd's noise.

"Do you sell the fish you catch here?"

"No, everyone on our tours keeps the fish they catch, and Brig and I release anything we won't eat."

"Then why are we—"

"Miguel!" A large, dark man covered in fish bits wrapped Miguel in a hug. "Who is your lady friend?"

"Brig's daughter. Claire."

Before she could stop him, the man pulled her into a firm hug, too. Slimy fish guts rubbed against her neck and arms, and she attempted to politely wiggle out of his grasp.

"Any relation of Brig's is a friend of mine!" he boomed. She wished he'd change his policy on friendship. "You here for the Steakhouse order?"

"Yep."

The man shook his head as he handed over a couple of bulging plastic sacks. "Does this really help you?"

"Doesn't hurt." Miguel saluted the man, the sacks now hanging from his hand, and they left the crowded fish market.

Claire wanted to ask what was in the sacks, but didn't want to appear too curious about his business. They walked several blocks before showing up at a nice restaurant. Claire followed Miguel around back, where he knocked on a large metal door.

An older Hispanic woman opened the door a crack, but

when she saw Miguel, pulled it wider. She grabbed him by his hairy face and kissed him on each cheek. "You're an angel, Miguel."

He snorted. "Hardly." He set the sacks on the ground by her feet and pulled some fliers out of his back pocket. "Still handing these out to your customers?"

"You question me, Niño?"

"Never." Miguel crossed his fingers over his heart. "Otis has one more fish delivery for you today. I'll bring it by in about an hour."

"No. I am not so old I can't get my own fish."

"I'm getting your order, Nana." His stance was unyielding.

She threw up her hands and glared, but Claire could see the twinkle in her eye. "He won't ever listen to me," she said to Claire. "Who are you?"

"Claire Bryson. Brig's daughter."

"Hmm." Her hands snapped out, and with a surprisingly strong grip for such a tiny woman, she yanked Claire toward Miguel. "You two will make pretty *ninos*. I know these things."

"What?" Claire blinked, glad she didn't have anything to choke on.

"Nana has dementia," Miguel said out of the side of his mouth.

Nana smacked him upside the head, and he reached up to rub where she'd hit. "My mind is as clear as yours. Get out of here, *loco hijo*. I've got some *fachendoso* customers out front. Nothing's good enough for some people."

The door shut in their faces, and they both stood there for a moment.

"So, that was your grandma?"

"No."

She glanced at him. "You called her nana."

"Everyone calls her nana," he said, as if it made sense. "This is the best restaurant in the area, mostly because of her cooking." He glanced down at his phone and began walking away from the building. "We've got to finish up. Our overnighters will be checking in soon."

"What's *fachendoso* mean?"

"How should I know?" He turned an accusing stare on her.

"I guess I assumed . . . I mean, because you're Hispanic . . ." *Right, Claire, because everyone who looks Hispanic speaks Spanish.* Her face was on fire.

A half-smile tilted the side of his beard up. "It means *conceited.*"

Claire barely resisted hitting him upside the head like Nana. Instead, she went for his arm. "I felt like such a jerk back there!"

"What is wrong with you women today?" Miguel rubbed his arm with a wounded scowl, but there was no way she could have hurt him.

"I don't think *we* women are the problem."

He laughed, and they spent the next hour doing the same sort of thing. They'd pick up fish from the marketplace then take it to a local restaurant in exchange for handing out fliers. Poorly made fliers. No way did they drum up enough sustainable business.

When they dropped the last fish order off at Nana's, she looked even ornerier than before.

"The *fachendosos* are still here. Those kind never tip," she said, her expression dark.

They left, and Claire had to jog to keep up with Miguel, but her legs stalled beneath her when she heard a familiar voice coming from the outdoor eating area in the front of

Nana's restaurant. Two familiar people sat there, heads lowered together over a laptop and a million papers.

She paused before dashing behind a rusty delivery truck parked beside the restaurant.

"Claire, we've—"

"Shhhh," she said, waving him over. He walked slowly, as if approaching a crazy person. She pointed at the couple at the table. "That's my mom," she whispered.

"Did you know she was here?"

"No. She must have followed me."

"Why would she do that?"

Claire hesitated before pointing to the man. Even at the beach, he wore a dark, pinstriped suit with a red silk tie. His hair was brushed away from his face, not a strand out of place. Objectively, she knew he was handsome, but he was also in her mom's pocket, one of the most unattractive places anyone could be.

"See that guy?"

"The one who belongs in a hair gel commercial?"

"That's Everett Pickford."

"That's an unfortunate name."

"He tried to propose to me yesterday."

"Tried? That seems like the kind of thing you either do or you don't do," he said loudly, taking Everett in.

She shushed him. "He knelt and pulled out the ring, but before he could say anything, I pretended to be sick and ran to my sister's house. I booked the first available flight to San Diego."

She still lived with her mom, so going home had not been an option. With Claire in panic mode, Jade had convinced her that she needed to get away. And of course, Everett ran straight to Mom when things didn't go according to plan. Jade must have sold her out. Not that Claire could blame her. Mom's skills for extracting information rivaled those of trained military personnel.

"And now he's here," Miguel said slowly. "With your mom." He seemed to be trying to piece it all together.

Mom laughed, bringing home the fact she was really here, not twenty feet away.

"They're both over-committed to the idea of me and Everett being in a relationship, okay? We have to get out of here. They can't see me." She looked up at Miguel, realizing he was only a breath away. If she bent forward a centimeter, his beard would brush her cheek. The thought propelled her backward.

Miguel smirked, like her reaction to his closeness amused him. "You're going to have to face them sometime."

"I'm not ready. Not like this." She motioned to the shorts and tank top she'd borrowed from Jade. Mom would be appalled if she could see her now.

"Fine." He let out a sigh, like helping her annoyed him to no end. "Follow me."

He took her hand and went back around the restaurant, the way they had come. As soon as they were out of sight, she dropped his hand.

"So I guess this means you don't want to become Claire Pickford any time soon."

"Ha. No. I never even wanted to date him, but Mom kept making us sit beside each other at work dinners and putting us on the same projects, and she had some strategically placed mistletoe at Christmas, and before I realized what had happened, he was down on one knee yesterday." She shuddered.

Only her mother could successfully ambush someone with a proposal. Mom believed Everett to be perfect for Claire—and perfect for the future of Integrated Design. And with the same tenacity that made her company successful, she'd convinced Everett of those things as well.

"If someone doesn't save me from them, I will walk into work one day and find myself in the middle of my own surprise wedding."

Miguel coughed, but it sounded like he was covering a laugh. "Can't you tell them to back off?"

Claire grabbed his arm—his very large arm—and shook it. "Have you met my mother? She's like a hurricane. She will come in and have her way with your life, no matter how much you protest, and leave wreckage in her wake. Hasn't Dad told you horror stories about her?"

To her surprise, Miguel shook his head. "He doesn't talk about her much, other than to say how worried he is about you working with her."

Claire folded her arms and kicked at the gravel beneath her feet. "I like what I do at Integrated Design. I'm good at it. And working with Mom, I get the opportunity to do what I love."

"Which is what, exactly?"

"Building websites, mostly. I help with logo design sometimes, but Mom sends the websites my way because I'm the best."

He gave her an appreciative nod. "Really. Maybe you should look at ours sometime. We don't get much traffic there."

"Where do you get most of your business from?"

"Mostly from local hotels and restaurants handing out our fliers."

"But if you had a great website, your reach could go so much farther."

He shrugged. "We get enough, usually."

"Yeah, enough that you both have to work seven days a week to stay afloat."

His jaw clenched, and she wondered if she'd accidentally hit on a sensitive topic. "We like what we do," he said. Then he flashed her a smile. "And we're the best, too."

Claire nodded, not surprised. "Once a Bryson puts their mind to something, they succeed. Which means I *will* get Dad to come home with me."

"That's interesting, because I'm determined to make sure your dad stays, and I never lose."

His shoulder bumped against Claire's, and her stomach did a tiny twirl of anticipation at his challenge. How long had it been since someone challenged her instead of trying to run her life? She held out her hand, and Miguel took it in a firm handshake.

"May the best person win," she said to close the deal.

He winked. "My thoughts exactly."

Four

iguel checked in a large family for their overnight fishing trip while Claire sat in the deck chair with her laptop, her packed bag beside her. The tour had fourteen people in total, including a three-year-old. Miguel hesitated allowing anyone at such a young age, but turning the family away meant losing everyone. They couldn't afford to lose this many customers at a time, not with Brig's creditors breathing down their necks.

"This website is crap!" Claire muttered for the hundredth time in fifteen minutes. "What is this, a blog template? Miguel, who set this up?"

He felt her waiting, but he was in the middle of running a credit card on their old, touchy machine. The slightest bump, and he'd have to start over. "A little busy here," he called, then forced a smile at the guy standing in front of him.

"My wife sent in all the paperwork for Grandpa last

week. Did you get it?" the man asked, his voice gruff. He wore a bright-orange Hawaiian shirt over a pair of blue plaid shorts. Sunglasses hung against his chest by a strap.

"Sure did," Miguel replied. "Everything is set for tonight." The machine connected to the internet, and the card finally went through.

"You can get an app on your phone for that," Claire said from right beside him, her arm touching his. "You have to buy an attachment that hooks to the top of it. They're pretty cool. Sends an e-receipt to your customer, saving paper waste, too."

"Don't you have a plane to catch?" Miguel counted the heads of everyone on the ship. Everyone was there except Brig. To stay on schedule, they needed to leave in fifteen minutes. Brig had never missed an excursion.

"I'm just trying to help, though I shouldn't because I want this business to fail. So please, keep using outdated equipment that makes you look cheap, and keep your unprofessional website. All the better for me."

"What would really help me right now is if you could go through the bin of life vests and find a child-size one for him." He nodded to the kid running around the deck as if he'd had nothing but sugar for breakfast.

"You let kids on tours?"

"Not usually, but this is a special case. Brig made an exception."

"Excuse me," one woman said to Miguel. He stepped away from Claire to listen to her concerns about a dairy allergy. From the corner of his eye, he watched Claire find the big roller bin of life vests and snag a small orange one from it. Miguel breathed easier after the kid was snapped into the vest.

"Dad!" Claire called.

Brig walked onto the boat, his face flushed. Miguel raised his eyebrows at him, hoping for good news, but Brig shook his head. That might mean they weren't approved for the loan . . .

"Miguel, get the boat ready for us to head out," Brig said.

Miguel saluted and dragged in the walking plank. The ship was anchored by a couple of ropes to the dock, and he undid the first one. On the way to the second, he walked past Claire and Brig, but paused when he heard their conversation.

"I ran into your mom in the parking lot," Brig said.

She grabbed her dad's arm. "She found me?"

"I told her I hadn't seen you, but that woman can sniff out a lie from across state lines."

"Crap! I'm not ready to talk to her yet."

Miguel piped in. "You may be able to sneak out the back way. Don't go through the parking lot. Walk on the beach then circle around. When you get to the main road, call a cab."

"That could work." Claire hugged her dad. "But I'm not giving up on convincing you to come home."

"I know," he said, the affection evident in his voice.

She turned to Miguel. "You haven't won," she said, but he only smirked in return. She was leaving his boat and probably wouldn't return for another four years.

She took a long breath of ocean air, as if she still wasn't quite ready to leave, but stepped toward her bag. "You already took the plank down."

"I'll lift you over," Miguel said. He didn't wait for her permission before placing his hands on her waist and lifting her onto the dock. He'd been in too much of a rush that morning to notice then, but she smelled nice. Like coconuts.

94

He reached for her bag, but paused when a shrill voice sounded.

"Claire Avery Bryson, where have you been?" A woman—it had to be Debra, Brig's ex-wife—stalked down the dock in shoes even more ridiculous than Claire's had been. Did none of the Bryson women have any sense? "Leaving poor Everett in the middle of a romantic proposal. I did not raise you like this. And Brig!" Her eyes went wide and scary. Nana would call them crazy eyes. Even twenty feet away, he could see the whites all the way around her irises. "You said you hadn't seen her."

Miguel checked behind him, glad that most of the passengers were already in their bunks, putting their bags away. The few remaining had climbed up to the second level and seemed completely oblivious of the drama taking place below them.

"I lied," Brig said, clearly relishing each word. Miguel couldn't help but smile when her crazy eyes narrowed.

Claire twitched, looking like she wanted to do nothing more than bolt. Miguel was surprised at the protective urge that rose in him at her distress.

"And what are you wearing? Are those *flip flops*?" she said, as if her daughter had committed a fashion abomination akin to murder. With every word, she drew closer to Claire like a lion stalking its prey.

"Miguel," Claire said so quietly that he hardly heard her. "Get me back on the boat."

He didn't move at first, unsure if he heard her right. Her mom was almost within arm's reach.

"Now, Miguel!"

She lunged toward him just as his arms came up and grabbed her. Her soft body landed against his with more force than he expected, sending him stumbling a couple of steps, but he managed to keep them from falling to the deck.

Brig, meanwhile, had untied the last rope and now pushed their boat away from the pier. With a jaunty wave at his ex-wife, he headed toward the cockpit.

"Get your hands off my daughter," Debra yelled, her face red.

Only then did Miguel realize his arms were still around Claire, but he only tightened his hold. Claire didn't seem to mind. The engine kicked on and drowned out the rest of whatever Debra yelled. She waved her arms back and forth, and Everett even ran up the dock beside her.

"Where's he been?" Miguel asked, his mouth close to Claire's ear. This close, her silky hair smelled even better.

"Probably didn't want to get sand on his leather shoes." She waved at her mom with a cheerful smile.

"Now you're just taunting her."

"Like you're not doing the very same thing?" She motioned toward his hands, still at her waist.

"Hey, I don't see you trying to pull away."

"I swear she can still see us," she said, with a small shiver, though her mom was little more than a speck in the distance. Slowly her mouth stretched into a huge grin, and she let out a loud whoop. "I did it! I stood up to her."

"Technically, you ran away from her." He squinted in the direction of the dock and was pretty sure he could still see the whites of Debra's eyes. "She'll probably still be sitting on the end of the dock when we get back."

"Don't ruin my moment. Also, your whiskers tickle."

He responded by rubbing his chin against the soft skin of her neck. With a squeal, she pushed her ear toward her shoulder and tried to wriggle away.

"Hey, Miguel!" Brig stuck his head out of the cockpit. "I know my daughter's irresistible, but I could use some help running this ship!"

"Duty calls," Miguel whispered in her ear before letting her go, loving the blush that stole across her cheeks.

"Looks like I've got twenty-four more hours to put you out of business," she called to him. The wind blew her long hair across her face. He couldn't help but appreciate her form as she lifted a hand and tried to capture the wild strands. She looked like she was born to be at sea.

Miguel grinned at her challenge. "You have more shark in you than you let on."

She flashed her teeth, and he laughed. Yeah, the next twenty-four hours were going to be very interesting.

Five

The screen of Claire's laptop tipped away from her and was replaced by her dad's large hands. "Step away from the computer."

She blinked a few times to let her eyes adjust to life away from the screen. Since Miguel had disappeared to help her dad, Claire had pulled up a screenshot of their website and decided to play with it a little bit. Not because she wanted to help or anything. It just physically hurt her knowing that such a bad website existed out in the web world. Especially a site attached to her family's name.

Some things she couldn't do without WiFi, but she could build something pretty great in a few hours using the existing programs on her computer. With what she'd already done, clients could book tours online, ask questions, post pictures after their tour, and talk about their experiences. Potential customers could take a virtual tour of the Double B and see the excursion schedule for the upcoming year.

"What time is it?" she asked her dad.

"Just past five. Miguel's cooking up some fresh bass for dinner." As her dad spoke, the savory scent of fish drifted up from the galley.

Three hours had passed since she'd made the split decision to jump back onto the boat to escape her mother, and she hadn't regretted it for a second. So what if her plane ticket for this afternoon had gone unused?

Yes, she still worked—and lived—with her mom, and would have to face her eventually, but she'd decided to take a page out of Jade's book and worry about tomorrow, tomorrow. Today, she wanted to breathe in the salty air and pretend she lived the kind of life where ocean adventures were more than the stories she and Dad used to read together.

"It's been a long time since I took you fishing," her dad said.

Claire closed her laptop and swung her legs over the side of the lounge chair. "Don't you have a lot of stuff you need to do?"

He nodded, but held his hand out to help her up from the chair anyway. "But I've spent the last four years doing 'a lot of other stuff.' I miss my daughter."

Her heart warmed as she followed him to the edge of the ship, where he already had a fishing pole waiting for her. He reminded her how to cast it and reel it in, then handed it over for her to try.

"I have done this before," she reminded him and flung the line into the ocean.

"Now we wait." Dad leaned his arms against the railing. After a moment, he leaned forward more, squinting. "See that?"

She followed her dad's finger pointing to a dark, shadowy spot below the surface of the water.

"Is that a whale?"

The tip of a fin came up then glided back under and dove out of sight.

"Shark," he said.

A chill ran through her, but the dark spot was gone. "Remind me to skip out on the evening dip."

He laughed and pulled her into a side hug, still favoring his injured arm. "I always knew you were the smart one in the family." He inhaled deeply. "It's been too long."

"It has," Claire said, content. She leaned beside him, using one hand to hold on to the pole so she'd feel if anything bit. Ocean mist sprayed her face and arms, cool on her sun-bathed skin. Gentle waves lapped the edges of the boat, rocking them in the water. The sun hovered several feet above the horizon; they still had a few more hours before sunset.

"Will we see fireworks out here?"

"The naval base does them about a mile that way as soon as it's dark." He pointed northeast. "One of the most spectacular shows you'll ever see."

"I haven't seen fireworks in years." She felt a small tug on her line, and for a moment, wondered if she'd snagged a shark, but it when she reeled it in, the line was empty. She put on new bait, threw her line out again, and watched it sink into the dark water. The wind blew against her face, taking most of her worries with it. She'd have to deal with Mom and Everett tomorrow, and things would be ugly after she'd run away today, but with how perfect everything felt at that moment, she had a hard time caring.

"Claire, remember the time we built that model boat of toothpicks?"

"Our dream boat," she said.

"We were going to buy the real thing and sail off as soon as you graduated from high school." He shook his head with a smile. "We spent hours on that thing, but before we could finish, your mom had the maid toss it."

She picked at something sticky on the railing, remembering how devastated she'd been when she'd discovered it was gone. "I still can't look at toothpicks without thinking about it."

"You and I—we used to have a lot of dreams."

Claire's back straightened, the levity of the moment gone. "And that's all they were, Dad. Dreams."

"What if they could be more?" He touched her on the nose like he used to do when she was little. "I shouldn't have left you with her."

"I was already an adult when you got divorced. It's not like you gave up custody or anything." And although that was true, part of her had felt like he *had* given up on her, that he'd walked away and chosen a life out here over being her dad.

He'd taken their dreams and left her out of them.

"In a way, I did give up custody. And your mom is still too quick to throw things away you care about." He sighed and pushed off from the edge of the boat. He never did like to talk bad about Mom, even when he had plenty negative things he could say. Meanwhile, Mom preferred to act as if he didn't exist, that Claire and Jade were the product of her and her alone.

Beside them, someone struggled to reel in their line, hollering with excitement. Dad watched them, eyes distant. "Your mom wants you to be like the hook on the end of her line—always going where she throws you, always ready to catch her newest goal." He stepped away from the side of the boat and turned to look at Claire, his eyes clear. "Your mom will take everything you give her and more. Don't give your whole life away just to make her happy."

"I'm not," Claire insisted.

But was she? She did enjoy building websites, but she hated being accountable to her mom, and having her mother run her life. Following Claire to San Diego had taken things too far.

"Okay," her dad said, and tugged her into a hug. "I'm glad you're here."

She breathed in the sun, the sweat, the scent of frying fish and finally released her resentment in one long exhale. She shouldn't have waited so long to come see him, but she'd stayed away because she'd known this would happen—the old longing would return for the kind of life she could never have. Still, for one night, maybe she could pretend that this was her reality.

Plus, she'd missed her dad more than she realized.

"I'm glad I'm here too."

Six

Claire finished putting away the spices and dishes Miguel had used to cook dinner. The sun edged closer to the water, and everyone on the ship had grown quiet and somber. Even Ethan, the three-year-old, was no longer running around as much as earlier.

Dad had asked her to clean up the galley, dress in something nice, and meet everyone on deck. With the dishes clean, she slipped into her room and put on a breezy, knee-length sundress she'd borrowed from Jade. It was a deep turquoise, nearly the same shade as Claire's eyes, with random bursts of peach blossoms. She slid her hair out of the pony tail it had been in all day then ran a brush through the wind-blown tangles. After swiping a bit of peach gloss across her lips, she headed up to the main deck where everyone was already gathered.

The tour group was quiet, mostly wearing shades of navy and gray, and the men were all hatless. Her dad stood in front of them all with a basket in hand. She came up behind the group and had to do a double take when she looked at the man beside her. Without warning, her heart skipped a beat.

Miguel had shaved his beard down to a goatee and trimmed his hair until it was tame—and he looked amazing. Gone was the wild, scary man from earlier, and in his place stood someone who would fit in at a model shoot. He wore a pressed white oxford shirt with navy slacks, and a serious expression on his face.

"You can stop staring any time now," he whispered while not taking his eyes off the basket. His mouth twitched with the promise of a smile.

"I'm not staring," she lied. Even after he'd called her out on it, she couldn't take her eyes off him. She swallowed and forced herself to face forward. "What's going on?"

"Burial at sea."

"Oh." All around her, the family listened to her dad explain the process of lowering a water-soluble basket to the bottom and releasing it. After time, the ashes inside the basket would become a part of the ocean itself, and they would always be able to visit this location again, like one might visit a grave in a cemetery. She nodded toward the basket. "Do you do this kind of thing a lot?"

"Maybe six times a year. Sometimes family comes, like now, and turns it into a huge trip. The deceased, Marty, loved nothing more than fishing with his family. They wanted to turn this into a memorial trip."

Her dad stepped aside, and one of the other adults—Marty's son—stood to share memories of his father. She hadn't known Marty, or any of his family, yet she felt herself growing teary as they recalled the fun things they had done together with Marty. She glanced at her dad and caught him watching her back. She swiped at her eyes, and Miguel thrust a wad of blue-tinted toilet paper at her.

"Thanks."

Her dad took over again and explained to the family how to lower the basket into the water. When the remains dipped beneath the surface, Marty's son grew emotional.

Miguel's hand rested on Claire's lower back, and she wondered if he realized that his thumb was rubbing up and down her spine, sending tingles through her body. He watched the basket as well, his own eyes suspiciously shiny. Everything she'd thought about him shifted. He still looked completely rough around the edges—definitely not the kind of person you'd want to run into in a dark alley alone—yet there was a softness to him she hadn't seen at first.

He'd retrieved her shoe. He delivered fish to old women. And he did everything he could to keep her dad's business running. Suddenly she was filled with an insatiable curiosity about the man beside her: What drove him? What made him who he was—this mix of pirate and gentleman?

"Should we give them some privacy?" he murmured in her ear.

The family stood in a solemn row along the railing of the boat and watched until the basket was swallowed up into the depths of the ocean. Claire nodded and followed Miguel to the other side of the ship. At some point today, he'd strung a hammock from some hooks on the second level. Now it swayed in the breeze. He plopped down onto it, his feet hanging off the side, and patted the spot beside him.

"Will it hold us both?" Claire asked, doubtful. In response, Miguel tugged her down beside him and shifted so they were both lying on the hammock, his arm behind her. "We're really close," she whispered.

"That's the point," he said, amusement in his voice. He squeezed her shoulders. "Relax. This is paradise."

She tried to ease the tension from her shoulders then ended up staring at the stars popping one by one into the night sky. The sea and sky stretched out around them, seemingly forever, and it was easy to feel as if she and Miguel were the only two people in the world.

"What would you do if you didn't work here with my dad?" she asked suddenly.

He shifted, getting more comfortable, and somehow she found herself snuggled up to his muscular side. The cool ocean breeze blew across her bare arms, and she was glad for the warmth. "You mean if the business went under?"

"Could that happen?" Her heart didn't lift at the possibility like she'd expected it to.

He didn't respond for so long that she thought he'd blown her off. But he finally answered. "It might," he said. "This morning, Brig did more than talk to the fishing and licensing people. He stopped at the bank. We need another loan to do repairs and keep this place going, but it wasn't approved."

She lifted her head to look at him. "You don't make enough to be self-sustaining?"

"Lots of companies like ours are out here. Ones that have several boats, unlimited free alcohol, and tons of advertising dollars. We have one boat, all you can drink soda, and fliers handed out by local businesses to people who most likely made their travel plans before ever even hearing of us."

"So most of your business comes from word of mouth?"

"All of it," he corrected. He turned his head toward her, bringing their faces really close. "Last year, our website got a little more than two hundred hits."

"You can't run a business nowadays without an online presence!"

"You know your dad avoids computers at all costs. I'm

lucky I even got my GED, okay?" A defensive edge had crept into his voice, and his body grew tense beside her.

She rested her head on his arm again, her mind whirling. "You could hire someone."

He let out a short laugh, but it lacked humor. "With what money?"

She almost offered to do it herself but bit the words back in time. She wanted Dad to leave this all behind. If she stepped in to help him, he'd stay out here forever.

"You didn't answer my question," she said instead. "What would you do if you didn't have this anymore?"

"I don't know. Probably follow Brig back to Colorado or help him open another business."

"You'd move with him to another state? What about your life here?"

"My life here," he repeated with a humorless laugh. Absently he rubbed his scarred knuckles against his chin. "It wasn't much of a life until I met your dad. He found me half dead on the beach. He cleaned me up and taught me how to run a ship even though I didn't want to learn. For the first year, I planned to steal the boat and sell it, maybe leave him to the same people I'd been fighting my whole life. But he never gave up on me," he said, his tone filled with awe.

"He doesn't give up easily," Claire murmured as she took in Miguel, now knowing a piece of his history. It wasn't too far from what she'd guessed already—that he'd had some sort of rough past. She just didn't know how far removed he was from the person who'd been in fights brutal enough to leave scars.

"After a while, I stopped trying to sneak back to my old life, and I got more and more involved in helping Brig. My dad kicked me out of the house when I was fifteen for getting into too much trouble, and that's the last time I stepped foot

in my high school, too. I've been in and out of jail, though."
He chuckled at some memory. "I yelled at your dad a lot.
Screwed with the ropes just to piss him off. One time I even
punched him in the jaw—left a huge bruise, too, but he never
made me leave. I have no idea why."

But Claire did. Her dad had always had a soft spot for
the underdog—one of the reasons she thought he connected
with her more than Jade, who almost never had a problem
standing up to Mom or living her life her own way, but
Claire had always struggled to take what she wanted.

"He paid for me to do night school and get my GED.
For the first time in my whole life, I knew that someone
believed I was more than a screw-up."

"Wow." Feelings of pride for what her dad had done—
and for what Miguel had accomplished—welled up inside
her.

"He used to tell me these stories," Miguel said. "Ones he
said he read to you as a kid. They were always about
adventures at sea—getting lost, finding treasure, fighting
pirates. He said the pirate stories were always your favorite."

"I can't believe how much he's told you about me."

"We've had a lot of time, just the two of us, over the last
four years." He paused, reflective. "If Double B's went under,
I would help Brig build up whatever kind of business he
wanted, and I would do everything I could to make it
succeed. I don't have many skills, but one thing I learned on
the street is how to be scrappy."

"And you're loyal to him." What would it be like to have
someone like Miguel care that much about her?

"He's like a father to me."

A comfortable silence fell, and somehow every bit of
space that had existed between them had vanished. His
minty breath fanned her cheeks, and her lungs stopped

working for a moment. His dark eyes shined with the reflection of the stars.

"You're different tonight," she whispered.

"It's the hair."

"No. It's more. You're softer."

He shrugged. "Burials at sea always make me reflective." He nudged her gently. "You're different tonight too."

"How so?"

"Less soft. Like you have some fire in you that wasn't there yesterday."

His words made her warm all over. No one had ever described her as having fire in her. She was always the compliant one, the reliable one. Not the kind of girl who defied her mom, who jumped onto a moving ship, or who lay in a hammock with a man she'd met only twenty-four hours before.

"I *feel* different." Her words were breathy as she searched his eyes, looking for some hint of his thoughts.

He smiled. "It's the magic of the ocean," he said, and then his mouth covered hers in a gentle kiss. She wrapped her hand behind his head and pulled him closer, loving the silky feeling of the dark strands between her fingers. His other hand came behind her back, so she was cocooned in his arms, their kiss awakening feelings inside that she'd never felt before.

Somehow they'd gotten even closer, when a loud crack over their head sent them reeling apart. Claire's heart pounded wildly, and her eyes darted frantically for the noise until she saw a firework explode in the sky above them. She couldn't stop the laugh that escaped from her chest—the full kind of laugh that used most of her body and released all of the tension that had built up inside over her over the past several days.

"I've kissed a lot of women, but I've never made literal fireworks go off. I am good."

"Not that good," she lied. Okay, maybe she *had* seen sparks behind her eyes before the literal ones went off.

He shook his head in resignation and drew his fingers across his goatee. "It's the beard. Or lack thereof. If I still had it, this would have been a much better experience for you."

"No, no." She shook her head vehemently, remembering the food caught in it earlier. "I like you this way much better."

"So I clean up good, huh?"

"You know you do." Claire smacked his chest lightly, but then left her hand there as she snuggled into his side. "Despite my first impression with the whole homeless, killer vibe you had going on, I like you, Miguel."

Even without seeing him, she could feel his smile.

"I've always liked you, Claire. From the first moment your dad started telling stories about you, I've wanted to meet you."

Now Claire was the one smiling. It stretched from ear to ear so wide, it almost hurt.

"Am I what you expected?"

He tilted her head up and placed the lightest of kisses on her mouth. "Better," he said against her lips. And while fireworks lit up the sky behind them, Miguel pulled her into another kiss that took her breath away.

Seven

"Some show last night, huh?" Claire's dad said from behind her.

She gave him a distracted nod and reeled in an empty line again. "Yeah. It was colorful." They'd be heading back to shore in an hour, and she was the only person on board who still hadn't caught a fish. Even little Ethan had pulled in a six-pound sculpin with his dad's help.

"I meant the one in the hammock."

Claire's heart dropped along with the pole in her hand. She scrambled to pick it up, then turned to him, face burning. "You saw that?"

"It was kind of hard to miss." He chuckled. "Came out when I heard the fireworks, ended up seeing more than I bargained for."

"Dad, I know it was irresponsible of me—"

"Hey." He held up a hand, and she was glad he'd cut off whatever she was about to say.

She should apologize for distracting Miguel and crossing a line, but she didn't want to. Last night was amazing, and even though she knew it would never happen again, she couldn't bring herself to regret it either.

Yet, she kind of regretted that her dad caught her making out on his boat.

"Don't overthink this. He's a good one." Before she could process her dad's approval, he yelled, "Miguel! My girl needs your help."

"No I don't!"

He winked and pushed away from the railing then went to help someone else.

Miguel came up from behind and wrapped his arms around her then placed a light kiss on her neck. She shivered despite the warm sun.

"My dad will see," she said, but didn't move out of his arms.

"I don't think he cares." His lips brushed against her ear. "Besides, he sent me over to help you, and he's the boss."

At that, Claire stepped away from him. "I don't need help!"

"How many fish have you caught again?" He folded his arms and raised one infuriating eyebrow. Without all of the hair covering his face, it was easier to see his expressions—and too tempting to stare at his lips.

"I have the blood of Double B himself flowing through my veins," she reminded him.

"Which is where all your orneriness comes from."

"No, it means I have a natural affinity for sport fishing." She pushed him away to have an excuse to touch him, something obvious when she kept her hands on his firm chest. "You're distracting me."

He smiled knowingly and stepped forward to give her a

welcome kiss on the lips. "Distracting you is something I could get very used to."

Me, too.

"Miguel," one of the customers called. "Can you come over here when you get a second?" Even from where she stood, Claire could see that his line had become hopelessly tangled. She sighed and recast her own.

"You guys make a cute couple," little Ethan's mom, Brianne, said with a smile.

"Thanks." Claire thought about explaining that they weren't a couple, not really, but she didn't want to have to get into the logistics of figuring out what to call the person you were trying to put out of business but really liked kissing.

"I can't believe he's the same guy as the one we saw when coming onboard, with all that hair. I think my husband's disappointed he shaved it all off. He was talking about growing his own beard out." She shuddered, and Claire had to agree with the sentiment. She glanced over at Brianne's husband—the one with the tangled line.

Miguel had cut it and was showing him how to restring it, his strong hands making intricate motions he'd surely done a million times before. She knew a dopey smile was spreading across her face but couldn't help it. He glanced up and caught her watching him, and his return wink made her heart skip a beat.

A flash of orange from the corner of her eye made her turn her head.

Brianne didn't see it and continued, "I don't know what it is with men and facial hair. Sometimes I think—"

In a blink, the orange object had fallen over the side of the ship. Claire knew immediately what had happened; the toddler had fallen overboard.

"It's Ethan!" she screamed at Miguel, cutting off Brianne, whose face had turned pale. Without thinking, Claire ran to the side of the ship, stepped onto the edge, and jumped into the freezing cold ocean. She scanned one way and then the other before she spied the bobbing life jacket twenty feet away. She could barely hear the little boy's frightened wails over the sound of the blood rushing through her ears.

Using muscles she hadn't used since swim team in college, she swam as fast as she could to Ethan, calling to him as she went. Within in seconds, she had him by the vest and pulled him to her chest.

"Ethan, it's okay. It's okay. I've got you, bud. We're going to swim back to the ship to see your mom and dad, okay? I need you to wrap your arms around my neck."

He held tight to her, but his life jacket made it awkward for her to swim. A dark shadow glided beneath the surface not far away. She couldn't tell if it was a shark, and she didn't want to wait around to find out.

"Side stroke," she whispered to keep her mind calm, then began the motions.

"Take this!"

She turned, surprised and relieved to see Miguel treading water beside her with a life preserver.

"I think—there's a shark—over there," she said, her words coming out in between gasps.

His expression grim, Miguel held out the preserver. She grabbed it with one hand, still holding Ethan with the other, and Miguel used the rope to drag them back to the ship. There, he led them to the stairs of the lower deck, where he helped lift Ethan up first before jumping up himself and reaching down to help Claire out of the water. She shivered, the chill hitting her worse that the coldness she'd felt after

Dad left. The Pacific was so much icier than she imagined. The wind kicked up, causing goose bumps to break out across her trembling body.

Brianne held a soaking-wet Ethan close in her arms. *Thank you*, she mouthed to Claire.

Claire gave her a thumbs up and headed to the upper deck to get some sun. Her dad was there waiting for her with a towel to wrap around her and another one for Ethan. Miguel took each of her arms in his hands and rubbed up and down to warm her up.

"You were quick," he said, his tone impressed. "You'd almost reached him before I even realized what had happened."

"I saw him at the right time," she said with a shudder. "Did you see something in the water?"

He nodded, and she decided not to ask what it was. His tense expression was enough of an answer. Ethan's parents hovered over their son, both of them in tears.

Miguel stopped rubbing her arms warm and pulled her into a hug.

"That was amazing," she said, looking up at him, feeling giddy now that some of the adrenaline was wearing off. She'd jumped into the ocean to save a little boy. She hadn't thought through it first or waited for someone else to do it, like she always did. Instead, she'd just jumped into the freezing, shark-infested Pacific to save a little boy. She was kind of a hero.

"You are amazing," Miguel said, his nose brushing hers. "And you're cold. Why don't you go change before we have to head back to shore?"

"If I don't change, does that mean we get to stay here forever?" The words fell from her lips before she could filter them. Being a hero made her say brave things. Or stupid

115

things, seeing as how they both knew that as soon as the Double B's was docked at the harbor, this romance between them would end.

"Yes," Miguel said fervently, a teasing twinkle in his eye. "You'll wear these clothes for the rest of your life, and we'll live off fish. It will be fulfilling to watch Ethan grow into an adult on this ship."

"I think so," she replied back. "Except his family might not like that."

"And if I had to be stranded in the middle of the ocean, I'd rather it just be with you."

Her stomach twirled. She placed her hand across it and took a deep breath.

Brig came up behind them, and Miguel reluctantly let her go. Brig gave her a kiss on her temple. "You did good, Claire. Ready to head back to land?"

Claire closed her eyes and took a deep breath. It had been too much to hope that she'd never have to face her problems again. Being on this boat with Miguel and her dad had been a fantasy. A dream.

And the thing about dreams was eventually, you woke up.

Eight

om was sitting in a lounge chair with a striped umbrella to protect her from the sun, sipping a margarita at the end of the dock. Claire had spotted the umbrella as soon as the boat got close, and she knew exactly whose it was.

Miguel whistled under his breath. "Your mom is insane."

"Little bit. Jade and I call her *intense*."

"That, too." He finished clicking all the fishing poles into their holders before turning to Claire. "You're really going to go with her?"

"I have to." Claire folded her arms and leaned against the doorframe while Miguel walked toward her. As soon as he was close enough, she wrapped her arms around his waist. She'd never wanted to be this close to someone so much in her life. In only a few days, he'd worked his way into her heart, but he was a part of the fantasy, and it was time to let go.

She hugged him and slipped away. He dropped his arms, but she could feel his stare as she walked away. Her dad hugged her and helped her onto the dock, where her mom glanced up from her phone with a smug smile.

"Have fun, dear?"

Claire waved at the chair, the drink, the fact her mother was sitting there waiting for her, as if she were still a teenager. "This is ridiculous, Mom. I can't even talk to you right now." She stalked past, her flip flops making loud thwacking noises against the dock.

Her mom grabbed her and yanked her to a stop, her fingernails digging into Claire's arm. "You will stop acting childish this instant. It's one thing to skip off for a little vacation, but to leave Everett hanging, to run from me yesterday? Unacceptable behavior. I might expect Jade to act like this, but never you."

"Is Everett still here?" Claire asked through her tight jaw.

"He's grabbing us some lunch. Oh, there he is." Her mother's hard face transformed into a smile when she saw Everett and waved him over.

He was tall, tanned, and blond. The perfect all-American man with two degrees and the kind of ambition that would quickly propel him to the top of Mom's growing company. His white teeth and sky-blue eyes sparkled first at her mom, then at her. Most people might have thought that he was more handsome than Miguel—the wild, unshaven Miguel, at least—but what Everett had in appearance, he lacked in passion, integrity, wit, and everything else Claire found attractive.

"You're back," he said with relief. He took Claire's hands and leaned in for a kiss, but she yanked away before their lips could meet.

"Claire!" her mom admonished under her breath.

A vision popped into Claire's head of exactly what awaited her for the rest of her life if she left this dock with her mom and Everett. She'd marry him, but he'd love success more than he loved her. Mom would always be there to make their life decisions—where they lived, how many kids they had, what she did at work.

Mom would set her lounge chair by Claire's front door then yank and cast and reel until Claire's life turned into nothing but a tool for everyone around her to use how they saw fit.

She couldn't face a future like that. Not now. Not ever.

"I won't marry you," Claire told Everett. His eyes widened in disbelief. She folded her arms to ward off any attempts he might try at persuasion. "My answer is no."

Mom gasped and grabbed Claire's arm. "She doesn't mean it, Everett. It's the sun getting to her. She must have heatstroke! Or it's her irresponsible father. That man—"

"Mom, stop," Claire snapped, and to her astonishment, her mom actually shut her mouth. "Don't talk bad about Dad. Don't follow me around like I'm a teenager. Don't try to run my life or set me up with people who only want to move up in the company. Better yet, don't set me up with anyone, ever. Let me live my life!"

Mom's eyes darkened, her mouth tightened, and it was as if a box had closed, tucking away every emotion but anger. "You would do well to remember that not only am I your mother, but I am also your boss. I'm the one who makes sure you get the assignments you love. Or don't love."

"I quit." Once she said it, a sense of rightness filled every part of her. "I quit," she repeated because she liked saying it so much. A huge weight had lifted from her shoulders, and she even laughed.

"You can't quit. You love your job!"

"I did. But working together isn't good for us. Being out here showed me that I have to go out, do my own thing for a while. Find out who I am and what I want to be."

Mom's eyes narrowed even further. "You sound just like your dad."

Even though Mom didn't mean it as a compliment, Claire smiled. "Thank you. Now if you'll excuse me, I have something to do." Adrenaline rushed through her body, much like when she'd jumped into the ocean to save Ethan.

Everett tucked his arm around her stunned mother, and walked with her toward the parking lot without even a goodbye. Claire knew this wasn't over—Mom wouldn't let her go that easy—but she was firm in her decision. She was jobless and soon to be homeless, but she was free, and right then there was nothing else she'd rather be.

"Hey!" she yelled at the empty ship. "Dad! Miguel!"

The men came out from the galley, Miguel still in his board shorts but no shirt, her dad wearing sunglasses and a floppy hat that a client had given him. The sun was too bright for her to read their expressions, so she couldn't tell how they felt about seeing her so soon after saying goodbye.

"Any chance you could use a crew member?"

Miguel let out a whoop, and Dad threw his hat into the air before helping her back onboard. "I knew if you came out here once, you'd never be able to go back."

On some level, Claire had known that all along. Maybe that was one reason she'd taken so long to get out here.

Before she could respond, she was wrapped up in Miguel's embrace, her face pressed against one of the tattoos on his chest—some kind of bird, though it was difficult to tell from this angle. Pulling ropes and working on a ship had been good for him. Very good for him.

"You still going to try to convince your dad to try to give this all up?" Miguel asked.

"Nah. Thought I might make you guys a decent website instead. I actually worked out an entire business model that has the potential to make Double B's very successful over time—"

Miguel's mouth dropped over hers in a thorough kiss, interrupting her explanation. Not that she minded one bit.

Epilogue

One year later

"You know, in romance novels, making out on the beach always seemed more romantic than it actually is," Claire said, tugging at the edge of her swimsuit to let some of the sand out.

Miguel laughed, the full-body kind that always made Claire's heart skip a beat. That was something she'd grown to love about Miguel—he was all in with everything he did, whether it was laughing, growing a beard, or building a business.

And relationships. He was pretty good at those, too.

They lay, tangled together in the soft sand of Flamenco beach, watching the sun set over the sparkling turquoise water near Culebra. Claire didn't know if she'd ever seen anything more beautiful.

"Is it weird that I wanted to go to a beach for our honeymoon?" she asked. They spent almost every day on a boat, working and living with her dad. Her awe of the ocean should have worn off by now, but instead, she fell in love with it all over again every time they went out to sea.

"No weirder than anything else you do." Miguel tickled her side until she laughed with him.

"So *I'm* the weird one?" she said, out of breath. "Who goes all recluse-bomber hairy once a month? Hmm?"

"You know you love the beard. Admit it. You fell in love with me because of that very thing."

"If I remember it correctly—and I do—it wasn't until after you shaved it off that I fell for you."

"Nope. We had a moment before then, when you jumped onto the boat to escape your crazy mom. I held you, you looked into my eyes, your heart leapt at the manliness of my beard, and you knew right then that you'd give up everything to be with such a manly man."

Claire groaned and brushed more itchy sand off her legs. Her mom had come to their wedding but still didn't think Miguel was good enough for her daughter. Too many tattoos, not enough degrees. Mom and Jade had come out together, but had left soon after the ceremony. Claire's relationship with her mom would never be the same, but in a lot of ways, that was okay.

"You're going to tell that version of how we fell in love to everyone we meet, aren't you?"

"It's the truth!" He placed light kisses along her jaw and neck, turning her mind to mush.

"We've come a long way," she breathed as his mouth continued to work its way down her shoulder.

In the past year, Double B's had expanded so much that they now owned two ships and had additional staff besides the three of them. A Double B's storefront was set to open in a month, complete with equipment for purchase and a real office. They'd even been able to take off a full week for their wedding and honeymoon without worrying what would happen to the business in their absence.

Well, Claire worried a little.

"Do you think Dad will remember how to update the website? He doesn't even have to worry about HTML . . ."

Miguel growled and tackled her back onto the sand. "I love it when you talk corporate to me."

Claire laughed then tucked her fingers into the silky strands of his hair. "I worry too much, don't I?"

"You do. He'll probably do it wrong, and you'll have to fix it when we get back, but who cares? I'm in paradise with the most beautiful girl in the world, and for some reason, she's in love with me."

"It's the beard," Claire teased, running her fingers along his stubbly jaw. "And the tattoos. Have I ever told you how much you look like a pirate?"

"A few times." He pressed his mouth into hers again, and Claire poured her entire heart into the kiss. Soon all thoughts of itchy sand and potential website disasters at home drifted far from her thoughts. Nothing mattered but this moment with the man who'd helped make her dreams come true.

There would always be a million things that could go wrong, but right now, she wanted to focus on what was perfectly right in her life. Miguel's arms held her close, and she knew that with him, she would have a lifetime of beards and banter, endless chapters of adventures at sea, and love like she'd never felt before.

Life couldn't get much better.

ABOUT KAYLEE BALDWIN

A glamorous day in the life of Kaylee Baldwin includes: chasing after her four children, obsessively checking her email, writing her latest book, trying to get motivated to train for that race she shouldn't have signed up for, hanging out with her seriously awesome husband, and reading in every spare second she can find.

She graduated from Arizona State University with a degree in English lit and currently lives in southern Arizona with her family. Her books include Whitney Award finalist Meg's Melody, Six Days of Christmas, and Silver Linings.

Kaylee blogs at KayleeBaldwin.com and loves to connect with readers on Twitter: @kayleebaldwin1

The Pier Changes Everything

Annette Lyon

OTHER WORKS BY ANNETTE LYON

Band of Sisters
Coming Home
The Newport Ladies Book Club series
A Portrait for Toni
At the Water's Edge
Lost Without You
A Midwinter Ball
Done & Done
There, Their, They're: A No-Tears Guide to Grammar from
the Word Nerd

One

To many people, the flight from Sky Harbor Airport in Phoenix to Long Beach would hardly have felt like a flight at all. In truth, as flights went, this one was short—only about 80 minutes. Alexandria Davis had certainly been on her share of long flights before, ones you counted in double-digit hours instead of minutes. But the truth was, she'd been so eager to leave Arizona that this time, the entire process of flying—from going through security, to boarding, to watching the instructional video, to takeoff, and finally, to landing—felt like it had all taken much longer than her flight to France.

Of course, traveling with someone you cared about to do something particularly fun beat the pants off of flying away to do something you weren't so crazy about doing. Even when it meant escaping nastiness at home.

The plane finally landed in California. She disembarked on an outdoor ramp instead of through a jetway. After getting her luggage, she'd rent a car, and then . . . She hadn't thought past that. Maybe she'd check into a hotel right away or get something to eat first. The beach—and Jason's ashes—could wait a few more hours, even if the screw-top jar in her big red purse felt as heavy as a barbell pulling at her shoulder.

This day had been in the making for five years. She rarely dwelt on the past—anymore, anyway. But this trip inevitably shone a spotlight on it, not exactly letting her forget everything that had led up to this point.

When she'd first made the promise to release Jason's ashes over the Pacific Ocean on their fifth wedding anniversary, the future had stretched before her like a long, meandering road through the woods. The end of that five-year path had seemed like it would always be a lifetime away. She'd even argued that she wouldn't be *able* to spread his ashes at their five-year mark, because of *course* he'd still be alive.

She'd even meant it, even though his bone cancer was terminal. Truthfully, Alexandria still had a hard time grasping the finality of death. And how fast time moved.

Did Einstein ever account for that kind of relativity? The kind that could make some years fly by like weeks and others feel like decades? Because even at twenty-three, she sometimes felt old enough to be checking for gray hairs.

From the ramp, she walked across the pavement and into the airport, following the other passengers as they headed toward the luggage carousel. She passed palm trees bigger and greener than those in Arizona. Out of habit, she took her phone out of her purse and checked for messages, only then realizing it was still in airplane mode. She turned that off and waited to make sure she didn't need to respond to anything urgent.

At the carousel, she quickly found her pink-and-white polka-dotted suitcase, something she used not because she loved it—the fuchsia polka dots bordered on overkill—but because it was easy to spot in a sea of blue and black suitcases. Some people thought her red purse clashed with her auburn hair as well as with the pink suitcase. Not that she cared. She rolled it behind her as she left the airport, crossed a parking lot, where she found a car rental. Inside the small building, a long counter ran down the length, separating the small office area from customers.

Alex stood in line behind the only other person there, a middle-aged man. The door jangled behind her at the same moment her phone began chiming over and over with incoming texts and phone messages, as if frantically catching up.

She sighed. It wasn't as if she'd been out of reach for long. But she was flying on a workday, so she couldn't exactly be surprised at the deluge. She just hoped most of her missed communications would be via email; those tended to be sent by non-panicked clients. Lots of texts and phone messages usually meant she'd be talking someone off a ledge.

She tossed her long braid over her shoulder and grabbed her phone from a purse pocket. Hopefully none of her clients had an urgent crisis, like a tech package missing major specs. That had happened only once, when she'd first started her pattern design business and before she'd fully learned the computer end of things. Instead of handing over a packet with every piece of information any clothing factory in the world could use to create her pattern, the client had been stuck until Alex frantically found the missing information and sent it over. She'd never made that kind of mistake again.

She thought through her current projects and decided that the most likely "emergency" would be from Charlotte, the owner of Isn't She Lovely Design, a line of clothes for little girls. She'd asked several times when the work would be done, in spite of the fact that the contract spelled out the delivery date. Alex never missed a deadline, and even when she finished early, she sometimes waited until the promised day to return the work to avoid these kinds of calls for future projects.

Her phone showed seven texts and four missed calls—probably all from Charlotte. She'd made contact in some way—calls, emails, texts—several times a day over the last month. Alex was ready to add a clause to the contract saying that any communications beyond fifty in the first month would be charged extra, if nothing else, than to rein in the Charlottes of the world.

She took a sip from her bottled water as she checked the phone log. Two people had called. Sure enough, Charlotte had called a little over an hour ago.

All three of the other calls were from Madeleine Kendall—Jason's mother. Technically, Alex's former mother-in-law, although they'd never had anything remotely approximating that relationship. No, theirs resembled more that of a velociraptor stalking its prey, and Alex could never prove that she didn't deserve to be eaten, consumed, and discarded.

It's not my fault that your son died. Or that he wanted to marry me. Or that I inherited his money. The thought had become almost an automatic response to thoughts of Madeleine Kendall.

To Alex, the woman was never just *Madeleine* or even *Mrs. Kendall.* During the few times they'd crossed paths in person, for better or worse—usually worse—she'd referred to Jason's mother as *Mrs. Kendall* but secretly wondered if she could provoke a heart attack by calling her *Madeleine.*

Alex stared at her phone, unwilling to listen to Madeleine Kendall's messages and not wanting to look at her texts, either. She was quite sure, now, that most of them were also from Madeleine Kendall.

More than once, Alex had considered changing her cell number just to avoid the woman, and she would have gone through with it in a heartbeat if it hadn't also meant antagonizing her further, confirming in her mind that some teenage hussy had brainwashed her only son and taken him from her.

But the biggest reason she kept her old number was the hassle a new one would create for business. Alex's company had grown a lot in the last eight months—she'd landed several contracts with international clothing companies—and she didn't want the pain of making sure a couple of hundred other people had her new number, printing up new business cards, and changing her website information, or risking losing word-of-mouth referrals from people who had only her old number, all because of a woman who harassed her a few times a year.

Most of the time, it wasn't too bad anyway; Madeleine Kendall went weeks—sometimes months—without any contact save for the occasional passive-aggressive Facebook post, interspersed with calls around big holidays and anniversaries. Jason's birthday in March. The anniversary of his diagnosis in May. The day he passed away in July, something Madeleine Kendall would never forgive Alex for, because as his mother, she had earned the "right" to be at his side when he took his last breath. She refused to believe that Alex hadn't known he would die when he did. That she'd kept trying to call Jason's mother but that Jason had kept begging her to hold his hand, to keep talking to him. And he'd passed away without Madeline Kendall's presence.

Probably as he wanted it to be.

But his mother had certainly made her presence known ever since, particularly on the anniversary of, in her words, "the biggest betrayal of her life," the day Alex and Jason sneaked off to a justice of the peace. He'd walked—slowly—on his prosthetic leg. She'd carried his medications in a bag over her shoulder. And they'd gotten married—on this day, April 25, five years ago. It had been more than a month before their high school graduation. Both of them were legal adults by then, so no one could stop them.

In her memory, their wedding day stood as a landmark for so many parts of her life, events she'd always think of as either *before* her wedding or *after* her wedding. Moments that made her head spin to think of all.

They'd married after Jason made almost a million dollars from three brilliant apps. They all still sold like crazy, with regular deposits into the account he'd moved all of his income into after turning eighteen so his parents couldn't touch it.

The understated wedding took place before he'd grown too ill to do basic things like walk around the grocery store or go to a movie . . . or eventually, feed himself, dress himself, brush his own teeth.

Yet when they wed, he'd already been given less than a year to live.

When Alex had said *I do*, her business was no more than a sparkly idea scribbled into a notebook, but Jason insisted that she pursue her company full throttle, fully believing she could succeed and insisting she use the money he'd never be able to spend and wanted her to have.

On their wedding day, she'd still been slim thanks to the fat camp, where her fourth foster family had sent her the summer they'd toured Europe. She regained the weight after

Jason's death, drowning her stress and depression with food. At least she'd lost the weight. Again. He'd be proud of her for that, and she hung on to that thought because the one other person who'd watched her transformation—a boy at fat camp who was her first kiss—had never contacted her again. She'd emailed him after camp, but the message bounced. She figured he'd given her a bogus address.

At one point, she'd thought of that boy as the person who'd first broken her heart—she'd considered him her best friend, until she got home and never heard from him again.

She knew better now; *that* wasn't loss, not really. Even though she'd cared about the guy, she couldn't really blame him, not really. Teens' emotions were fickle things. Even though what they'd shared that summer was real—she still believed that—he'd probably forgotten about her and moved on, like normal people did.

On her wedding day, she'd felt whole for the first time since middle school. In a sense, she'd gained a family in Jason. Her older sister, Joe, aged out of the foster system long ago but never had a stable enough situation to get custody before Alex, too, aged out.

She hadn't thought about so much of her past in years, yet as she contemplated her wedding day, so many things that marked *before* and *after* tumbled back into her mind. She really could split her life into Before Jason and After Jason. BJ and AJ.

"How may I help you?" the young man on the other side of the counter said, tapping on his keyboard as the other customer left with a key to his rental.

Alex blinked. Thoughts of Madeleine Kendall, Jason, the last year of his life, all swirled in her mind. For a moment, she couldn't find any words to say, couldn't pull herself back to the earth, to this moment. She looked at the employee again and blinked once, twice.

"Miss? May I help you?" He didn't sound annoyed. If anything, he sounded concerned.

Finally, the situation crystallized in front of her, and the past faded again. Not entirely, of course; it never did. But it slid to the periphery, where it hovered, letting her focus on the now.

"Yes, sorry." She fished inside her purse for her credit card and driver's license. "I need to rent a car. A compact, preferably."

She assumed those would be cheapest. Not that she couldn't afford something nicer, but she took care with how she spent Jason's money. Each month, she spent less of his and more of her own. In spite of what Madeleine Kendall believed, Alex hadn't married Jason for his money. With every purchase, she tried to prove that, if only to herself.

The next fifteen minutes were a blur as she answered questions, filled out paperwork, then finally put her suitcase into the trunk of a silver Corolla. After climbing into the driver's seat, she let out a deep sigh, then pulled up the hotel's address on her phone. But as she was about to start the GPS navigation, her finger hesitated over the icon. She glanced at her shoulder bag on the passenger seat, as if she could see through the red leather to the jar inside.

I'm a widow. The term felt off, like it belonged to a great-grandmother who played Bingo on Saturday nights at the senior center. A widow wasn't supposed to be approaching her five-year class reunion. At the age a lot of women were finishing college, she'd created a successful career.

As she sat in the rental car, her phone stared at her with accusation. Instead of starting the navigation directions, she checked her texts. Sure enough, most were from Madeleine Kendall—all but two. One from Charlotte, the other from her sister. That was the one Alex tapped first.

Today must be hard on you. Hang in there! Remember that Jason would be proud of you. Don't let MK get you down. Love ya tons! No worries—I'll take care of the cemetery!

Then an emoji of a red heart.

Her sister knew what today meant *and* that Madeleine Kendall would try to cause problems. Alex smiled and decided to not even look at the texts from "MK," as Jo called her, not until later. Not until after she finished what she'd come to California for.

At a sudden tapping on the car window, Alex jumped. The young man who'd helped her—Chad, his name tag said—called through the glass. "Miss? Are you all right?"

"I'm fine, thank you." She gave him her best fake smile, then clicked her phone off and slipped it into the cup holder—MK's texts unread, voice messages unheard—and started the engine.

Chad waved and walked away a few yards, but then stopped, clearly waiting to make sure she got off all right. She pulled out of the lot and into traffic, only then realizing that she had no idea where she was headed because she hadn't started the GPS. She stopped at a light, then pressed the button on the bottom of her iPhone to get directions to the one California beach she knew by name.

"How do I get to Santa Monica Pier?" she asked Siri.

Her phone pulled up a map, and Alex was off, heading for the beach where she'd free the last physical part of James she still had. *Then* she'd check in at the hotel, get a big dinner from room service—with a decadent dessert, because she deserved it—and then collapse, hopefully into a deep, dreamless sleep, unless she could dream of happier times with Jason.

Before he'd grown really weak at the end.

But after they were husband and wife: the trip to France,

137

the late-night movies. Laughing so hard they cried. The times they'd been happy—really happy.

The traffic light turned green, and she was off.

Two

ichael Montgomery paid the exorbitant fee to park at the Santa Monica Pier, then found an empty spot for his Mustang—one facing *away* from the ocean. He put the top back up before getting out and locking the doors, studiously avoiding the moment he'd have to look at the water. At least it was at a distance. Beyond the parking lot was a bike trail that was practically a thoroughfare where pedestrians had to look both ways or risk getting cursed out. Past that was maybe a hundred yards or so of sand before the rolling waves of the Pacific.

The timing of this whole thing couldn't have been more ridiculous. He should have come on a day he wore his usual casual clothes to work. But today, he'd had an important meeting with label execs, so he'd dressed up.

So I should have gone home to change first. Yet he knew that if he'd taken a detour, he probably wouldn't have kept his promise to come.

Not wanting to scratch up his dress shoes, he walked to the front of the car to take them off. That way, his back was still to the beach.

Why are you avoiding it? He chastised himself as he untied the second shoe. *The beach hurts. That why I'm avoiding it.*

After peeling off his dark-gray socks, he stuffed them into the toes of his shoes, then rolled up the cuffs of his slacks. He took a deep breath, locked the car with the key fob again—just to make sure—then headed for the sand.

As expected, the sight of the pale sand with the seemingly endless ocean beyond twisted his gut. He stood there, looking out over the vast ocean. The scent of salt reached him, bringing back memories, and with them, pain. Coming out here had been a dumb idea. He no longer cared that Nate, college-roommate-turned-therapist, had suggested he come as an exercise in letting go. Nate might have a Ph.D., but that didn't mean he knew what he was talking about when it came to Rachel.

Just thinking her name hurt. He gritted his teeth. This was a dumb idea. Dumb, *dumb* idea.

But agreeing to come here now, at the very hour Rachel was walking down the aisle and making vows with another guy? That was downright asinine.

Cathartic, Nate had called it. *It'll bring closure,* he'd assured Michael.

Sure, if *closure* meant ripping open old wounds and pouring alcohol on them. That's about what this felt like. He stood there, ostensibly waiting for a few bicycles to pass, but his mind had drifted to the fancy church wedding Rachel had always wanted. He could see himself waiting at the end of the aisle as she walked down it, smiling through her veil and looking angelic as she reached his side and they took hands to face the minister.

Angelic? Yeah, right.

On the heels of that thought came Nate's voice echoing in his mind: *Bitter, much?*

Hell, yes, he was bitter. Isn't that why Nate had insisted on this charade?

And Michael had come, taking off the rest of the work day. He had nothing better to do today than finish this cathartic exercise or whatever. Only one thing made him walk across the sand instead of cruising up the Pacific Coast Highway with the top down for the rest of the day. That one thing: Nate wouldn't forget. At next week's pickup game, he'd grill Michael about it—before, during, and after the game. Nate would see to it that a fun game would turn into a therapy session. The games were a stress outlet for Michael, something workouts didn't always provide.

In theory, he could skip this week's game, but Nate would still hound him. Better to get the job done, go to the next game, and report back. But to do that, he had to face the past.

As Michael walked across the sand, he felt distinctly out of place. Ahead were groups of children frolicking in the water and making sand castles, adults lying in the sun—all in swimsuits. And then there he was, a white-collar professional wearing a suit and tie to the beach. As he drew nearer, he could almost hear the *Sesame Street* song "One of These Things Is Not Like the Other." He was asking for stares.

With each step in the soft sand, his bare feet slid a few inches backward. He still had quite a distance to walk; the shoreline lay even farther ahead than he'd remembered. His suitcoat felt heavy, as if it held in extra heat. He took the darn thing off and draped it over his arm.

This is crazy.

That wasn't what Nate wanted him to think about.

"You haven't dated anyone in a year," he'd said in the locker room after their last game.

"Yes, I have," Michael had insisted. "Lots of women."

"Okay, you've had *dates*," Nate conceded. "That's not the same as *dating*. How many second dates have you had? Third dates? Any girlfriends?"

At that point, Michael slammed his locker shut and would have stalked out to his car if Nate hadn't called him back.

"Michael. Hey. Don't."

He stood there, his back to his best friend, wanting to ball up his fists and yell. He didn't say a word. But he didn't leave, either.

"You need to find a way to move on, and I think going to the beach on Friday may be exactly the thing to help you do that. Close the book on Rachel, then put it on a shelf, never to be opened again."

Michael remembered the image of the book, of closing it and putting it on that mental shelf. Of letting it gather dust for the rest of his life. That's not how he'd lived the past year. Rather, he'd flipped through Rachel's "book" often, and each time the emotional knife drove into his chest further.

I don't break promises. Unlike some people I could mention.

Maybe there was something to the old folk myth that redheads had no soul, because that would explain Rachel's heartlessness. Not so much her tears, though.

The farther he walked, the more aware he became of the sounds from the pier—the unintelligible chatter, thrilled shrieks of kids on the Ferris wheel and other rides, the occasional thump on wood as people went up and down the stairs or something hit the pier, like a dropped skateboard. He intently avoided looking at the pier itself. He'd go onto the pier and into Rusty's Surf Ranch another day. Maybe. That's where he and Rachel had had dinner on a night he'd known he would remember forever.

He was right, of course. He'd remember it. But not for the reason he'd thought at the time.

Even when he was quite sure he'd passed the restaurant, he kept his eyes straight ahead, never veering to the left, not wanting to see vendors selling all kinds of goods, from jewelry to cell-phone cases to California- and Santa Monica-themed t-shirts and more. On that day a year ago, after their dinner at Rusty's, he'd bought Rachel a Santa Monica t-shirt before taking her on a walk along the beach, hand in hand, until the sun had dipped and the light came at the perfect angle. Then he'd dropped to one knee and proposed.

She'd squealed, cried, and said yes, and he'd slipped the perfect ring—a carat and a half—onto her finger.

How exactly had so much changed so fast? He hadn't known anything was wrong until she stopped returning his texts and calls. Two weeks into her odd silence, she'd showed up at the recording studio, where he worked as a producer. There had been a time when she used to drop in for lunch unannounced, so at first he hadn't thought much of it.

Not until she spoke. "I met someone else." She never explained more than that.

What had he done to kill their relationship? What *hadn't* he done to make it thrive? What had she needed from him? What had he done to make her look for someone else? He still had no answers to any of it.

Nothing but, "I'm sorry, Michael. So sorry." Then tears as she handed over the ring, covered her mouth with one hand—her left one, which already had another ring on it. And she ran out. He'd always wondered if she'd gone out of her way to be sure he saw her new ring. He'd never know. Not that it really mattered.

Their only contact since had been the wedding invitation, which arrived only three weeks ago—apparently, she'd taken almost a year to plan her perfect day. He assumed she'd sent it more out of a need to inform rather than as an actual invitation. He didn't bother RSVP-ing his regrets. He just crumpled the invitation into a ball and threw it away.

Then he'd turned into a raging lunatic at the basketball game that night, which was when Nate stepped in. Why the guy thought that coming here of all places, and of all days, would be healing—

Several yards ahead, a woman stood alone—red hair, and a long braid down her back. Rachel? He stopped dead in his tracks, too stunned to move. What was she doing here? Had she run from her own wedding? If so, why didn't she have her hair in some fancy up-do instead of the long braid down her back? Why did she wear a long skirt instead of a wedding dress?

Maybe his eyes were playing tricks on him, and this was just some woman here to enjoy the beach. Except that she didn't look like a typical beach-goer. She didn't wear a swimsuit or carry a towel and beach bag. Just a red purse over one shoulder. She looked like she'd come here alone too.

If that woman was Rachel, then she'd left another man at the altar, which meant she really was cruel and heartless. Some poor schmuck was waiting at the end of the aisle, about to be humiliated in front of hundreds of people. For the first time, Michael actually pitied the other guy.

At least she broke my heart before the wedding day. What an odd comfort: realizing that things could have been worse.

As he walked, his gaze stayed on the red braid. Now that

he was closer, the hair seemed to be the wrong shade of red—darker than Rachel's. But the woman stood there, hugging herself in the same way Rachel used to. He had an impulse to walk up from behind and wrap his arms around her. She'd lift her head, smiling, and he'd give her a kiss. It was the most natural thing in the world.

Rather, it *used* to be.

His arms physically ached from emptiness. He missed being able to hold someone he loved—who loved him. Someone he *thought* loved him back, anyway.

He stopped a few feet to her side and made an effort to look casual as he waited for her to notice him. Finally, out of the corner of his eye, he saw her turn his direction and look him up and down. His heart rate sped up as he waited for her reaction.

"You must be drenched in that suit." Definitely *not* Rachel.

He glanced over quickly, barely catching a glimpse of her profile. She was pretty. Very pretty. And not Rachel. As he tried to come up with a witty reply, she sighed and stared out at the sea again, apparently lost in thought.

She was right, though; the heat was killing him. At least he'd taken his suitcoat off.

"You're right," he said simply. He draped his suit coat over the other arm. "I'm a bit overdressed for the beach."

Her only response was a nod. He couldn't help but look at her again, surreptitiously. She looked nothing like Rachel. Now that he'd seen this woman up close, he marveled that he'd ever mistaken her for Rachel. Their hair colors weren't remotely the same—Rachel's was a dramatic red with strawberry-blond highlights. He'd always suspected that she got the look with the help of a bottle. This girl, though—her hair was dark red and obviously natural. No way could those

145

highlights be from anything but the sun kissing her hair and lightening a few strands. She wasn't an orange ginger, either. Her red hair was more like burnt sienna—less flashy than Rachel's vibrant red, but warm and attractive—and *real.* Her cheeks had a light sprinkling of freckles. Rachel's did too, but she caked on enough makeup to cover them and give her complexion the look of porcelain.

He'd never given Rachel's makeup much thought, but seeing this woman look so much like Rachel, yet so *unlike* her at the same time, he found this stranger possessing a natural beauty that women like Rachel could only pretend to have.

The girl turned and looked over at him, her brows raised in question. Her eyes were slightly bloodshot, and she sniffed as if she'd been crying. "Do I know you?"

Now that she faced him full on, he couldn't help but stare at her eyes—deep brown. He'd never known a redhead with brown eyes. Rachel's were green. Or were they hazel? Not brown, certainly. He would have remembered the striking combination. This woman's lashes were thick and long, and while she wore makeup, it only highlighted her features; it didn't cover them.

When he didn't answer, the woman tilted her head. "Have we met before?" She licked her lips uncomfortably. "See, I'm, um—I'm kind of in the middle of something."

"Oh. Sorry to interrupt," Michael said, taking a step away. "You just look like someone I used to know. I'm kind of here . . . for something too."

She eyed him up and down again, then nodded with the hint of a smile. "Yeah, you don't look like you came to the beach to surf."

"Not exactly." He slipped his hands into his pockets. He didn't want to leave, even though standing by a pretty girl wasn't what Nate had in mind for this. She'd come here for something private too, it seemed. He took a step toward her, narrowing the distance between them, and stuck out a hand. "I'm Michael, by the way. And I don't usually come to the beach dressed like this."

She hesitated for a second before shaking his hand. "Alexandria. And I've never been to the beach." Her small hand clasped his with a firm grip. He didn't want to let go.

"Alexandria," he said, trying the name out on his tongue. "Do you go by your full name?"

"Nah," she said, shrugging and letting out a deep sigh and looking back at the ocean. "Five syllables is a lot. My sister calls me Dria, and so did—" She cut off and quickly added, "Friends usually call me Alex."

Michael nodded in understanding, then couldn't help but say, "So the first two syllables and last syllable are all covered. Anyone ever use the third one as a nickname?" At her confused expression, he clarified, "Anne. Although I guess that technically, it would be spelled with just an A and N, and that would just look weird. But it's a thought."

"Someday, maybe." She laughed. "So the middle syllable doesn't feel as left out."

Huh. He'd had thoughts like that as a kid. It's why he'd sometimes played with the action figures he liked least, so they wouldn't feel bad because they weren't Spider-Man and Batman, his two favorites. He'd never found anyone else who gave human qualities to inanimate objects—or, in this case, to sounds and syllables.

They both faced the ocean again, Michael making a point to stay where he was—to not step away again. He liked this girl, felt drawn to her. Not because she reminded him of Rachel, but because within a couple of minutes, she'd proven to be entirely unlike Rachel in a dozen ways. Their brief conversation felt like a breath of fresh air.

This is the kind of girl I could take on a second date. The thought should have terrified him, and after it crossed his mind, he waited for the familiar sick feeling in his chest. It never came. Of course, he didn't verbalize the idea. Any sane girl would freak out at hearing something like that.

"So," he said, trying to rock on his heels in an effort to be cool, but failing utterly. "Should I call you Alex? Anne? Dria?" He mentally said her name again—Alexandria—just to be sure he didn't miss a syllable.

"Call me Alex," she said with certainty. "I wouldn't know who you were talking about if you called me Anne. And Dria is . . . well, only a couple of people have ever used that."

"Of course. People you randomly meet on the beach definitely don't fall into that category."

"Right." She seemed to be watching the waves as they broke on the shore, but Michael could sense her gaze still on him, possibly sizing him up. "What about you? Do you go by Mike? Or is it always Michael?"

He opened his mouth to answer but hesitated. There had been a time, many years ago, when people called him Mikey, back when he was a very chubby fifteen-year-old. The name felt like it belonged to another person altogether.

"Not for years," he finally said. "Michael is all I go by now, although sometimes when my mother gets really upset, I'm Michael Lorenzo—Lorenzo after a great-great-grandfather. I couldn't ask for a more dated name."

"I don't know," Alex said. "I think my middle name could give yours a run for its money as far as old-fashioned ones go: Bertha."

"Alexandria Bertha. Wow. That's a mouthful. It's amazing you weren't bullied into oblivion as a kid but instead grew up to be the well-adjusted woman you are today."

She gave a sardonic laugh at that. "Whether I'm well-adjusted is up to debate in some people's eyes."

Michael watched her smile fade as she looked out at the massive expanse of water again; he wanted to bring the smile back. Nate and any therapeutic homework were shoved aside. He nodded toward the pier. "Do you want to get some ice cream or a churro or something?"

She looked in the direction he'd indicated, and he immediately wanted her to turn back to face him. Or he could reach out to touch her thick braid—it was gorgeous. She looked at him again. "Straight sugar doesn't usually—"

"Or, you know, something more like a meal. Do you like crêpes?"

She spun back around, her eyes alight. "I do, but good ones are hard to find."

"I know the perfect place," he said. "It's a bit of a drive, but if you don't mind that . . ."

She hesitated, biting one side of her lower lip. She looked out to the ocean, glanced at her purse, then back at the ocean. "I . . ." She didn't voice any objection; her voice simply trailed off.

"I'll drive," he offered. "Then I'll bring you back to your car so you can finish . . ." This time it was his voice trailing off. He gestured between her and the beach, twirling his hand. "Finish whatever I interrupted. I'm sure it's important."

He wanted to spend an hour or two with this pretty girl, who seemed quick and smart and fun—someone he felt comfortable around in spite of just meeting her. It was as if he'd found an old friend. An old friend who happened to be hot.

He'd come back later to drop her off, then find his own closure at the beach. Who said it needed to happen at the

149

exact hour of the wedding? *Nate did.* But Michael brushed the intrusive thought away.

"I'd love to have a good crêpe." Alex patted her purse. "I can take care of this later."

Three

This is crazy, Alex thought as she rode in the car of a perfect stranger through the streets of L.A. *He could be a serial killer or something.*

So why didn't she feel scared or anxious? In the oddest way, she almost felt as if she'd come home, but to a place she'd never been. Her sister would have a conniption if she could see her now. But Becca never needed to find out.

And if Michael posed some threat, wouldn't she feel it?

Maybe I'll end up as a Dateline *unsolved case.* She chuckled at the thought.

He glanced over and gave her a puzzled half-smile. "What?"

"Nothing," she said. "Doing something like this . . . It's so unlike me."

"Doing what, specifically?" He navigated a turn and continued down the street.

"Going out to lunch with a perfect stranger." *A perfectly*

gorgeous stranger. "Maybe I'm having a midlife crisis." She furrowed her brow. "Except, twenty-three is a bit young for one of those."

He grinned at that. "I doubt my friends would believe me if I told them about this either. Maybe we're both having a midlife crisis. Maybe we should do something shocking to freak them out." He waggled his eyebrows, then laughed, and Alex joined in.

She couldn't help but picture Jason's mother scowling at a news report about whatever mischief Alex and Michael decided to get caught up in. The texts, voice messages, and emails she'd get after the fact—no, MK would *not* be hearing about this . . . *outing.* Or whatever it was.

During the rest of the drive, she wanted to ask questions about him, but then he'd ask questions about her and why she'd come to the beach, and . . . She let the conversation lapse into a surprisingly easy silence, until Michael looked for a place to park.

He shook his head. "Nothing close. I've never had to park here before."

At her puzzled expression, he explained. "I used to work at the crêpe shop." He circled the block, looking for spots again. "Back then, I rode the bus."

"And when you're on the bus, you don't pay attention to parking."

"Exactly," he said. "Let's just park in here." He pulled into the lot of a big grocery store with plenty of parking. Soon they were headed across the street.

People packed the passageways between the small buildings and booths of the market, and Michael moved quickly. Just as Alex began to worry that she'd lose him, he slowed and reached for her.

"Here," he said. "Take my hand."

She did, and as their hands touched, she felt a flutter in her chest. He squeezed, smiled, then continued, weaving them through the throng with confidence. At last they reached the crêpe booth; Alex couldn't have found her way back to the car without help. She looked up at the red menu boards, which had a ton of options—combinations she'd never considered for crêpes, both sweet and savory. She completely ignored the waffles and sandwiches; why get those when visiting a place specializing in French crêpes?

"What do you recommend?" she asked, genuinely having no idea what to order.

She'd said she didn't want anything sugary, but the difference between a churro and a dessert crêpe was a culinary chasm. Yet she'd worked hard to lose the weight she'd regained and prided herself on the fact that she weighed seventy-one pounds less than she had in eighth grade.

"Each one is pretty big," Michael said. "I could order a savory one, and you order a sweet, and we could split them."

"And we each get a full meal, including dessert," she finished. "Brilliant."

"You don't mind sharing?"

"I'd prefer it. See, I—" She cut off. No need to reveal things like how there had been a time when she would have wanted both a savory crêpe and a dessert one and could have easily polished off both. As much as she still enjoyed food, she never wanted to go back to everything the weight had brought with it. A preteen shouldn't be bullied, for starters. But a preteen should also never have joint pain or be pre-diabetic.

In her case, those things were results of being shuttled between foster homes. The chaos of constantly moving, never knowing what the future held, frequently changing schools, trying to make new friends again and again . . . it all added up to food being the only "love" she could count on. Unlearning that had taken far more work and time than she'd ever imagined possible. Chances were good that she'd always hear food's siren call, would always have to fight to keep her health.

"You okay?" Michael asked.

"I'm great," Alex said. "Just trying to decide." She purposely put her hands on her hips as she thought; feeling them was a tangible reminder of how far she'd come. "Honestly, all of the savory crêpes look great, so you pick your favorite, and then we'll split a strawberry and Nutella dessert crêpe. That's calling my name."

"Mmm. Berries and chocolate," Michael said with an approving nod. "Can't go wrong there." He looked over the savory menu. "How about the veggie crêpe?"

She found the description, and immediately her mouth started watering. "Sounds divine. But you're welcome to get a whole one for yourself. You don't have to share with me. I can always get a box for what I don't eat."

"Nah," Michael said. "I don't eat that much." He stepped forward to order, adding offhand, "Not anymore, anyway."

Wait, what?

But the forty-something man on the other side of the counter turned to them and exclaimed, "Michael, is that you?"

"Sure is, Carlos." They shook hands, and Michael introduced the owner to Alex.

After starting on their order—ladling batter onto hot metal rounds—Carlos reminisced with Michael about when he hired Michael and they worked together in that very booth.

"Still don't know how you didn't put on pounds like the rest of us." He took a wooden tool—a thin handle with a dowel attached perpendicularly at the end, which he used to shape the batter into perfect circles. "I mean, even after spending a summer at a fat camp, most people wouldn't be able to keep it off, let alone being surrounded by things like Nutella and whipping cream all day."

"It'll always be battle," Michael said with a shrug. "But I won't go back there."

Alex stood frozen in place, not believing her ears. How in the world could this hot guy have ever struggled with his weight? How had someone who looked like *that* ever been sent to a fat camp?

She'd thought the only thing they had in common was a love of crêpes. Apparently not.

He'd experienced something few people ever had. Suddenly, she wanted to tell him about her past, something she rarely did, because most people couldn't handle even one part of her history, let alone the crazy mess that was being orphaned, bounced among foster families, and having a brief marriage to a dying teen.

Back at the pier, she'd welcomed the attention of a good-looking guy who clearly had money. At the time, she'd had no intention of telling him anything about herself beyond vague things like how she lived in Arizona, where she'd grown up—keeping past cities out of it, because she'd lived in at least eight. Maybe she'd mention that she had her own company in the fashion industry. She'd become adept over the years at avoiding uncomfortable topics and focusing on areas she could talk about easily.

She couldn't help but let her eyes trail from Michael's shoes up to the back of his hair. *He* used to be fat? She understood his words better than his friend across the counter did. They both fought the urge to medicate with food and always would.

After Jason's death, she'd given up the fight for a year, regaining more than half of the weight back. On the first anniversary of his death, she'd promised herself to lose it all again, for herself as much as for Jason. And she had. As of two months ago, she'd lost the last pound—it had taken her three years. She wouldn't throw in the towel again.

Michael laughed at something Carlos said, then waved, ending the conversation as he turned to Alex and gestured around the corner to one side of the booth, where four stools stood beside a short counter. She climbed on one, and he took another. "I've always loved sitting here instead of at one of the little tables," he said. "You can watch the magic from here."

She got to see how the savory crêpe was expertly folded and slipped onto a plate. With her feet on the bar at the bottom of the stool, she pointed as Carlos used a metal spatula to fold up the berry one, using quick, precise movements as if the spatula were an extension of his own hand. "You know how to do that?"

"I'm a bit rusty, but I used to make one mean crêpe."

They waited as the final garnishes were added, and during that time, Alex felt as content as she could ever remember being. Only one thing would make it better: Michael had released her hand to pay but hadn't taken it again. She wanted his strong, warm grip around hers, leading her confidently through the crowd. If she'd had the guts, she would have taken his.

Yeah, right. She'd never been so forward. And she'd met the guy not an hour before. *So why do I feel so comfortable around him?*

The savory plate was slid to them first, with the crêpe

cut in half. Carlos held out two forks, which Michael took, handing one to her. "Dig in," he said. "But I warn you, you'll never be the same."

She cut off a small piece and took a bite. Sure enough, the veggie filling melded into a paradise of flavors. She closed her eyes with pleasure. "Oh, wow."

"Crazy, huh?" Michael said, cutting off a piece only after watching her reaction.

They made short work of the crêpe, then turned to the berry-chocolate one, which sat on another plate, also cut in half. Two clean forks rested beside it. Michael slid the plate over and handed her a second fork. "We'll pretend that this is healthy because of the strawberries."

Alex nodded with mock solemnity. "And because of the real whipping cream. The real stuff's healthier than the fake whipped topping crap."

"Oh, absolutely," Michael said with an equally serious tone.

This time he cut into the crêpe first, but Alex's bite followed shortly behind. She ate more slowly with this crepe, taking smaller bites as her appetite waned. She felt utterly satisfied, but comfortably so, even though several bites remained. Michael offered the rest of his half to her, and when she turned him down, he pushed the plate away and stood. Alex stared at the remaining food; she had a hard time grasping the reality of a man who didn't put away twice as much food as the average woman, even if he did work out.

They walked back, through the maze of stores and booths, this time side by side and at a more leisurely pace. Alex couldn't help but wish he'd take her hand again, then reminded herself that she didn't know the guy and was being ridiculous. Out of the corner of her eye, she took in his body and wondered how on earth she happened to meet someone with such a significant similarity in his past, someone who knew what a weight struggle felt like and had come off conqueror.

She had to ask, but the thought of bringing it up made her jittery. Not everyone wanted to talk about past hard times; she knew that firsthand. They had to stop to wait for a group of people to move along a cross-corridor. He looked over and caught her eye—and winked. Instead of finding the action cheesy, she felt her face warm and her cheeks round with a smile. She turned away, hoping he wouldn't see her blushing.

When they kept walking, she decided to force out the burning question. She had to know, and if she didn't ask soon, she might never know. He'd take her back to her car, and she'd never see him again. She had to clear her throat—twice. "What did you mean back there?"

"About working there? It was a long time ago, when—"

"No, not that." Now that she stood on the topic's precipice, she wanted to wimp out. How did you bring up something potentially painful from the past without upsetting the other person? Then again, Carlos had talked about it almost like a joke. "I mean about—summer camp."

"Oh, that." He took a few more steps before answering, but he didn't seem upset, only pensive. He ran the fingers of one hand through his hair, making it look adorably tousled.

"Did you really go to a fat camp?" she pressed.

"I sure did." Michael tilted his head to one side and then the other. "Of course, they didn't call it that. But yeah, I spent the entire summer before my junior year of high school at a camp meant to help obese kids lose weight."

"How awful." She knew all too well.

"It was pretty miserable. You wouldn't believe the rules. Every calorie we ate had to be accounted for. We had to take one bite at a time, put the fork on the table, and chew a specific number of times before swallowing. I couldn't even go the bathroom alone—worry over bulimia or sneaking food out of the cafeteria and eating it there, I guess. Privileges had to be earned, stuff like being able to bring snacks to your room. There were daily weigh-ins. Group therapy." He shook his head. "Rough, rough summer. And most of the rules didn't really help."

"But something obviously did," she said, remembering fat-camp rules all too clearly. "Something must have made a difference, because look at you—you made a change . . ." She gestured up and down his lean frame from shoulders to feet.

"A few things helped. The nutrition classes were big. I hadn't grown up understanding what food was made of and how it fueled the body—you know, basic stuff you can't be healthy without knowing. My trainer and counselor were both great. But the biggest thing . . ." His voice trailed off, and when he didn't go on, Alex looked up to see him blushing. His cheeks had bright pink spots on them.

"The biggest thing . . ." she prompted in what she hoped was in a casual tone.

"I've already told you a lot more than I usually tell anyone." He shrugged and seemed to be ready to change the subject.

But Alex didn't want him to. She playfully nudged him. "So what's one more deep, dark secret?"

He eyed her skeptically, raising one eyebrow and laughing. But not, she noticed, answering the question.

"Fine," she said. "I'll spill something about me first." She paused in her step and held out one hand. "Deal?"

Michael ran his fingers through his hair again—it looked better and better every time he did that, as if the action released some of the gel or whatever it was that held his hair in place, letting out waves and gentle curls. She'd always been a sucker for curls on guys. She made a mental note to take a selfie with him before they said goodbye at the pier just so she could see his hair again any time she wanted to.

"*Maybe* it's a deal," he said, eying her hand. "Depends on how deep and dark your secret is."

"Okay," Alex said lightly. But her insides tightened at the idea of verbalizing the past. If she could have emailed the information to his brain, that would have been so much easier that saying it all.

They kept walking, and with each step, she had to remind herself that telling Michael shouldn't be scary. He'd gone through the same things she had; he wouldn't judge. Besides, they'd say goodbye soon, likely to never see each other again. Today would be a pleasant memory during an otherwise difficult time, when a man happened to notice her, and she got the chance to flirt a little and feel feminine.

"Okay," she said as they left the market. "Here's my big secret: I went to a fat farm too. It was the summer before my sophomore year, and I weighed well over two hundred pounds. Those places must all be the same, because it was just like you said. It totally sucked, but I learned enough to keep myself healthy."

The truth, if not all of nitty-gritty details.

"So," she said, nudging him again. "Finish your story. Camp didn't totally suck because of your nutritionist, your trainer, your counselor, and ..."

Michael's step slowed to a gradual stop on the sidewalk. He stared straight ahead, his expression suddenly intense. "This is going to sound completely nuts, but humor me, okay?"

"Okay," Alex said, unsure what type of shift his mood

had taken. "What is it?" She wanted to add, *You can trust me.*

"Where was your camp?"

"Tahoe," she said. "Wellness Meadows for—"

"Teens," he finished, and nodded as if he'd expected the name.

Alex felt her eyes widening with surprise. "Yeah."

She suddenly felt as if someone had drawn back a curtain, but instead of revealing some grand truth, she couldn't make out what she was looking at. A crucial detail still hovered at the edge of her peripheral vision. She narrowed her eyes and tried to picture Michael younger and chubby. Maybe with his hair a bit longer, not as held in place, curlier . . .

The pieces clicked into place. "Mikey?" she said with wonder. Her hand moved on its own toward his face as if she needed to feel what she was seeing to make it true, but her hand stopped a few inches short.

Before she could pull away, he reached for her hand and held it. His thumb traced the inside of her palm, sending her middle into a flurry of butterflies. His mouth curved into a smile, revealing perfect teeth instead of braces. Yes—there was the cleft in his chin. The same freckle below his right eye. She searched his face, not entirely believing, but wanting so much for the man before her to be the boy who had made that otherwise awful summer endurable.

The first person she could almost call a boyfriend. Her first kiss.

Finally, he spoke, wonder in his voice too. "Al?"

She nodded, unable to speak for a second. "Yeah." She couldn't manage more than that. Camp was the only place she'd ever gone by *Al.* She'd wanted a different identity there, a new start. No one there knew her as Alex or Dria. Back then, both names *felt* fat. She'd introduced herself to everyone as Al. And then she'd fallen hard for the boy with the curly hair and braces.

Michael—no, Mikey—reached over and brushed a loose strand of hair from her face. "I've always been a sucker for gingers."

They stood there, gazing into each other's eyes as if time itself had stopped. Her mind spun, around and around. Was this really Mikey? How could they have found each other again after all this time? This kind of thing didn't just happen. But maybe it had. And if it so, it was as wonderful as it was unbelievable.

"Why didn't you ever email me back?" he asked.

She shook her head adamantly. "I would have—if you'd ever emailed me. When I tried emailing you first, it bounced. I still have your old email memorized: mikey66@dragon-slayer.com."

Now he was the one shaking his head. "No way. I cannot believe that my bad handwriting kept us apart all these years. It wasn't six-six; it was zero-zero. I've kept that address all these years, on the off chance . . ."

His gaze held hers now; however their messages had crossed in cyberspace, they were here now, together. His eyes slowly moved from her eyes to her lips, and then he stepped nearer and lowered his face to hers. She held her breath and closed her eyes, waiting to feel his lips again after so long. It would be the same and yet oh, so different.

But sudden loud sounds burst the bubble—a loud squeak followed by the roar of an engine. They startled, pulling away to look across the street, at the sound in the store parking lot.

Where a tow truck was driving away with Michael's car.

Four

They took off running for the traffic light; Michael hoped it would change so they could cross the busy road. When they got there, the light was still red. He mentally cursed; they had no way of catching the tow truck now. It turned a corner and went out of sight, pulling his Mustang behind it. They stopped at the intersection, trying to catch their breath.

"They can't just tow your car," Alex said, clearly upset. "You didn't break any law. And how are you supposed to know where they took it?"

"I don't know." Michael groaned and ran the back of his wrist across his forehead to wipe off the sweat from their sudden sprint. His brain couldn't keep up with this day. First he'd gone to the beach to get over Rachel, only to end up finding the girl he'd first fallen for so long ago. And then his car got towed.

He didn't know what to think or feel. Or what he'd tell Nate. *That* would be an interesting conversation.

When the light finally changed, they hurried through the press of pedestrians, and when they reached the parking lot, they walked straight to the now-empty parking stall. Even though he'd seen the tow truck, Michael could scarcely believe his eyes. His car had been here a few minutes before, but now it was just—gone. He blew out some air and looked around, not knowing what he was looking for.

Alex seemed to do the same, only instead of coming up empty, she pointed at a hut that advertised key-copying services. "Maybe that guy knows something."

Michael looked over. Sure enough, a portly man inside watched them, wearing a knowing smirk. As soon as he saw them coming in the hut's direction, he came out of the side door and waited for them. He reached for his back pocket and pulled out his wallet.

Michael spoke first, skipping any pleasantries. "Did you see a tow truck take a black Ford Mustang a few minutes ago?"

The man nodded, then flashed a grin filled with yellow teeth. "Sure did."

"Why did it get towed?" Michael asked.

Alex jumped in. "And where did they take it?"

The man slipped a business card out of his wallet and handed it to Alex. "There. That's the address. Go there, pay the fee, and you'll have your car back."

She handed the card to Michael, who asked the question again. "Why did it get towed?"

The man slipped a toothpick between his teeth and chewed on it. "Did you cross the street?" They both looked toward the market, and he laughed. "That's why. This lot is only for store customers. The sign says so." He pointed to one mounted on a light pole.

Michael stepped closer to read the small print. Sure

enough—parking was for customers of the grocery store only. But it wasn't as if the store's customers were hurting for places to park; the lot was half empty.

"Great way to make money," he said. "I bet the store gets a nice kickback from each tow."

The man shrugged. "Maybe. Don't know. I *do* know that they're always watching. Cross the street, and I guarantee that your car won't be here when you get back."

Alex grunted in annoyance. "It's like they're deliberately trapping people to make a few extra bucks."

The man laughed. "Try several *hundred* bucks."

They exchanged looks of shock. Michael regained the use of his tongue first. "So how far away is this place?" he asked, pointing at the card in Alex's hand.

"A fifteen- or twenty-minute drive," the man said. "Assuming traffic isn't bad."

Alex took a step forward, as if the guy had crossed a line. Michael put a hand on her shoulder to be safe; he didn't want her getting hurt by anyone, least of all a slimy key-copying guy. Then again, Alex seemed to be holding her own. She always had, even back at camp.

"How can we *drive* there without a *car*?" Her face had a spark of anger to it, making her brown eyes even prettier.

The guy didn't seem at all perturbed, which seemed to annoy her all the more. Michael had to stifle a smile; he liked seeing her this way. A common phrase from fat camp group sessions came to mind.

Anger is a secondary emotion covering the primary emotion.

Among the primary emotions were frustration, embarrassment, shame, hurt, and fear. What was Alex's primary emotion was right now?

He surreptitiously admired her figure; she, too, had learned how to stay trim and healthy, whether from *anger is a secondary emotion* or some other tool. He liked to think that whatever her key to overcoming her weight had been, that maybe she'd found it at camp too—because that would mean he'd been there, that maybe he'd been part of her success, as she'd been part of his.

The key man pointed down a side street. "Taxis always wait over there. Tell them your car was towed; they know where to go." He held out his hand as if asking for the business card.

Michael took the card from Alex before the man could take it, wanting to tear it up or let it fall to the ground—or maybe do that under-the-chin flick the cop did to Ren in *Footloose*. But that was anger creeping up. *Secondary emotion*, he reminded himself. In this case, his primary emotions were frustration and worry. He took a deep breath, held it, then let it out slowly—another tool he still used from camp. Alex noticed, and her eyes crinkled with amusement; she recognized the calming exercise. She joined him, breathing in, holding it, then breathing out.

Both of them calm once more, Michael spoke. "May I take a picture of the card first? In case we need any information from it."

The man shrugged as if to say he didn't care.

"Good idea." Alex held her hand out, and he placed the card on top—a simple action, barely a touch as his fingers skimmed her palm—but enough to send a zing through him.

A powerful emotion followed. Not anger or anything else secondary, just attraction, pure and simple. Much like the summer they'd first met, but somehow better. He pulled up the camera on his phone and focused on the card. The camera clicked, and Alex handed the card back to the man, who tucked it into his bulging wallet and half waddled, half strutted, back to his hut.

Michael looked in the direction of the taxis and gestured with one arm. "Shall we?"

"Let's," Alex said, not seeming upset anymore, maybe because they didn't really have a choice in the matter. Or maybe for her, the key man had been the trigger for her primary emotion—a desire to find justice for Michael. Or her trigger had been the unknown, and now that they both knew how to find his car, her emotions leveled out.

Even my thoughts are starting to sound like a shrink. Thanks, Nate.

They walked side by side, and before he realized it, Alex's hand was in his again. He couldn't remember consciously taking hers, but he didn't think she'd taken his, either. Maybe they'd both reached for each other. However it had happened, it felt right, inevitable.

As if Michael's subconscious were a prophet, he could hear Nate's chastising voice as they walked toward the taxis along the curb.

You aren't ready for a relationship, Nate would say. *Don't go falling for another girl when you're still vulnerable; you'll use her as a rebound, and you'll both end up hurt. Take some time to be on your own, without a woman.*

Intellectually, he agreed with pseudo Nate's lecture. *This entire day could still turn out to be a monumental disaster.* It was already pretty bad; he'd gotten his car towed, for one thing. But he'd also taken a gorgeous woman to his favorite crêpe place when he should have been mourning his ex. Instead of facing his emotions, he'd turned not only to a different woman, but to food. His old camp counselor would flip out if he could see him now.

Or maybe Nate would be thrilled that Michael had found Al after all these years.

Oh, right, he could hear Nate saying. *And puppy love*

from one teen summer will totally still be alive and well today. Not only that, but I'm sure it's morphed into something grownup all on its own that can sustain a long-term, adult relationship. Of course. Excuse me while I snort. Finding love with this girl is about as likely as Krispy Kreme donuts never being a temptation again.

Stupid Nate and his stupid advice.

Michael glanced over at Alex nervously, unsure how long it had taken to reach the taxis and hoping she hadn't minded his silence. She hadn't attempted conversation either, so maybe she felt as comfortable with him as he did with her. They fit together like puzzle pieces.

He and Rachel had been more like puzzle pieces you want to fit, ones that even look like they *should* fit, so you try to cram them together, but it's all wrong. But this felt right.

That word again: *right.* As odd as it seemed—and as unlikely as it was—this *did* feel right. And even more unbelievably, it felt *possible.*

That thought made something big twist in his middle, and not unpleasantly. He opened the back door of the first taxi. Alex smiled up at him, then climbed inside. He followed and found her not near the window, but in the center of the bench so he had no choice but to sit close to her. He told the driver about the tow. Sure enough, he knew exactly where to go.

As they pulled away from the curb, Alex's hand slipped into his. And even though he knew he was about to fork out enough money to cover a car payment just to get his car back, for the moment, he didn't mind. Somehow, it even felt worth it. He glanced at their hands, rested his head against hers, and smiled.

Yep. This feels right.

Five

*a*lex found herself talking about camp during the entire drive to the impound lot, which took a little over fifteen minutes, just as the key guy had predicted. Suddenly she felt like camp had ended last week. As if they'd never been apart.

Except that they were both adults now. She was a size six—or four, depending on the cut. He'd undergone a similar transformation. He still had the same curly hair, though he wore it shorter and somewhat tamed. He had the same quirk in his smile. The same laugh.

"Remember the counselors' skit where Dot pulled that practical joke?" Alex asked.

"You mean when Dot made Steven laugh so hard that he spit water all over the campers? Or the time she replaced Tate's punch with that baby gum medicine?" Michael laughed.

"I'd forgotten about the water," Alex said, laughing too. "I think Jenny had Coke shooting out of her nose. I meant the numbing medicine. Man, the look on Tate's face after drinking it . . ."

"And how he talked afterward with his tongue half numb—"

Alex caught her breath between chuckles. "I almost peed my pants right there in the amphitheater." Her eyes widened with embarrassment at having lost her filter. "I mean. Forget I said that. I—"

"I almost did too." Michael shrugged as if she hadn't mentioned something awkward. "It's me—Mikey—remember?" He playfully put an arm around her shoulders, as he'd done so often at camp. Back then, the gesture had begun as a buddy thing, but it had quickly become something more, and it had remained something more for the rest of the two months they spent at camp.

Now, as soon as she felt the warmth and weight of his arm, she turned to look at him, wondering what the gesture meant all these years later. He returned her gaze, seeming to study her eyes. For several seconds, neither of them said a word—and Alex couldn't breathe.

That is definitely not a buddy look. The thought sent her emotions into the twists and turns of a roller coaster.

What was she doing? She still hadn't done what she'd come to California to do. And it's not like this could turn into anything; she lived hundreds of miles away. Spending the day with some guy, even if he turned out to be a friend from her vulnerable adolescence, couldn't be a good idea.

She opened her mouth to speak, to put a voice to her doubts, to let him know that she would be heading home to Phoenix the day after tomorrow, likely to never return to the L.A. area, that—

But before she could say a word, he'd pressed his lips to hers. His other arm reached around her, and she couldn't help but melt into his embrace as she kissed him back. At camp, their kisses had been unsure, shy. This kiss eclipsed those ones in every way.

We've both grown up in this area too.

They didn't pull apart until the cab rolled to a stop and the cabbie cleared his throat loudly. "Uh, here we are."

They flew apart, and Alex flushed, feeling conspicuous and not a little sheepish at being caught making out in the back of a taxi—but not the least regretful over it. To her relief, Michael just grinned. He didn't seem to regret it either—and may have enjoyed it as much as she had.

After he paid the tab, they headed for the front door of the company. Michael was the first to speak. "If you aren't sick of me yet, I know this Italian place down by Venice Beach that's to die for. I could take you there for dinner."

"Sounds great," Alex said. Venice Beach meant nothing to her; she had no idea how close it was to Santa Monica Pier or anywhere else in the L.A. area. Jason hadn't ever said specifically *where* along the Pacific Coast his ashes should be spread. He'd been to Santa Monica before and had talked about how beautiful it was, so she'd just always planned to spread his ashes there.

Thoughts of Jason sent her heart yelling at her to put a stop to this day before either she or Michael did something to regret. Instead, she said, "I imagine their bread is fattening."

"Oh, man, yes. They're called Killer Garlic Rolls for good reason," Michael said, holding the door to the tow shop open for her. "You have to pace yourself. You could easily eat a thousand calories before the entrée ever shows up. Not that I speak from experience. At least, not from *recent* experience."

She loved how he admitted to slipping at times. In spite

of appearances, he was still, in fact, human. As he went to the counter to pay the fee, Alex's phone vibrated with an incoming text. She checked it, hoping to find nothing from Charlotte or from Madeleine Kendall.

Only a text from Becca—relief. Alex opened it.

Delivered the flowers. Saw J's parents parking as I left. Don't think they saw me. Hopefully they'll think you left them.

Below the text was a photo of a pretty arrangement of purple daisies beside the stone marker with Jason's birth and death dates. Alex stared at the small dash, knowing it represented everything that had happened between those dates—it represented his entire *life*. Part of her life, too. All boiled down to a little straight line.

She reread the text, hoping Becca was right, that after seeing the flowers, the Kendalls would assume they'd missed Alex's personal visit. That would give them one less reason to hate her. They wouldn't understand why she hadn't come today, that she'd flown to the coast for their son. Just as they didn't understand why Jason hadn't wanted to be embalmed and buried.

They still hated her for supposedly "seducing" their son—a belief they clung to because they couldn't accept the idea that he'd wanted to leave them and that *he'd* proposed to her. The whole thing had been his idea. As much as they loathed having a daughter-in-law, they'd been doubly shocked when Alex hadn't taken his name. But that was also Jason's idea. Knowing that they wouldn't be together for long, he'd insisted she keep her maiden name as a way of making sure that when he passed, she would really be free.

That she wasn't a possession—not his, not his parents'. She was her own person, capable of making her own decisions. One of many gifts Jason had given her.

But inability to understand the other side didn't lie only

with the Kendalls. Maybe one day she'd understand why they put up a marker when nothing of their son was buried below it. Maybe you had to be a parent to understand that one.

"Al?" Michael said, turning from the teller. The transaction had either gone awfully quickly, or she'd been staring at her phone for a really long time.

She blinked and looked away from the screen. "Oh, um . . ." She shook her head, trying to clear it of the images of her former in-laws and the flowers and the cemetery. She couldn't think of anything to say except, "That went fast."

Michael squinted in confusion. "You okay?" He went to her side, brows furrowed with concern, and read the text over her shoulder. She didn't mind. In fact, she was kind of glad he'd find out this way so she wouldn't have to find a way to tell him everything.

"Who was . . . J?" He looked at her phone again, at the photo of the flowers and the marker. "James C. Kendall," he read aloud. "Wow. He was young." He looked over, a question on his face.

So much for this being the easy way. Of course a text and a simple photo didn't tell the whole story. Yet how did you tell someone—someone like Michael, no less—that you'd been widowed? She wasn't ashamed of Jason, or of their brief marriage. But the whole thing was just so emotional, and complicated, and . . .

"Jason was, um . . ."

"Never mind. It's none of my business." Michael waved off the question. "Let's go."

Crap. She could feel him putting both a physical and an emotional distance between them. He turned toward the door, and she hurried after him, wanting to explain, but not in front of the cashier. When she got outside, Michael was already heading for the corner, where the teller had said

173

they'd have to walk around to reach the huge metal gate to reach the car.

"Mikey, wait."

At hearing his old nickname, he slowed his step and then stopped. He cocked his head to the side but didn't quite turn around.

Alex ran to catch up. She wanted to take his hand but clasped her own anxiously instead. "Jason . . . was my husband. He died of cancer almost four years ago. We were young, only eighteen. He knew he was dying, and . . . Some people think I married him out of pity, but it wasn't like that at all. I wasn't *in love* with him, but I loved him very much. He was my best friend."

Michael's face softened, showing concern and understanding, both of which gave Alex the courage to go on.

"We both had hard backgrounds. He had the money to support us, and, well, it felt like the right thing to do." She watched cars pass by, letting her mind drift so she could avoid thinking about how Michael hadn't taken his eyes off her since she started telling the story. She struggled as she went on. "I helped Jason have some happy months before he died. And he helped me too." She wrapped her arms around herself, suddenly feeling a chill in the spring air. "See, we were married . . . five years ago . . . today."

At Michael's widened eyes, she hurried on.

"We weren't stupid teens; I swear. We weren't poor kids living in his parents' basement or anything. He'd made money as a developer, and he wanted me to have it so I could start my own business."

"And you did, didn't you?" he asked, with a tone full of trust and confidence.

"Yeah, I did. And it's doing really well. But that's why

his parents think I'm a gold digger and why they pretty much hate my guts." She shrugged. "They blame me for creating a rift between them and their son, but the truth is, they created the rift long before I met Jason." She shrugged. "He wanted an escape—and some happiness—before he died."

"Wow." Michael put out a hand, she took it, and they slowly walked to the back of the lot. "You came to California on your anniversary," he said with wonder in his voice. "Did the beach have some special meaning for you as a couple?"

"No." Her free hand brushed her purse and felt the shape of the jar inside. "To him, the ocean meant freedom and joy. He visited the beach once when he was a kid, and he said that was the place he felt most free and alive. He asked me to release his ashes into the largest ocean in the world on our fifth anniversary. And then he'd be free forever."

"That's . . ." Michael said, seeming to struggle with words. "It's just . . . beautiful."

"You don't think it's . . . weird? Or that I'm taking the last piece of him away from his parents?"

He shook his head. "Not at all. I think it's awesome. Besides, it gave you a much better reason for being at the pier today than I had." He squeezed her hand.

She grinned at both the action and his words—and at the unspoken invitation to ask the obvious. "So why were *you* at the beach today—in a suit?"

He tilted his head one way and then the other, considering. "Let's get the car. I'll tell you as we drive."

Six

en minutes later, inside the Mustang and with several miles behind them, Michael finished telling the bare bones of his story.

"Oh, I'm so sorry," Alex said.

He looked over and smiled. "You know, it's okay. She wasn't the one."

Oddly, Michael hadn't found talking about Rachel to be hard. Maybe Nate hadn't been entirely off his rocker, although there was no way Nate could have known that Michael would run into Alex there—*the* Al, the one person on the planet who could pull him out of this funk.

He asked questions about Jason, her company, her dreams, how long her trip would be. In return, she asked about his job as a music producer and so much else that had happened since their summer together.

He told her how he'd tried to find her online after camp—several times—but failed, likely because he hadn't remembered her full name, he only now realized. And he'd misspelled her last name, too. He'd searched for Al Davies and variations—Alex, Alexandra, Lexi, but he had the last name wrong. And he'd forgotten about the last *I*, which gave her name one extra syllable: Alexandria.

They reached C & O Trattoria, the Italian restaurant he'd told her about. He purposely hadn't mentioned how the place was open air—no roof—or about how the adobe-style walls were hand painted. How at night, tall burners throughout the restaurant kept the ambiance warm and enjoyable. He hoped she'd join in when the servers came in to sing "That's *Amore*." The lyrics were on the back of the menu, so anyone could sing along, and when they did, the whole restaurant felt like a group of old friends.

He suspected she wasn't hungry yet, but he had an idea for something to do before dinner.

The sun dipped below the horizon as he pulled into a parking stall in front of the restaurant's green awning. As he killed the engine, Alex had her eyes focused down the street, on the sunset in the distance, a pensive look on her face. Michael looked the other way down the street, at C & O Trattoria, back at the sunset, then back at Alex.

His stomach rumbled with anticipation of the best fettuccine alfredo he'd ever had, even though the crêpes couldn't have been long ago. He checked his watch and realized that they'd parked at the grocery store almost three hours ago—almost long enough to justify eating again already.

But Alex had a far-off look in her eyes, and he knew why. He'd mentioned Venice Beach being nearby, and while it wasn't as nice as Santa Monica, it was still the Pacific Ocean. Alex still had a job to do today, and he wanted to be sure she got it done before the sun fully set on her anniversary.

"Want to walk down to the beach?" he ventured.

She blinked as if the action clipped her thoughts. She looked apologetic as she nodded. "Would you mind? I really need to—"

"I know." And he did. Nate was on to something about finding closure. Of course, stumbling upon your crush from the best summer of your life certainly helped. He jerked his head the direction of the beach. "Let's go."

He got out of the car and took his suitcoat with them; the evening air was getting a bit chilly. With the jacket over his arm, he opened her door. Then, hand in hand, they walked to the beach, neither saying much. Alex shivered at the cooling evening, so Michael stopped and put his suitcoat around her shoulders.

She pulled it close with one hand and smiled, flushing. "Thanks."

With the water just coming into view, Michael couldn't help but think that reconnecting with Al—Alex—after so long couldn't be a coincidence. Yet she didn't live here. She'd be heading back to her life in Arizona soon.

They reached the sand, where Michael walked at her side for some time, but then, as they drew closer to the shore, he instinctively released her hand. She looked over with a question in her eyes. He nodded toward the ocean. "This part's not for me. Go. Set him free."

A wide smile broke over her face, sending warmth through Michael as if he'd been injected with it. She slipped off her flip flops and pulled a jar out of her purse—Jason's ashes. She walked out farther, her figure silhouetted against the fading orange-gold of the sun. Only when she stood ankle-deep in the water did she open the jar. And then she paused. He couldn't tell for sure, but he imagined that she was communing with Jason one last time. With her free hand, she pulled her long skirt up a few inches, then took a few more steps into the water—almost to her knees—then flung the ashes in a wide arc and stepped back, watching the ocean disperse them and take them away. She stood there for a moment longer, watching the ashes in the water.

Then, with quick steps, almost running, Alex returned to him. Sand stuck to her wet feet, and she still held the now-damp bottom of her skirt in one hand. "I did it," she said, breathing heavily. A yellow halo from the sun glowed behind her. She put the jar back into her purse, then took both of his hands in hers, reaching up for a kiss—the last thing he expected in that moment, but one he was happy to indulge in. Fettuccine could wait.

After a nice, slow kiss, she pulled back, smiling broadly, and picked up her flip flops in one hand. "Let's go."

As they walked back the way they'd come, their feet seemed to eat the distance far faster than when they'd gone the other direction. Michael checked his watch and was startled to see how fast the time had gone. The day had completely flown past; before he knew it, they'd be saying goodbye for the evening, one day closer to her flying home and away from his life again, and—

No.

"So," he said, trying to sound casual but knowing he was failing. "Are you based in Arizona for a reason?" An urgency to find a way to hang on to Alex, to test these new waters, to see if they had a future, burned inside his chest. He clung to the fact that Mikey and Al were together again—not a coincidence. "I mean, is Phoenix a hub for the fashion industry or something?"

Alex chuckled at that. "Hardly." She began swinging their hands as if being together was completely natural, as if they'd always been together. "I grew up in Arizona, that's all. It's the only state I've ever lived in."

"So you have a lot of ties there."

"Just my sister. But she's married now and lives in Tucson, which is a bit farther away. We don't see each other as often as we used to. Besides, her husband joined the Air Force, so they'll probably be hopping all over the world soon."

"Interesting."

She nudged him with her elbow. "What?"

He lifted one shoulder in a shrug. "I can't help but think that if nothing is keeping you there, then . . ."

Her step slowed, and she stopped, facing him. She took his other hand too. "Then . . . what?" Pink had returned to her cheeks like twin rosebuds—like they used to so long ago when she grew emotional. A good sign?

"Then maybe you could move here." Michael ran his thumbs over the tops of her hands. So soft. "We found each other again after all these years. You're free. I'm free. It's like fate expects us to . . ." But he couldn't quite get the words out.

"Give it a shot?" she finished, stepping closer. She pressed her hands to his chest and smoothed his shirt with her fingers.

Goose bumps broke out all over his arms. He nodded dumbly, then managed, "Yeah." He cleared his throat, then tried again. "And maybe you'll find even more business out here. L.A. probably has a slightly bigger fashion scene than Phoenix."

"But the cost of living is astronomical, and—" Her words cut off as if she couldn't find another argument.

"Being here could lead to huge company growth. It could be a very good career move." As if *that* were the reason he'd brought up the idea. The truth was, careers and money didn't matter; those things could work themselves out.

She lifted her face to his, seeming to study every feature. Now it was his turn to feel heat creeping up his neck. When she spoke next, her voice had lowered to almost a whisper and was full of emotion, "Maybe I will move west. But if I do, it won't be for my career."

"It wouldn't?" His voice turned into a whisper too. His throat started to tighten as hope and anxiety warred inside him.

She cocked her head to one side, holding his gaze with hers. "Not *wouldn't*. It *won't* be."

"Are you serious?" he said, unable to stop himself from tightening his grip on her hands. "You're really considering a move to L.A. and—"

She squeezed back and stepped even closer. "And maybe it'll help my career . . ."

He took a matching step, until their bodies almost touched. "And maybe we'll find Mikey and Al again . . ."

"And maybe it'll turn into something pretty awesome."

Michael reached out and cradled her face in his hands. She closed her eyes and sighed at his touch. He leaned in and pressed a kiss to her lips. One kiss, and then another, soft at first, and then with more intent. Alex reached up and threaded her fingers through his hair, kissing him back. After a long, deep kiss, Alex took a breath and pulled back, smiling wide. He rested his forehead against hers.

In the distance, the strains of "That's *Amore*" floated down to them from the restaurant.

Alex bit her lower lip. "You know, it's already been pretty awesome. And you're right; we owe it to fate to give it a try."

ABOUT ANNETTE LYON

Annette Lyon is a Whitney Award winner, a two-time recipient of Utah's Best of State medal for fiction, and a four-time recipient of publication awards from the League of Utah Writers. She's the author of more than a dozen novels, about that many novellas, over 120 magazine articles, and other publications. It's safe to say that she uses her cum laude English degree pretty much every day. In addition to fiction, she writes about grammar and chocolate, but she prefers eating the chocolate.

Find her online:
Website: AnnetteLyon.com
Blog: blog.annettelyon.com
Twitter: @AnnetteLyon
Facebook: Facebook.com/AnnetteLyon

A Hero's Song

Jennifer Moore

OTHER WORKS BY JENNIFER MOORE

Change of Heart
Simply Anna
Becoming Lady Lockwood
Lady Emma's Campaign
Miss Burton Unmasks a Prince
The Sheik's Ruby
Spring in Hyde Park

One

AnneMarie peeked through a crack between the heavy curtains. The size of the audience filling the theater made her heart pound and her throat go dry. A trickle of sweat rolled down her back, and she hoped the thick layer of deodorant she'd applied in her dressing room would live up to the advertiser's guarantee.

Feeling someone come up behind her, she turned to see Bob, the stage manager.

"Remember to look at the camera once in a while, smile, be yourself, and relax." Bob spoke in the routine tone that indicated he'd given the same instructions hundreds of times before. "No coughing or sneezing once your mike is on, and remember, don't stare at the playback screens while you're onstage." He fiddled with the small microphone attached to her collar, then pointed at the cameras where AnneMarie watched the ageless face of Clyde DeVille, the host of *The After-Hours Show* joking with the audience.

His monologue ended, and at the sound of audience applause, AnneMarie's heart tightened.

"Our first guest," Clyde went on, "is a prize-winning author of four novels in her best-selling series, *A Scoundrel's Embrace*." He paused and waggled his eyebrows.

A woman yelled, "I love you, Gaston!"

The audience laughed.

"Sounds just like my wife," Clyde said, and the audience laughed again. "The final book of the series, *The Rogue of the Masquerade Ball*, will be released tomorrow . . ."

The stage manager adjusted the box attached to the waistband at the back of AnneMarie's skirt, then raised a finger in front of his lips to indicate the microphone was on. "You ready?" he mouthed, and without waiting for a reply, parted the curtain and gave her a gentle push onto the main stage.

At her appearance, Clyde gestured toward her. "Everyone, please welcome AnneMarie Sinclair."

AnneMarie blinked at the bright stage lights and the noise of applause. She faltered, momentarily paralyzed as her eyes swept across the large crowd, all watching her. How had her agent, Sue, managed to arrange something like this? She'd never done a television interview before, let alone a late-night talk show, even if it was only a local cable station.

Remember, this is an amazing opportunity. She scolded herself, trying to restart her brain. *Please don't faint in front of the citizens of California.* Another bead of sweat slid down her spine. Taking a deep breath, she clenched her trembling hands into fists and smiled, walking as confidently as she could across the stage, up the few steps to the raised sitting area, where Clyde, his perfectly coiffed hair, and signature white smile waited for her.

He is *that handsome in real life.*

The host shook her hand, fake-kissed her cheek, and swept his palm graciously toward the couch, waiting while she took her seat before sitting in the chair next to her.

AnneMarie crossed her legs, then uncrossed her legs. She scooted forward, smoothing her skirt, and turned her knees to the side. Glancing at the playback screen, she slid back on the seat, crossing her legs again.

Get ahold of yourself and stop fidgeting. She took another deep breath and held her hands in her lap as the audience finished applauding.

"Thanks for being on the show, AnneMarie." Clyde said.

"Thank you for having me." She hoped her smile didn't look as phony as it felt. What she wouldn't have given to be watching this from the comfort of her own couch with a cup of cocoa and her fuzzy slippers. She glanced at the playback screen again, *it was nearly impossible not to*, and sat straighter to keep her blouse from bunching around her waist, then turned to Clyde.

"So how are things?" he asked.

"Things are good." *That's how he's opening his interview?*

"So, have you been to Los Angeles before?"

She nodded, putting on the animated public-speaking face. "I have, a few times. I love the city and the beach, but California's quite a culture shock for a farm girl from Aberdeen, Idaho."

"I believe it." He leaned his elbow on the arm of the chair between them and nodded with a casual smile, obviously trying to put her at ease. "So, this is your first time on the show, and from what my producers tell me, you're an intensely private person . . . which means we have *so* much to talk about." He chuckled at his own joke.

His cheeks didn't wrinkle when he smiled.

AnneMarie wondered if he was going to ask anything about her writing. Her high-school journalism class had conducted better interviews.

"Would you tell us a little about yourself?"

"Well, as I said, I live in the same small town where I was born. Let's see, when I'm not writing or reading, I like to go to movies, or for long walks, or out to dinner with friends." She nearly rolled her eyes at how supremely boring it all sounded. Too bad she didn't have the nerve to just make something up. As a fiction writer, she could have come up with hundreds of interesting scenarios. She kept the smile on her face and watched Clyde expectantly, waiting for his next question. She hadn't given him much to work with.

"Some of your books have exotic settings. Do you travel for research?"

"Not really. I do most of my research in the library and on the internet." And by *most* she meant *all*.

Even more boring.

"And are you single? Married? Seeing anyone?"

She shook her head and uncrossed her legs, tucking one ankle behind the other. "No, not right now."

"But I'd imagine you don't become a best-selling romance novelist without having any experience with love. Am I right?"

AnneMarie squinted and tilted her head slightly; her smile started to feel strained. *Where is he going with this?*

Clyde reached behind his chair and picked up a copy of one of her books: *Fires of Destiny*. He showed the cover to the audience, waited for their applause to die down, then opened it, pulling out a strip of paper that marked a page. "My wife chose something for me to read." He twisted his lips in a playful smile, which elicited an appreciative chuckle from the audience.

AnneMarie kept her pathetic imitation of a pleasant expression on her face, but her insides writhed. Nothing was worse than hearing someone else read your words aloud.

How did Sue talk me into this?

Clyde cleared his throat. "'Emeline swooned, and Rowan caught her easily, sweeping her into his strong embrace. She leaned her cheek against his powerful chest as his stallion galloped toward the chateau. Though he was a wealthy baron, and she but a milk maid, from the first moment, as their eyes had met across the crowded tavern, their souls were bound, and true love had intertwined their destinies.'" He closed the book, and swept one arm as he bowed to the applause and good-natured laughter at his presentation.

She tried to hold her smile, knowing full well that he'd read the words with a hint of sarcasm. *Remember, this is an amazing opportunity.*

Clyde turned back to her. "I'm sure the one question on our viewers' minds is this: Do your words come from personal experience? Have you ever been in love?" He rested his elbow on the arm of the chair and his chin on his palm.

AnneMarie considered a moment before answering. "Well, first of all, my novels are fiction, but it would be difficult to write about feelings I've never experienced." She slid her hands under her legs and raised her shoulders in a shrug. "Yes, I *have* been in love."

"Let me guess—a sizzling affair with a cowboy from back home? A fling with a professor in college?"

"No, nothing like that." She took a breath, wondering exactly how much to say. Here was one area where she wasn't completely uninteresting. And it had been ten years ago, so why not share it? "It was a summer romance right after high school."

"Your high school sweetheart?" Clyde prodded.

AnneMarie shook her head. "We met at a fine arts workshop at California State in Sacramento. They drew students from all over the country on scholarship. He played the guitar, and I took a poetry course." She could feel heat spreading over her cheeks and wondered if her skin looked splotchy on camera. "He was perfect, and I was crazy about him." She gave a small smile at the memory.

"And what happened?"

"Summer ended, and we . . . went our separate ways." The constriction in her throat surprised her. "I went to college. He focused on his band. And that was it." She shrugged and tried to smile, forcing herself to look at Clyde and pretending that she didn't still feel an ache in her chest and a burn of guilt. But would anything have changed if she'd gone to his concert that night?

The audience *aah*-ed.

"And you never saw him again?" Clyde spoke in a soft voice, which just made the itching behind her eyes worse.

Seriously, am I going to ruin this whole interview by crying?

She cleared her throat. "I wanted to keep in touch, but . . . well, it got complicated. Anyway, you asked about inspiration and that's where a lot of mine comes from. That's why I write romance. Reality doesn't always end happily ever after. Even when you meet your soulmate. Even when you fall in love. Sometimes it doesn't work out. Sometimes life gets in the way."

Sometimes you're too afraid.

"What about since then? Who was the next lucky guy to break your heart?" Clyde opened his eyes wide.

Back to boring. She cursed the blush on her cheeks. "Well, I've dated and had a few semi-serious relationships, of course, but he's the only one I would say I was ever in *love* with."

"Did this long lost love of yours become the inspiration for your hero, Gaston de Vaux?"

"Partly, I suppose." She was relieved that the subject had returned to her writing. "My characters aren't directly based on anyone, but it's hard not to let bits of people I've known creep into their personalities."

The interview continued for a few moments longer, and at last, AnneMarie felt herself relax as she told her journey of becoming a best-selling novelist, where she found her ideas, and what was next in her career.

I got this.

"And tomorrow is your grand release at the Beverly Hills Hotel," Clyde said. "Why don't you give us the details for those viewers who want a signed book?"

"The book's actual release is at midnight tomorrow, but my publisher has made special arrangements with Vroman's bookstore to have copies available tomorrow evening. I'll be speaking at seven in the grand ballroom and then signing books afterward." A rush of panic flowed through her at the reminder that she was giving a speech. Then again, if she survived *The After-Hours Show*, a speech at her own event should be a piece of cake.

"And do people need tickets to get in?"

"Yes. Your ticket reserves a copy of the book, and there will be plenty available. You can get them at the door, or at Vroman's."

"Well, AnneMarie, it's been delightful to meet you. You're a beautiful young woman, which was a pleasant surprise—most authors we have on the show are a little more on the stuffy side." He winked. "Good luck tomorrow, and I hope you'll come back sometime."

"Thanks again for having me." She shook his hand and smiled at the audience, then sat back and sighed in relief as the camera turned off and the monitors went to commercial.

I survived.

Clyde leaned toward her. "You were great," he said, then closed his eyes and rested his head back as a woman put a paper collar on him and touched up his make-up.

AnneMarie turned away, glad that her interview was over. Now for the easy part: sit here and smile while the next guest gets the uncomfortable questions.

During the break, a crew rushed around the stage, adjusting lights, and setting up for the musical guest. Earlier, AnneMarie had been too nervous to pay much attention to the behind-the-scenes action. Now that the interview was over, she watched it with fascination.

The crew worked efficiently on the other side of the studio, attaching cables, setting up musical instruments and equipment, until the stage manager called out, "Fifteen seconds, people . . ."

AnneMarie was still watching the crew—moving cameras and silently holding cue-cards—when she realized that Clyde was talking. She straightened and glanced at the screen as the camera zoomed in on his face.

"Ladies and Gentlemen. Well, mostly ladies. Our next guest needs no introduction. He has two platinum albums and is here to perform his new hit single, 'Lovin' my baby tonight.' Please welcome . . . Lance Holden!"

AnneMarie's head snapped up, and her heart flew into her throat. She thought she might have made a groany-squeaky sound. Did she hear him right? She couldn't have. But after one look at the cue cards—then at the stage where *he* stood, adjusting the microphone—she felt the blood drain from her face.

He looked up, and their eyes met. Lance gave her a crooked smile. Her heart squeezed so hard that she gasped. His too-familiar gaze held hers as he began to sing.

Clyde chuckled. He leaned close to her ear, holding one hand over the microphone pinned to his tie. "You and every other female on the planet."

At his words, AnneMarie realized that she was gaping, open-mouthed, at Lance Holden. She snapped out of her daze and shifted in her seat, giving Clyde a smile that she hoped made her look only like a sheepish, star-struck fan. Her mind churned. How could this be happening?

Had he listened backstage as she basically confessed that she'd never gotten over him? AnneMarie wanted to sink through the floor. She didn't dare look at the stage again, and turned to watch the playback screen instead.

Lance stood, hands gripping the microphone, singing a song she heard nearly every time she got into the car— singing it, to a studio full of screaming women and girls. He wore tight, designer jeans with tennis shoes. The sleeves of his black button-down shirt were rolled up to the elbows, showing arms colored with tattoos. A fitted vest complimented his lean torso. Chains and cords hung from his neck, and thick leather bands were strapped around his wrists. His hair was the same: gelled, messy, a little too long, and nearly black. A few days' growth of whiskers darkened his jaw.

She watched him on the screen, his deep-brown eyes drawing out the memories she'd refused to think about for years.

Sitting on a plaid blanket while he played his guitar and sang. His warm hand, holding mine as we walked down a rocky path. A timid kiss in the moonli—

The stage manager waved his hands to get her attention.

193

AnneMarie blinked herself out of the daydream and realized that the man was motioning for her to scoot to the other side of the couch. The idea of bolting from the stage flitted through her mind, but she followed instructions. What else could she do?

The song was over, and Lance walked toward them. Clyde stood to greet him.

AnneMarie slid to the far corner of the couch—which she now realized was more of a loveseat—as Lance sat beside her. Seeing him on TV and on magazine covers was hard enough. But sitting next to him . . .

Could the microphone pick up the thumping of her heart?

Clyde waited for the audience to quiet, then took his seat and turned toward his newest guest. "Lance, it's good to see you again," he said with showman aplomb.

Lance rested an ankle on his opposite knee. *He* didn't look the least bit uncomfortable. "Thanks for having me back."

"I'd like to introduce you to AnneMarie Sinclair," Clyde gestured toward her.

Lance put out a hand, and she took it. "Hello, AnneMarie." As they shook, he tipped his head the slightest bit, and his eyes held hers.

Could he feel her pulse racing? Would he admit he already knew her—that he . . . they . . . He was so relaxed and appeared completely unfazed by her presence—all of which humiliated her beyond belief.

She tried to tug her hand away, but Lance didn't let go.

"And AnneMarie, as I'm sure you know," Clyde continued, "this is Lance Holden,"

"Hello, Lance," AnneMarie managed to squeak out. *Please don't say anything about us.*

"She has a thing for guitar players," Clyde waggled his tweezed eyebrows, eliciting an appreciative chuckle from the crowd.

This can't be happening.

One side of Lance's mouth lifted as he continued to study her face. Did he realize he still had this effect on her? He finally released her hand and turned back toward Clyde.

"You've been pretty reclusive over the past year," Clive said. "So we're particularly delighted that you agreed to come on the show. So, tell me what you've been up to lately."

"Well, the band's getting ready to head out on tour, starting here in L. A. in two days. The new album's set to drop next week." He smiled as the audience cheered. "It's different from anything I've done before. The music is more personal."

AnneMarie watched him speak. He was so at ease; so confident in front of the crowd. Completely the opposite of how she felt, and it was another reminder of how different their worlds were. He looked older, of course, but he seemed to have aged more than ten years since she'd seen him last. His expression carried a hardness that hadn't been there before, and his mouth and eyes had fine lines around them. Seeing him up close now, he looked tired and worn. But he was still so handsome that she had to tear her eyes away and look around the stage for something else to focus on. Luckily, the camera had zoomed in on the two men.

"You've had a tough year," Clyde said. "Trouble with the law, a long stint in rehab. Did any of that have an influence on your music?"

Though he didn't show it outwardly, Lance's body had gone tight.

AnneMarie looked up, and a rush of defensiveness rose inside her at the insensitivity of Clyde's question.

"I'd like to think that the mistakes I make don't define me. Hopefully I can learn from them. I think I've changed—at least, I'm working on it." His jaw tightened. "Rehab's rough. I'd never wish addiction on anyone. But my experiences have definitely created who I am, and that person is reflected in my new album."

The lines on his face deepened as he spoke, and she wondered what he'd gone through. She felt guilt twisting inside over the fact that she hadn't once considered how taxing his lifestyle had been on him in the ten years since he'd made it big.

Clyde apparently sensed Lance's tension too, and changed the subject. "Earlier, AnneMarie and I were talking about love, and she shared a personal experience with us that now has me curious about your romantic interests."

AnneMarie's stomach turned over. *Kill me now.*

"You have quite the reputation of a playboy; your name's been associated with models, movie stars. And I heard that you recently broke up with Evangelina Porter." He looked at the crowd and winced dramatically.

The audience let out a groan.

AnneMarie's small bit of pity for Lance evaporated at the mention of his relationship with the gorgeous starlet. The twist of jealousy made her insides cold.

Clyde turned back to Lance. "So, how are you holding up? I mean . . . *Evangelina*." He let out a low whistle. "That had to be rough."

AnneMarie stuffed her hands under her legs.

Lance leaned forward, his fingers interlaced. Clyde leaned forward, too—looking delighted to be able to get some firsthand Hollywood gossip. AnneMarie leaned back, simmering and wishing there was an ejector seat built into the couch.

"Evangelina is an amazing woman," Lance said. "But we decided it would be better if we were just good friends."

Clyde's smile didn't fully cover his disappointment at the lack of a scandal. "Well, you're sitting next to the romance expert. Maybe you could get some relationship advice from AnneMarie—then next time, you won't end up in the friend zone."

Lance turned toward her and laid his arm across the back of the couch, raising his eyebrow. "So, AnneMarie Sinclair. Do you have some advice for a bad boy like me?" A lazy smile spread across his face. For a moment she thought she saw a hint of vulnerability in his eyes, but it vanished so fast that she wasn't certain it had been there at all.

He could mock her all he wanted, but she'd give him a serious answer. AnneMarie did her best to hold his gaze. Her throat was dry, and her palms were sweaty. She might be a farm girl from Idaho, but she had things she'd have liked to tell Lance Holden over the past ten years, and this would probably be her only chance to say anything to him. A decade of frustration and pain bubbled under the surface, so she tamped it down, feeling dangerously close to exploding all over the man in front of millions of viewers.

"I do have some advice. It's pretty simple, and at the same time, it's the theme of nearly every love story: a villain remains a villain until he cares about a woman enough to become a hero. She has to know there's nothing he wouldn't give up for her, nothing he wouldn't change."

She kept her eyes locked on his, hoping he understood how hurt she'd been, but at the same time, her stomach was hard with self-reproach. He hadn't been the only one unwilling to sacrifice. But he *had* been the one whose picture graced tabloids touting his relationships with a new woman in every issue. He'd probably been glad to be free of her.

Any trace of lightheartedness left his face. Lance's mouth moved as if he wanted to say something, but before he could, Clyde broke in loudly. They both turned their attention to him.

"Well, there you have it, folks—romantic advice from today's premiere romance novelist. Thank you both for coming tonight ..."

AnneMarie sank back into the couch not even caring that her blouse bunched around her waist. The gamut of emotions she'd experienced over the last hour left her feeling exhausted and shaky. She needed to get out of here. The camera zoomed in on Clyde's face while he ended the show.

The closing music started to play, and stage techs descended onto the stage. A man motioned for AnneMarie to stand and she shifted around as he unclipped the microphone from her collar and unhooked it from the back of her skirt. Looking up, she saw Lance studying her. He brushed her arm with the back of his fingers. "Hey, I wanted to talk to you. I—"

"Great show," Clyde interrupted.

AnneMarie shook Clyde's hand, thanking him again for the interview. When he turned to Lance, she bolted, practically running across the stage, through the curtain, and into her dressing room. She grabbed her purse and jacket from the vanity table before hurrying down the hall toward the back door that led to the alley where the station's limo waited to take her to the hotel.

"AnneMarie Sinclair?" a woman's voice called behind her.

She stopped and turned as a middle-aged woman in a pencil skirt and cardigan hurried toward her.

The woman had a colorful scarf tied around her neck, a bob haircut, and a cheerful smile. A badge that said "visitor" was clipped to her sweater. "I'm so glad I caught you. Will you sign my book?" She pulled a copy of *The Debutante's Surrender* out of her purse. "I can't wait for *The Rogue of the Masquerade Ball* to come out tomorrow. I've got a copy reserved."

AnneMarie darted a glance back down the hall, still feeling frantic to escape, but seeing she hadn't been followed, took the book and opened it to the title page. She fished around in her purse and found a pen. "Whom should I make it out to?"

"Marilyn," the woman said. "I'm a huge fan."

She wrote a greeting, signed her name and handed the book back, smiling but wishing she wasn't running from a situation fraught with humiliation. Marilyn seemed like someone AnneMarie would have liked to talk to. "I'm so sorry, but I'm really in a hurry. Please excuse me, Marilyn."

From the corner of her eye, she saw Lance step into the hall. She turned toward the doors behind her.

"Lance!" Marilyn called.

AnneMarie hesitated for an instant, glancing backward as Lance approached. Was Marilyn a friend of his?

"You were perfect." He reached them and Marilyn kissed his cheek then brushed the lipstick mark away in a maternal way.

"AnneMarie, this is my manager, Marilyn Daniels." He took a step toward her.

His manager? Aren't managers usually messy-haired hipsters with trendy suits, dark-rimmed glasses, and fake smiles?

"Good luck with your tour, Lance," AnneMarie said. "And Marilyn, it was nice to meet you. If you'll excuse me, I was just leaving." She nearly sprinted for the door.

"AnneMarie, wait," Lance called.

She didn't stop. Pushing on the metal bar, she opened the door and stepped out, heading toward the waiting limo.

Two

*L*ance shot a grateful look at Marilyn before he hurried out the door behind AnneMarie. No way would he let her leave without talking to her. Not after all the work he and Marilyn had put into making sure that they were on the same show. He could never have dreamed that she'd tell their story on air. And hearing it lit a fire under him.

Maybe something still lingered between them after all.

He'd read about AnneMarie's success, but as the years passed, he'd known that she'd never have anything to do with him. Not with the mess he'd made of his life, of his career . . . of everything.

But that was all in the past. He'd changed. Early on, he'd been so busy making a name for himself, and then he'd had to fight to maintain that hard-won success. He'd thought that booze and drugs were the only way to keep up in a world where one day you were a king and the next, nobody remembered you. The last four years were almost a blur; his addiction had become a way of life. He hadn't even been able to think for himself, but now he was clean. And the small spark of hope for another chance with AnneMarie flickered and grew.

He caught up to her and slid in front of the open limousine door, blocking her way.

She looked up, tossing her blonde curls over her shoulder with a flick of her wrist.

A jolt shot through his chest at the gesture that was so familiar, even after so long. Her expressions, her mannerisms—everything about her was so *her*. A flood of memories washed over him, and the emotions that came with them took him by surprise with their intensity. With no substances in his body to dull them, the feelings were nearly too much to handle. He breathed deeply.

I need to hold it together.

"Is everything all right?" AnneMarie's blue eyes lifted to meet his.

He thought his heart would crash through his ribs. He brushed a finger on her earlobe. "You still wear pearls."

She tilted her head to the side, her eyes narrowing, but the expression didn't fully hide the softness in her face.

The fact that she hadn't jerked away or pushed past him gave him courage to go on. "And I bet you've got a tube of some kind of fruity lip gloss in your purse."

"*That's* why you chased me down? To point out that I'm still boring and predictable? And wearing outdated accessories?"

He shoved his hands into his jean pockets and lifted his chin, studying her. "Not boring. Maybe *constant* . . . And, didn't you always say that pearls are classic?" He lifted both shoulders. "I'm glad you haven't changed."

Glad was an understatement. He couldn't think of anything more comforting than her steadiness. And she looked fantastic. Her face had lost its youthful roundness, while her body had done the opposite—filling out and curving in exactly the right places.

She darted a look at the limo driver, who had stepped away and waited a polite distance. "Well, I'm glad you hurried out here to tell me that."

She wasn't making this easy on him, and he didn't blame her. Why hadn't he come up with a better plan to reconnect? Had he seriously thought that after all this time, she'd just fall into his arms? His mind scrambled for something to talk about to keep her here longer.

"How are you doing? How's your family? You still live in Aberdeen?"

She nodded and raised her brows. "I'm fine, we're all fine, and yes . . . still in Aberdeen."

"You still write poetry? Or have you completely converted to steamy romance novels?" He winked.

AnneMarie blushed at his teasing and lowered her eyes, untwisting her purse strap.

He realized that though she tried to put forward a self-assured persona, she was still shy, and likely lacking in confidence when it came to her talents. The realization stirred a fresh wave of nostalgia, making him want to pull her into his arms, to reassure her as he used to.

"Maybe just a little steamy." She glanced up through her lashes before looking back down and running her fingers over the strap. "As far as poetry, I don't—at least, not much anymore. Not a lot of people are really interested in that sort of thing."

He reached out and tapped his finger beneath her chin, raising her face. "I always was." He spoke in a quiet voice, hoping she could feel the sincerity of his words.

She looked at him for a moment but then stepped back quickly. "I should go." She crossed her arms, looking everywhere but at him. "I have a big day tomorrow and . . ." She gestured with a flapping hand for him to move out of her way.

A wave of panic went over him. Why was his charm not working? "Wait. Can we talk? You want to grab a bite to eat? I know a great Thai place close by."

She glanced at the limo driver again. "I really can't. Tomorrow's my launch, and I still have a few things to get done for it. I need to get back to my hotel."

"How about I ride with ya?"

AnneMarie paused, seemed to consider, then looked down and nodded, her cheeks turning pink. He remembered how he'd loved making her blush, and wished she would look at him again.

She climbed into the car and scooted all the way across the seat to the opposite door.

He slid in beside her. The door closed, and out of habit, his gaze moved to the limo's bar, locking onto the bottle of champagne sitting on ice. He breathed heavily, and his mouth watered as he fantasized about grabbing it, popping the cork and drinking straight from the bottle.

Annemarie's gaze followed his line of sight. She lifted the bottle from the bucket and opened her door, leaning out and setting it on the curb. She moved back inside without saying anything.

He slumped back in relief now that the temptation was out of sight. Did she have any idea of the craving that raged inside him every single second and was held at bay only by an immense amount of self-control?

AnneMarie looked out the window, leaning her chin forward to look up at the skyscrapers as they drove through Los Angeles.

Lance knew their time was short, and he wouldn't have another chance. He had to know if she meant what she'd said on Clyde's stage. He took a breath and plunged in.

"About what you said on the show . . ."

AnneMarie winced. "I shouldn't have called you a villain. I'm sorry if that embarrassed you." She held his gaze for a moment, then looked away quickly.

She knew damn well that wasn't what he was talking about.

"I mean, what you said before that—about our summer."

She rubbed her hand up and down one arm and turned her body toward him—but not her eyes. "I don't know why I said that. I was caught up in the moment with the audience and everything, I guess."

"But you meant it. Didn't you?" He had to know.

"Lance, I've never kept my feelings for you a secret. But why do they matter now? So you can feel sorry for me? Chalk it up as another conquest?"

"That's not it at all. I . . . I miss you." He didn't think he'd ever laid his feelings out like this, ever made himself so vulnerable.

"I have a hard time believing that's true," AnneMarie whispered. She pushed a curl behind her ear and looked out the window. "I have a TV and a computer. Maybe you haven't been to a grocery store in a while, but judging from the tabloids, you don't seem to have missed *anything*."

He looked out the other window, trying not to let her see how her words—how the anger in her eyes—stung. He knew what she'd seen, and although some of it was true, most was exaggerated. The media loved to portray him as a player. But AnneMarie should have seen through the headlines, known the image wasn't all true. She knew him better than anyone.

The silence stretched uncomfortably between them. He kicked himself for not knowing what to say. She was going to leave, and all of this would be for nothing. Why had he thought that this might work? Did he really believe things could be the same—as if the past ten years had never happened? He shoved his fingers into his hair and rested his elbows on his knees. When she'd talked to Clyde, he'd had so much hope, but now he had no idea where to start.

AnneMarie cleared her throat. "It's been awesome to see your career take off. I have your albums."

He turned to her, grateful for the change of subject. It was just like her to take away his discomfort, even if he deserved to wallow in it. The spark of hope grew again when Lance realized she'd followed his career, as he'd followed hers.

"Thanks."

She smiled at him. "I especially love 'When You Say My Name.' I'd have to say it's my favorite song of yours."

His heart warmed. "When You Say My Name" was a ballad, and one of the only released songs he'd actually written himself. Of course AnneMarie had picked that one out. It was probably the least downloaded of any. Most of his fans skipped over it, but he should have known a person that knew him—the real him, not his fame—would love it.

"My manager wanted me to bury that one."

"Marilyn?"

"No, the manager before her."

"Marilyn seems nice," AnneMarie said.

"She's amazing. She's the closest thing to a mom I've ever had. I don't know how I would have gotten through the last year without her."

AnneMarie's brow wrinkled at that, but she stayed quiet.

A Hero's Song

The limousine pulled into the curving drive in front of the hotel, and Lance's pulse sped up as he tried to think of a way to keep her from leaving. He couldn't remember the last time he'd had to work so hard to get a woman to be with him. The car stopped.

AnneMarie touched his arm and smiled. "It was good to catch up, Lance." The attempt at cheerfulness didn't fool him; her smile didn't reach her eyes.

He studied her expression, trying to find any sign that she'd be willing to see him again. "So, you in town for a while? Maybe we could get coffee or dinner or something, I mean, we're both here in L.A., we haven't seen each other in years."

The driver opened her door. AnneMarie studied him for a moment before her eyes tightened and she lowered her shoulders. "Sorry. I'm leaving the day after tomorrow. My flight is Saturday morning. It was good to see you, and I'm glad you're doing so well." She turned away. "Looks like you've got everything you ever wanted." She stepped out, and the door closed behind her.

He leaned his head back against the seat. *Not everything.*

Three

The next morning, Lance climbed out of the water and wrapped a towel around his waist. He glanced around, thinking how strange it was for his entire pool area to be empty. Since he'd gotten sober, it wasn't just his pool that was empty. Once partying wasn't his only goal in life, the people he'd thought were his friends simply disappeared into the woodwork.

He grabbed another towel and rubbed it over his hair, smiling wryly. *Friends.* Did any of those people know the barest facts about him? They'd all known when he'd be hosting a party, which girls would be there, and that they'd be seriously tanked by the time the night was over. Many of them had spent days at a time here, drinking and partying. But he would have bet that none of them knew the name of his hometown or his favorite candy bar. They'd been content to ride the wave of his fame as long as it lasted, but when his world came crashing down, they'd had no problem bailing on him.

A Hero's Song

Even when his house had been filled with music and models, drugs and liquor, he'd still felt lonely. Those things had just made it easier to ignore the feeling—they kept his mind in a constant haze. His addictions had pushed away everyone who had ever cared about him, driven a wedge between him and his family. They'd brought his career to a crashing halt when he hadn't been able to so much as arrive at the studio sober.

He looked through the Plexiglas fence surrounding the pool area then down to the beach below. This time of day, some surfers still rode the late-morning waves, but most of the diehards had left hours ago. Now families spread out towels, opened umbrellas, and applied sunscreen. The sight made him feel more alone. He owned a multi-million dollar house, one of the most exclusive residences in the county. But though the location was amazing, the view staggering, and everything inside top of the line—he was still alone in a world where he didn't feel like he belonged anymore.

He remembered how hard he'd tried to invite AnneMarie into his life ten years ago. Anger welled in his chest as he thought of how she hadn't come to his concert that night. And pain. He'd waited, hoped . . .

He leaned back on a lounge chair and closed his eyes as the morning haze burned off under the California sun, which warmed his skin. He heard the sound of the sliding-glass door and Marilyn's heels clacking on the stone tiles behind him.

He felt her shadow across his face as she stood over him. "Are you gonna tell me what happened yesterday?"

He didn't sit up or open his eyes. "What happened is we wasted our time. She's not interested." His face burned as he said the words, and he hoped his voice wouldn't crack. He needed to learn to cope with his newly rediscovered emotions.

"I don't think so. We both heard her interview. So unless there was another guitar player at that summer camp—"

"I'm not that guy anymore." He sat up and twisted around, slapping his bare feet on the ground. He couldn't help but think of the hurt in AnneMarie's eyes before the car door closed behind her yesterday, and know that he was the reason. It made his chest ache. "I'm not the guy she remembers."

His manager handed him a t-shirt, which he obediently put on. She refused to conduct business when he was half-dressed. "You're not giving up this easily. Not when I had to pull the big shot rock-star card to get you on *The After-Hours Show* the same night she was. It's going to take a little work to win her back, but you know how to work hard. And she's worth it, right?"

Marilyn folded her arms around her iPad. She wore slacks and a starched white blouse. He liked how she was always professional and didn't try to look like a twenty-year-old. Unlike most managers he'd seen, she was comfortable with who she is. Her light hair had a few grays showing, but that didn't seem to bother her in the least.

He squinted as he looked up at her. Firing his old manager, Rudy, and hiring Marilyn Daniels had probably been the best decision of his life. Not that it was much of a contest. The bad decisions he'd made over the years stacked so high that it had taken lawyers, bankers, and, of course, his manager to dig him out from under all of it. Without her, he'd either be in jail, broke, or dead. Maybe all three. Marilyn had figured out that Rudy was robbing him blind. She'd convinced Lance to go to rehab, and she was the only one allowed to visit while he sobered up and took a good, hard look at his life.

She'd seen him hit rock bottom. She stood firm while he threatened, screamed, and cursed and told her he'd fire her if she didn't get him a hit of something *now*. She hugged him when he sobbed on her shoulder. And once he was clean, she helped him figure out where he wanted his life to go. He would never have made it this far without her.

His old manager had been ridiculous. A smooth-talking, Armani-wearing slime ball who constantly yelled into the Bluetooth on his ear. He made a career of telling Lance exactly what he wanted to hear, feeding him lies and flattery until he didn't know what the truth was anymore. When Lance had wondered about his career path, Rudy had thrown so many girls and drugs at him that after a while, Lance had stopped caring, and let him have free rein with his money. Marilyn was probably the only person in the last ten years to speak to him with complete honesty—something not always easy to hear, but he loved her for it.

"Yeah, AnneMarie's worth it. But that's the problem. I'm an addict with a rap sheet and one of the worst reputations in Hollywood." He held his hand up to shade his eyes. "Nice girls don't want to get mixed up with a mess like that."

Marilyn pulled a chair closer, and sat across from him. "You're a great guy who's had some bumps in the road. But you're getting your life back together. That's nothing to be ashamed of. If anything, you should be proud of how far you've come."

"I'm sure she doesn't see it like that."

"Why not?"

Lance hung his hands between his knees. "She had goals too. She followed her dream, but she kept her head. She didn't sell out. She didn't let other people flatter her to the point of forgetting who she was and nearly losing everything." It was when he was at his lowest point that he realized the need for a slower pace and stability. But maybe he'd realized it too late.

He glanced at Marilyn. Her face showed compassion, but not pity. Yet another thing he loved about her. She wouldn't let him feel sorry for himself.

"We all have to grow, Lance. And people do change."

He blew out a breath. "*She* hasn't. And what if I've changed too much?"

Marilyn crossed her legs and set the iPad on her lap. "You're back on track now and deserve to be happy. But you also have to be willing to work for it. In the last decade, I'll bet you never had to do more than show that crooked smile to get any woman you wanted to come running." She raised her brows. "And how long did any of *them* last?"

Lance didn't answer. His gut burned with shame when he thought of the memories—she was right, of course. How could she speak so calmly about the appalling life he'd led?

She leaned forward to catch his eye. "But trust me; a woman you have to work for—she's worth the effort." She nudged his leg with her toe. "And you'll never forgive yourself if you don't try."

Did he dare try again? AnneMarie had seemed so angry yesterday in the limo. His mind moved back to the summer ten years earlier. How enchanted she'd been by Glass Beach and the picnic that turned into late-night stargazing. She'd whispered the words of a poem she had written but was too shy to say aloud. He'd played his guitar and sung to her as she lay with her head propped on one hand, watching him with a look that melted his youthful heart. Her hair had been longer then, and it glowed in the moonlight, just like her eyes.

A tune started in his mind. Lance jumped up. "I need my guitar."

A Hero's Song

"I know that look." Marilyn pointed her finger toward him.

Lance hurried into the house and down the hall to his studio. The melody was growing more insistent; if he didn't get it down on paper, his brain would explode.

For the remainder of the day, he lost himself, chasing words, experimenting with chords, and filling page after page with notes. Finally, he played the song through, singing as he strummed the tune that had hijacked his thoughts. The lyrics weren't his, but he remembered them as clearly as if he'd heard them every day of his life.

And in a way, he had. They'd sounded in his memory so often that they'd somehow wedged themselves deep into his psyche. He hadn't realized how difficult they would be to hear again after so long, not until he sang them. He played the last note and closed his eyes, relieved to have it all down, and swallowed at the tightness in his throat.

Hearing a soft knock, he looked toward the doorway, where Marilyn leaned against the doorframe. "It's amazing, Lance." She wiped at her eyes. "We have to put it in the set tomorrow."

His neck heated. He hadn't intended for anyone to hear, especially with his voice cracking as the lump in his throat had grown. "That would change the entire lineup."

"It wouldn't require much adjustment. The acoustic version is beautiful all by itself. Nobody else would need to rehearse with you."

"I don't know. It's still pretty raw."

"It's a hit, Lance. When something comes from your soul like that, it speaks straight to the heart."

"Yeah, but the person whose heart I want to speak to won't even know it's for her."

Marilyn tilted her head and was still for a moment. She

pulled the phone out of her pocket and glanced at it. "I don't know if you're up for it, but there's a romance author signing books downtown for another two hours." She tapped a finger on her lips.

If he went, would AnneMarie be happy to see him? Would it do any good? Had he blown his chance? Her words from the show sounded in his head.

He's the only one I'd say I was ever in love with.

He jumped up and hung his guitar on the rack, then ran out of the room. "I can be ready in ten minutes," he called over his shoulder.

His heart pounded as he hurried into the shower. Marilyn was right. Winning back AnneMarie's heart would take some work. But he could do it.

Years ago, her soul had touched his through her poem. His song might do the same, right? His chest tightened with doubt but softened again when he remembered that AnneMarie loved "When You Say My Name." She saw through the years of music and fame and picked out the one part of his career that was really *him*.

She was definitely worth it.

But was he?

Four

AnneMarie let out a relieved breath. She stepped away from the podium on the raised stage where she'd just finished speaking and answering audience questions. As much as she loved hearing from fans and talking about her writing, she preferred doing it through email. Standing in front of a crowd turned her brain into mush—and kicked her sweat glands into overproduction.

She had to admit, though, that she was delighted by the turnout. Every chair was filled; the hotel ballroom was standing room only. Journalists were on hand, snapping pictures, and a cameraman wearing a jacket with a local TV-station logo stood in the back, filming. She glanced at her agent, Sue, who was speaking to a man in a suit who held a microphone.

AnneMarie pulled at her blouse to get some airflow, hoping the silk wouldn't stick to her skin. She thought through what she'd said, wincing at some of her dumb answers. At least when she was writing, she could go back and edit her words.

"That was great," said Christy, the event manager, who met her at the bottom of the steps. "I don't know what you were so worried about."

AnneMarie gave her a grateful smile. "Thanks." She looked around the noisy room as the two of them walked to the side of the ballroom where a line was already forming at a table stacked with books.

Sue hurried over and wrapped her in a hug. "Did you hear? We had to send someone to Vroman's for more books." Her literary agent looked practically giddy.

"That's wonderful." AnneMarie's eyes traveled over the crowd. The other, smaller events she'd done had always been in a library or bookstore, and had been much more subdued. The crowds and attention here were exactly what had intimidated her—exactly what had come between her and Lance. She felt sick as she thought about yesterday and blowing him off, though she knew it had been the right thing.

But he misses me? At the time, his words—and the sincerity of his expression—had stolen her breath, but now that she'd distanced herself, she realized he couldn't have been serious. He had his choice of women and must be either bored or on a rebound.

Her smile must have looked forced, because Sue squeezed her hand. "You're almost done, and then you can go back to hiding in your little farmhouse in the middle of nowhere." She rolled her eyes, joking. Sue loved to tease AnneMarie about her quiet life, and even more about what she considered to be a mind-numbingly small town. Sue was used to the activity and excitement of New York City and couldn't understand why AnneMarie would choose such a solitary existence.

AnneMarie watched her agent hurry away and start a conversation with a reporter, then turned back to the table.

Enormous posters of her book cover leaned on easels, and AnneMarie grimaced at the not as enormous, but still horrifyingly large author photo on a poster next to them. She sat on the designated chair and picked up the pen, smiling as the first woman in line stepped forward and held out a book.

Someone squealed, and the woman in front of her spun around, nearly running into the tanned pectoral muscles of Gaston de Vaux—or, more precisely, the cover model who depicted him. Lenny was dressed in full medieval costume, shirt open and long hair cascading over his shoulders. He looked as if he'd just arrived on horseback straight from the Middle Ages. The woman pressed her hand to her chest and sucked in a breath, her face turning crimson.

AnneMarie couldn't help the giggle that escaped.

The woman turned toward her and fanned her face with her hand. "Oh my."

They shared a laugh as the cover model moved on. He strode through the crowd, stopping to take pictures with swooning, giggling women—he had to be loving it—just like his character would if he'd been transported to the twenty first century.

For the next two hours, she signed books and chatted with fans about Gaston de Vaux, movie rumors, and what she planned to do next. After each person left, she glanced at the far end of the room, looking for the end of the line, but it didn't seem to be getting shorter. She was humbled that so many people would wait for so long to see her, and found that in spite of her earlier reservations, she was actually enjoying the night.

Sue sat next to her and placed a bottle of water on the table.

AnneMarie took a drink. "Thanks."

"Sure thing, honey." Sue opened her compact and checked her lipstick. "I can't believe this turn out." Sue struck up a conversation with the next woman in line.

AnneMarie scrawled her name, closed the cover, and held out the book. But the woman had stepped away and looked toward the door. A change came over the room like a shift in the energy. A wave of whispers spread through the crowd. She shrugged at Sue, who seemed as confused as she was.

The line became irregular as people craned their necks to see what was going on. Someone squealed. And the already noisy crowd became noisier. *Is Lenny flexing or something?* The whispers got louder, and AnneMarie started to pick out phrases.

It can't be.

Can you really see him?

Why would he be here?

The crowd moved so that the line was nonexistent.

It is him!

Oh my gosh! Lance Holden!

AnneMarie's heart raced, blasting hot blood throughout her body and settling in a flush over her skin. *He's here.*

Another squeal sent the crowd rushing for the door. AnneMarie stood, trying to see through the throng of people.

"I'll go check it out." Sue smoothed her hair and hurried away.

AnneMarie stepped to the side, watching the crowd, which had stood patiently in line to get a book but had suddenly turned chaotic. Women pulled out their phones and screamed things like, "Someone find me a Sharpie," or "I can't believe he touched my shoulder."

In the middle of the frenzy, she caught a glimpse of

Lance, and the sight sent another jolt through her. Her pulse sounded in her ears, and her breathing sped up. He'd come to see her.

Their eyes met. He looked like he was trying to move toward her. But a teenage girl stopped him, throwing her arms around his neck and whispering something in his ear. Lance smiled back but pulled her arms away, even as another woman grabbed him around the waist, putting her face next to his and snapping a selfie. Someone shoved a piece of paper and pen in front of him. He shook his head, turning back toward AnneMarie.

The orderly line was reforming, but in the opposite direction, as people waited to get their picture taken with Lance. Women far too old to justify the behavior pressed against him and exposed body parts, hoping for a signature.

AnneMarie looked around. Her side of the room had emptied except for the bookmarks and other paper products littering the floor. She stood alone next to a giant picture of herself, behind a table stacked with her books. The biggest night of her life had become a disaster.

Her initial elation at seeing Lance sank. Her insides twisted, and angry heat flushed through her. Why was he doing this? Was he trying to prove something? To show her how famous he was? His obvious play-acting frustration as he "tried" to escape enraged her further. He knew exactly how a crowd of women would react to his appearance.

Her breathing became uneven, and she clenched her teeth. Lance and his stupid fame had ruined her night. Suddenly she couldn't stay in this room and watch women fawn over him for another second. She looked around for an escape and spotted a service door. Without a backward glance, AnneMarie fled.

Five

ance watched AnneMarie rush through a side door. Panic at losing her spiked through him. He pushed his way through the crowd, doing his best to keep his smile on and not shove anyone to the ground, but his frustration was building. She looked furious, and he was desperate to reach her. He had to explain.

As gently as he could, he pried another woman's hand off his arm and dashed toward the door, which was just closing. From the corner of his eye, he saw a reporter and a group of fans hurrying after him, but he didn't stop.

He slipped through the door into a service hallway, pulling the door tight behind him, and hesitated. Which direction to go? Doors on one side led to what he assumed were other meeting rooms, and on the other, to a large, stainless-steel kitchen. A movement at the end of the hallway, a flash of pink like AnneMarie's blouse. He hurried that direction.

When he caught up to her, AnneMarie turned around. Her eyes darted back to the row of closed doors.

"I'm sorry," he said. "I really didn't mean to . . ." He took a careful step, feeling as if he'd trapped a bird, and one false move would send her flying away. "AnneMarie, if I had any idea that coming would have turned your night into such a circus, I never would have—"

The door behind them banged open and the noise of the ballroom floated into the hallway.

AnneMarie turned. She *was* going to bolt.

Without thinking, Lance opened the nearest door, grasped her arm and pulled her inside.

He glanced back at a group of reporters, fans, and hotel staff hurrying toward them, then closed the door, plunging the room into darkness. He clicked the lock, and ran his hand along the wall until he felt a light switch and pressed it. He turned around and realized that they were in a small custodial closet.

AnneMarie stood a few feet behind him, her arms folded and her eyes wide.

He couldn't believe he'd screwed this up so badly. He raised his hands. "I'm not trying . . . I mean . . . I just wanted to get you away from . . ." He motioned to the door behind him, then dropped his arms. "I'm sorry I ruined your night and shoved you into a closet. I just wanted to talk to you."

She pulled her brows into a scowl. She didn't say anything; she didn't have to. Her glare could have melted steel.

He rubbed his palm over the back of his neck "Listen, I really didn't mean to ruin your event. I really thought I was coming at the end when most people would already be gone. I would never have—"

The door handle rattled, and they both stared at it.

221

AnneMarie looked from the door to him. "I have to get back out there. People will be wondering where I am."

"Not yet. We need to talk." He didn't know what to do with his hands, so he stuck them into his pockets. "Please, can we just . . . talk?"

She remained silent, her lips pursed, but her eyes didn't look like she still wanted to commit murder, which he took as a good sign.

Lance slid two buckets from beneath the shelves and turned them over. "For an evening out, I usually prefer a location with fewer toilet scrubbers, but this isn't bad." He grinned and swooped his hand toward the makeshift chairs.

AnneMarie looked at the buckets then at him but didn't smile at his attempt to lighten things up. "Why are you here, Lance?" She folded her arms.

"I saw you leave the ballroom and—"

"No, why are you *here*? Why did you come tonight?" Her lips were pressed together tightly and she looked away. "Why are you doing this?"

Lance reached toward her. "I thought it was obvious—to see you."

She shifted her weight to one side, avoiding his extended hand. "That's not what I mean. It's been so long . . . *Why* do you want to see me? Why now?" She darted a look at him then stared at a shelf of glass cleaner. "Is it because of what I said on the show? Are you feeling sorry for me . . . or are you just bored between super-model girlfriends?"

Someone pounded on the door.

Marilyn was right; this wasn't going to be easy.

"Just listen, okay?" He tried to think of the perfect words to say but came up blank. How could he explain that he'd always missed her? How he'd been so caught up in partying and fame that he'd lost sight of everything, even the best thing in his life?

"I'm listening."

The gentleness in her voice threw him off balance. "Why didn't you come to my concert that night?" The words burst out of his mouth, surprising them both.

"What? Is that why—"

He scrubbed both hands over his face. "I waited . . ." It was a relief to ask what he'd wondered for a decade, even if his brain wasn't consulted before his mouth spewed the words. "My first stadium concert as the main act. I— dammit . . . Why didn't you come?" He felt like he had something in his throat and tried to clear it as the memory of standing at the backstage door returned.

The guys in the band begging him to hurry onstage because they should have started twenty minutes ago. His manager yelling. But he knew if he just waited a bit longer . . . And she never showed.

AnneMarie sat on the bucket and her shoulders slumped. "I didn't think you'd notice. You stopped calling, you cancelled dates, and when I called you, someone else always told me you couldn't come to the phone. You were so busy with your new life and didn't have time for me anymore."

"Yeah, I was busy." He sat next to her, resting his elbows on his knees and leaning forward. He tipped his head to catch her eye. "But I wanted you to be a part of all of it. I was . . . I loved you."

AnneMarie looked down at the tile floor, but not before he saw that her eyes were wet. "I guess I was scared. Your world was so big and so different, and I was an eighteen-year-old, small-town girl. I didn't think there was a place for me in it."

"I'm sorry. I just got caught up in everything. I should have—" His chest was tight. The hurt from her rejection had started him on the road to self-destruction, using drinking and girls to cover up the pain. But it wasn't all her fault. Looking back, he could see more clearly. Their lives had been so out of sync, no wonder she had felt scared. "I wanted you there. I wanted it so bad, it hurt." He brushed his hand up her arm, smiling when she shivered, and emboldened when she didn't pull away. Her skin was hot and her eyes locked on his. He skimmed his thumb over her chin, and AnneMarie closed her eyes.

He ignored the sounds from the hall and leaned close, brushing his lips over hers. "Remember Glass Beach?"

A small smile lifted her lips. "Yeah, I remember."

He pushed the hair back over her shoulder, combing his fingers through the soft strands. "Do you remember what you said that night? Your poem?"

AnneMarie pulled away. "Stop." Her voice grew louder and took on an edge. She shook her head, slowly at first and then more firmly. "Just stop."

He stared at her. What had changed?

"Lance, I'm sorry. I can't do this again." She waved her hands through the air as if to push away the memories. "I know what I said then, and what I said yesterday. When it comes to you, my feelings were—*are*—so complicated." She dropped her arms. "I care about you, I really do. It's just been too long."

Lance's heart pounded and his skin felt tight as desperation overcame his thoughts. He was losing her.

The door handle shook again, and she stood. "I have to go."

"But we can figure it out. It's not too late." He wasn't above begging.

"No, Lance, we can't." Her expression was set. She bit her lip and rubbed one arm but didn't look at him. "It *is* too late."

Lance watched her for a moment then pulled his phone from his pocket. "Marilyn can get security to clear the hall." He sent a text and stood next to the door, his mind scrambling to find out a way to fix this. AnneMarie's chin trembled, and when he saw it, Lance's heart felt like it was being squeezed. "AnneMarie?" He lifted his hand toward her.

She shook her head. "I'm sorry." Her voice was hardly more than a whisper, but it might as well have been blasted from a blow horn. The two words said it all.

Before long, the noise in the hall stopped.

His phone vibrated, and he read the message then looked up at AnneMarie. "You're good to return to the ballroom. Marilyn and someone named Sue have everything under control." His chest was heavy. Marilyn had been wrong. It *had* been too long and there was too much to forgive. Why had he let himself hope?

"Thanks." AnneMarie moved past him and opened the door. She took a step but then turned back, keeping her eyes on the floor. "Lance, I wish . . ."

"Yeah me, too." He closed the space between them and pulled her against him.

Lance held her, and she sank into him, burying her face against his chest and returning the embrace as if she meant it, as if the ten years and the gulf between them had never existed. She fit in his arms. *This* felt right.

He tightened his arms and spoke against her hair. "I didn't want to say goodbye to you again."

She nodded, barely moving her head. He brushed his fingers over her hair, wanting every detail of the moment to last: her scent, the feel of her in his arms, the way her body molded to his . . . everything seemed so perfect. But, all too soon it ended.

AnneMarie stepped away and hurried out without a backward glance, leaving behind an ache he remembered all too well.

He closed the door, sinking down onto one of the overturned buckets, and rubbing the skin around his eyes. He'd blown it. Another chance had been too much to hope for.

The closet door opened.

Lance didn't glance up. Of course Marilyn would find him. "I'm taking the song out of the set," he told her.

Marilyn didn't ask what he was talking about. "Leave it in."

He looked up and rested his arms on his knees. "It's too late. We're pulling it."

"I'm your manager. It stays in."

Six

nneMarie folded her cardigan and laid it over the other clothes in her suitcase. She set her toiletry bag in an empty corner and fastened the straps to hold it all in place then closed the suitcase and zipped it.

She sat on the small couch and rubbed her temples, glancing at the digital clock. Not quite 7:00 a.m. Her head ached—no surprise after a long sleepless night. Leaning back, she closed her eyes and let out a heavy breath. She felt anxious and unsettled. It would be good to return to her comfortable life in Aberdeen, where everything was familiar. She could sit at her tidy desk, pet her cat, and immerse herself in work without having to think about Lance Holden or the emptiness that had filled her heart yesterday after she'd walked away from him again.

At least, that's what her brain kept telling her. But her heart longed for something completely different. *Doesn't that dumb organ know I'm trying to protect it?*

The entire situation had been a weird coincidence—the two of them appearing on the same show on the same night. Without that strange twist of fate or her confession to Clyde, Lance would never have given her a second thought—she was sure of it.

But he *had* thought of her. And for just a moment, it had seemed like there was a chance to go back to the past. Lance's reminder of Glass Beach had brought back a surge of memories that AnneMarie had thought she'd successfully locked away.

Glass Beach. He'd kissed her that night, and with her poem, she'd laid her heart open. They'd made promises to each other. She'd thought it was the beginning of something that would last forever. She'd been so young and hopeful; she would never have believed that it would all be torn apart a few months later. She hitched up her shoulders, and, with some effort, pushed the memories back where they belonged—deep inside, where they couldn't hurt.

What had happened was for the best. But she resented the "what if" that dug into her like a splinter she couldn't remove.

The now-famous tabloid picture of Lance Holden waist-deep in the ocean, kissing a curvy, bikini-clad starlet, popped into her mind and pushed away more of her regret.

"I don't belong in his world," she said aloud, hoping to convince herself. She slid her feet into her shoes and let out another breath. It was over. But had she thrown away a second chance?

Mercifully, her fitful musings were interrupted by the sound of the bedside phone ringing.

She reluctantly crossed to it. "Hello?"

"AnneMarie? Hi. It's Marilyn Daniels."

Marilyn, as in Lance's manager? AnneMarie's heartbeat quickened. "Uh, hi."

"Listen, sorry to call so early, but I hoped to catch you before your flight. Do you have time to meet me for coffee? I'm down in the lobby."

"Why exactly are you here?" She didn't want to sound rude, but she also didn't want to think any more about Lance—or his manager, or his career, or his bikini-clad minions. She wanted to go home and pretend that the past 48 hours had never happened.

"I just wanted to talk. I won't take up much of your time. Fifteen minutes, tops."

"Did Lance . . ."

"He doesn't know I'm here."

The line was silent as Marilyn waited for an answer. How to reply? AnneMarie felt uncomfortable with the idea of meeting Lance's manager, but she had to admit that a part of her was curious about the woman's motives. Besides, it would be awkward if she hung up then walked past her a few minutes later on the way to breakfast. "I'll be right down."

AnneMarie rode the elevator with a pit growing in her stomach. What did Marilyn want? Did Lance truly not know she was here? If so, had Marilyn come to scold her for the way she'd treated her client? She seemed protective of him, and AnneMarie was sure she hadn't come to bid a fond farewell.

By the time she stepped into the lobby, her emotions had leapfrogged over uncomfortable and landed on annoyed. Who did this woman think she was?

Marilyn waved from a small chair in the lounge area. When AnneMarie reached her, Marilyn gestured toward another chair.

AnneMarie took a seat across the table, and sat with clenched muscles, braced to defend herself.

"I ordered us both a café au lait, if that's all right," Marilyn said.

Her smile caught AnneMarie off guard. Instead of accusatory, her expression was sympathetic. "Thank you." Looking closer, she noticed that Marilyn's eyes, which had seemed bright when they met at the studio, were now bloodshot and red-rimmed. "Are you feeling all right?"

"Just tired," Marilyn said. "Stayed up all night reading." She yawned, and her friendly smile turned a bit sheepish. "I just had to know what happened with Gaston and Scarlett."

AnneMarie didn't know what to say. Was Marilyn just making small talk? Had she really come to the hotel first thing in the morning to talk about AnneMarie's book? Well, fine. She could talk books. "Did you like the ending?"

"Loved it. I don't think it could have been any better. I got pretty worried there for a while. I didn't think there was any way the two of them could ever end up together. Not with all they'd been through. He'd messed up so badly, but once he'd changed and become the man she needed . . . and she saw that and forgave him . . ." Marilyn placed her hand on her chest. "It was just perfect."

And there it is. AnneMarie's skin heated in irritation at the pointed comparison between the book and Lance. Even so, she couldn't help but smile at Marilyn's effort. She'd obviously put a lot of thought into her approach.

They both looked up as a server placed steaming mugs in front of them.

Marilyn took a sip and sighed. "Thank goodness for caffeine."

AnneMarie ran a finger around the rim of the cup. "Listen, I appreciate your not-so-subtle allusion to my situation." She smiled and looked at her foamy drink. "I know what you're trying to do. You care about Lance. So do I. But our lives are just too different."

"You know, I would do anything for that guy," Marilyn

said. "He's like a son to me. Last night, he was so devastated that I was going to come straight over here to convince you to give him a chance." She wrinkled her nose. "But the amazing speech I planned doesn't sound so brilliant after a few hours of sleep, so I'll spare you."

"I appreciate that."

"Now you're headed back home?

AnneMarie nodded. "Yep, back to good old Aberdeen, Idaho."

"Your safe place." Marilyn took a sip of her coffee.

AnneMarie studied the woman's face but sensed no censure, only kindness. She was grateful that Marilyn hadn't gushed with sympathy, or anger, or expressed any kind of judgment. She seemed to understand what AnneMarie needed was someone to listen, and she found herself wanting to confide.

"I live in the same small town where I was born. I've had very few romantic relationships, I rarely travel, and my life is slow and dull. Pathetic, isn't it?" She sat back, surprised at herself for opening up to a stranger.

But Marilyn didn't seem at all surprised. For a moment, AnneMarie wondered if Lance found his manager easy to talk to as well.

Marilyn swirled her coffee in her cup. "I don't think it's pathetic at all. Sounds heavenly—a slower life in the country, away from the confusion and stress. To Lance, it sounds like salvation. He wants the kind of life, where he can be grounded and move at a gentler pace with the one person who cared about him before all the fame made him doubt everything and everyone around him—even himself."

AnneMarie's pulse sped up as Marilyn spoke.

"You knew I couldn't resist bringing the conversation back around." Marilyn shrugged sheepishly.

AnneMarie was grateful for her honesty, but it didn't change anything. "Was that the brilliant speech you prepared?" She spoke in a light tone, hoping that Marilyn couldn't see that just speaking about Lance sent her insides trembling.

"Give me a little credit," Marilyn said with a grin. "The best part is the conclusion."

"By all means." AnneMarie raised her palm. "Please continue."

Marilyn cleared her throat and dramatically laid a hand on her chest. "It wasn't easy for Scarlett Rose to trust Gaston de Vaux, but in my opinion, Lance's saying 'I'm sorry, I messed up, I miss you and can we give it another try?' is every bit as brave as Gaston's climbing a castle wall and challenging the evil warlord to a duel to win back his true love."

She winked, and as much as AnneMarie wanted to be annoyed at her interference, she was warmed by Marilyn's understanding.

"It might not seem as heroic," Marilyn went on. "But I thought that Lance's plan to have the two of you on the *After-Hours Show* on the same night was splendid. He didn't plan for Clyde to ask you such a leading question, but your answer gave him a little bit of hope—"

"Wait, did you say that having us both on the show was Lance's idea?"

Marilyn nodded. "They've been pestering him to come on for months, but he didn't want to. Clyde's questions are always unpredictable, and rehab was hard on the guy. He didn't want to relive the struggle in front of an audience."

It was all AnneMarie could do to breathe in and out as her mind turned it all over.

Marilyn leaned her forearms on the table and tapped

her fingers on her cup. "In rehab, you take a hard look at yourself—and it's not easy. Lance hated what his life had become. He'd been so intent on building his image that he didn't know who he was without the drugs. He felt like everything about him was a lie. Aside from me, nobody knew the real Lance Holden."

She looked at AnneMarie and gave a half-smile. "Except for one person . . . *you*. Talking about you and how you'd cared about him before his fame was the one bright spot in those long hard months. I heard you were coming to the show, and I mentioned it, sort of teasing. But that sparked something in him I'd never seen before—he was nervous and excited and . . . hopeful." Marilyn tipped her cup to drink the last of her coffee then put it back on the table. "It took a bit of negotiating by his extraordinary manager to work it all out with the show."

AnneMarie's heart beat so hard she could hear blood rushing in her ears. So the show wasn't a coincidence. He'd planned it—arranged the whole thing to see her. The events of the past few days took on a new shade, as if someone had placed them behind a colored lens, making her see everything in a different light, from the first second their eyes met on set until she ran away from the custodial closet.

She put her elbows on the table and rubbed her eyes. Suddenly her decision to run away didn't seem so black and white. Was Lance really trying to start again? Did he actually—

Marilyn put some bills next to her empty mug and stood. "I appreciate your meeting me. I need to get going; I have a busy day. We have a concert tonight to get ready for, which reminds me . . ." She pulled a concert ticket from her purse and set it on the table, sliding it toward AnneMarie with her fingertips. "Just in case you change your mind."

Long after Marilyn had left, AnneMarie still stared at the ticket. She remembered another ticket from ten years ago, one she'd tacked to her bulletin board next to a picture of Lance. She'd been so excited to go to his first concert, but the time got closer, and they spoke less often . . . and then not at all . . . As she thought of Lance's face yesterday, she realized how she'd hurt him by not going. She'd only thought of her own insecurities. Her heavy stomach soured with guilt.

She pulled her boarding pass from her purse and placed the two papers side by side, looking back and forth between them. Whichever decision she made would turn her life onto a specific course. One would be safe, where she knew what to expect. The other would be a risk. It could lead to more heartache. She rested her head in her hands.

Was there a chance? Was she brave enough to risk her heart?

Seven

nneMarie walked down the steps of the Staples Center, second-guessing herself for the millionth time since rescheduling her flight. What in the world was she doing? She wasn't a cancel-my-flight kind of woman, and knowing that she'd spend the next few hours watching Lance perform made her knees tremble so badly that she hung onto the railing to steady herself. She glanced at her pink cardigan and jeans, wishing she'd bought something new to wear.

She found her row as the opening act was finishing up. Her seat was near the stage, a few rows back from the mosh pit of teenage fans. She had a perfect view when the lights dimmed, and with a blast of noise and explosion of lights, Lance's band took the stage.

Lance strummed a chord on his electric guitar, and the arena erupted in cheers and screams. He grinned at the audience, then pulled the microphone closer and started to sing. AnneMarie felt like a giddy fan-girl.

Lance was completely at ease moving around the stage as he sang. He held the entire stadium enthralled. The way he moved, his confidence, his talent—he *belonged* onstage.

She realized her hands were clasped beneath her chin. Her heart pounded along with the music. AnneMarie glanced around at the audience; the same adoration she felt shone out of the eyes of every woman and girl around her. They all loved him. She was no different than any other fan. AnneMarie suddenly felt small and insignificant. She was a shy, small-town girl with a crush on a rock star.

How could she have thought that she'd ever be a part of this life? How could she compete with all of this?

The longer she watched, the more obvious it was that this was a mistake. This was Lance's world, not hers. He lived for the spotlight. He fed off the crowd's energy as they hung on every note he played. Why had she ever thought he needed her? That there was room for her? She had nothing to offer someone who already had it all.

Her chest felt empty, and the bass of the music pounded in her head, shaking her from the inside out. AnneMarie stood and scooted past the other fans, toward the aisle. As she started to climb the stairs, the song ended. She was running away again, as she always did whenever she was the least bit unsure. The thought made her angry with herself, but that didn't negate her need to hide, to get away and stop living in a fantasy world.

Lance's voice sounded in the microphone behind her. "How about we slow it down a little?"

How could merely the sound of his words melt her insides? When she reached the landing, AnneMarie glanced back and saw him alone on the stage with just his acoustic guitar. He adjusted the microphone, strummed a few chords, and the crowd settled down as if under a spell.

He played a few more notes. "I wrote this song for a girl. It's about regrets and second chances, but she probably won't ever hear it." He cleared his throat. "Because some people change too late."

And he began to sing.

A lonely villain tired of his wasted days
Given another chance, he'd never have walked away,
Never let her go,
Never said goodbye
Never made her cry.
Would she come back? Would she open her door? Does he dare to even try?

His words chipped away at the walls AnneMarie had built around her emotions, making all of her reasons for leaving seem insignificant. The lyrics were heartfelt and the melody soft and beautiful. The song was so much like the ones he sang to her at Glass Beach that it made her breath catch. A flood of memories assaulted her, and she pressed her hand against the cement wall.

The tune changed subtly and the song moved to the chorus.

My heart was just a part
Missing pieces to be whole.
You see the me
Nobody else can see.
And make it full.

Those words—*her* words. The poem she'd written for him. He'd remembered them all . . . the sentiments of a young girl falling in love. They pierced her heart. AnneMarie's body shook, and her breath came in hysterical bursts. She closed her eyes as Lance's voice released the memories she'd kept locked away: catching his eye across a classroom, laughing over milkshakes, finding bits of colored glass on the beach, her first kiss . . . and with the memories, all of the emotions that accompanied them, both good and bad, which she'd pushed down anytime she'd been reminded of Lance. It all returned with a vengeance. She didn't know whether to laugh or cry.

The song ended, and she stumbled through the auditorium doors into the hallway, leaned against the wall near a concession stand and tried to get herself under control.

She felt an arm around her shoulders and didn't need to open her eyes to know that Marilyn had found her. "I told him that song was a keeper."

Eight

*L*ance's ears were ringing as he left the noise of the stage and stepped into the below-ground tunnels that led to his dressing room. The concert had gone better than anyone had expected. Being onstage again felt so good, and performing with an alert mind, actually singing the right lyrics and playing the instruments instead of relying on recordings to convey the illusion? Amazing. He'd forgotten the rush that came from standing in front of a pumped crowd.

The cement corridor felt cool against his damp clothes and hair. He was exhausted.

But the tour promised to be a success. The band had performed the songs the way they'd rehearsed, and all of the equipment had worked beautifully. The fans seemed to like the new songs—even the brand new one was well received.

If only the one person who was meant to hear it—

He hated the pang that always accompanied thoughts of

AnneMarie. He shook his head, rounding the corner to his dressing room.

He opened a door and stepped into the suite. A few roadies sat on couches in the common area, and Lance tried not to look at the brown bottles they held. He hurried to the adjoining doorway leading to his private room.

Marilyn stepped out before he could enter. "Great show. Feel good about it?"

"Yeah, really good."

"Someone wants to talk to you." She motioned her head toward the door behind her.

"I'm not up to hanging with fans tonight; one of the other guys might—"

"Not this time." Marilyn's lips twisted into a smile. "Trust me."

Lance studied her. Marilyn had never been the type to bring a girl to his room. Was she trying to make him feel better because AnneMarie had left? That didn't seem like her.

As Marilyn watched confusion cover his face, her smile grew. She stepped back and opened the door.

Lance looked inside, and time stopped. His gaze met a pair of brown eyes that he never thought he'd see again. "AnneMarie?" His voice cracked like a fifteen-year-old's, but he didn't care.

"Great show. I . . . I heard the song." Her voice shook slightly, and her brow was furrowed, but she held his gaze steadily, offering her trust. Giving him a chance.

He saw the girl he'd left behind ten years earlier and knew that because she was really here, and if she was really willing to try, he'd never betray that trust again. He could do it. They could make it work. A house in Aberdeen and an apartment in L.A. Maybe a writing desk in the tour bus . . .

"You came," he said.

She rubbed her arms and looked at the floor. "I made a mistake." Her voice was so quiet that he stepped closer to hear.

He barely registered that Marilyn left, closing the door behind her.

"What mistake?" He took another step and reached a finger beneath her chin, lifting her face.

AnneMarie's expression set his heart racing. "I said that a hero has to be willing to give up anything for the heroine, but the truth is, if she wants him to step into her life, she has to be willing to take a step into his, too."

"Are you . . . sure?" His throat was dry and his voice raspy.

She hesitated for an instant and then took a step, closing the space between them. She nodded and placed a hand on his chest. "I thought I'd left behind a villain, but he was actually my hero."

His throat tightened as he placed his hand over hers. "Are you scared?"

"Terrified."

"Me, too. But that doesn't sound very heroic, does it?" He brushed his fingers over her cheek.

AnneMarie closed her eyes and leaned against his hand.

"What's the hero supposed to say now?"

"Nothing." She looked at him through her lashes, and the vulnerability he'd seen in her eyes was replaced by a warmth that lit his nerves on fire. One side of her mouth pulled into a smile, and a blush spread over her cheeks. "At this point in the story, there's really not a whole lot of talking."

Lance slid his hand beneath her ear and pulled her toward him. When their lips met, all of the apologies, regrets, and shame evaporated. AnneMarie was giving him a second chance.

She entrusted him with her heart, and he'd spend the rest of his life guarding it well. That's what heroes did.

ABOUT JENNIFER MOORE

Jennifer Moore is a passionate reader and writer of all things romance due to the need to balance the rest of her world that includes a perpetually traveling husband and four active sons, who create heaps of laundry that is anything but romantic. She suffers from an unhealthy addiction to 18th- and 19th- century military history and literature. Jennifer has a B.A. in linguistics from the University of Utah and is a Guitar Hero champion. She lives in northern Utah with her family, but most of the time wishes she was on board a frigate during the Age of Sail.

You can learn more about her at AuthorJMoore.com.

Stay with Me

Shannon Guymon

OTHER WORKS BY SHANNON GUYMON

My One and Only
Free Fallin'
At Last
Falling for Rayne
Tough Love
Dreaming of Ivy
Be Mine
A Passion for Cleo
Makeover
My Sweetheart
I Belong With You

One

FAIRY FACE

Jo grabbed her beat up suitcase off the conveyer belt and surveyed LAX. This was her first time in California, and she wondered if maybe she should turn around and get back on the plane. She hadn't even left the airport, but she already knew three things about California: it was crowded, it was loud, and she didn't belong here.

"*Jolie?*"

Jo turned around and saw a man staring at her with a slight smile. He looked harmless enough, but in California, anyone could be a serial killer. They just looked better holding the knife and duct tape. He was dressed in jeans, brown work boots and a white t-shirt, which looked clean and soft. His hair was perfectly California though—thick, a little out of control, with the perfect amount of curl, as if all he had to do was run his hands through it, and he'd be camera ready for a modeling shoot. His face seemed genetically designed by a top modeling agency: high cheekbones, sculpted lips, and dreamy brown eyes under dark slashes for eyebrows.

What kind of people hired a model to pick up their nanny? Talk about throwing out the welcome mat.

"Ah, you're hard of hearing," he said. "Sorry, they didn't tell me." His eyebrows rising in question as his mouth quirked on one side.

Jo cleared her throat and blushed at being caught thinking instead of opening her mouth and using words. "No, my hearing is fine. I was trying to figure out who *you* are . . ." She let the sentence drift off as she raised one of her own eyebrows.

The man grinned, his eyes gleaming in amusement as he held out a hand. "Call me Fitz. Short for Fitzgerald. I'm the driver-slash-man-of-all-trades for Bax and Lila James. Please tell me you're Jolie Barrett. I've been sitting here for a half an hour looking for a girl with brown hair, big hazel eyes and freckles. You'd be surprised by how many women fit that description."

Jo grimaced. "Yeah, I don't exactly stand out. And call me Jo." She glanced around the constant movement of people around her and could almost feel the pulse of energy flowing around her. She felt somehow diminished by it, deflated. She swallowed back a wave of nervousness and straightened her shoulders. She was here to be a nanny, not to audition for a TV show. She didn't have to compete with these people. All she had to do was be the nanny to two little angels. At least that's how her cousin Lindsey had described them.

Fitz grabbed her suitcase. "Okay then, *Jo*, follow me."

As Jo walked outside, the instant heat and bright sun made her grab for her sunglasses, a going-away gift from her mom. Jo didn't want to think of the tears on her mom's cheeks as she'd waved goodbye in Denver. Kim Barrett had a new life now. She had a job she loved at the hospital, and she had a new boyfriend. She didn't need an adult daughter hanging around, mooching off her. No, it was time to grow up and do something besides send out resumes every day, hoping to get a job.

But Jo wished somebody had told her how hard it would be to actually *get* a job after graduation. She'd never imagined she'd end up being a nanny. But here she was, one of the unemployable, educated masses with a hefty college loan weighing her down.

Lindsey's call had come at just the right moment, when she'd been seriously considering a job as manager at the local McDonald's. Spending the summer in Santa Monica, watching two kids, had to be better than working fast food.

I'm hoping. Lindsey had been the Jameses nanny for the past year but quit when she'd married her high-school sweetheart. Donovan was a Marine, and he'd been transferred to a base in Maryland. Lindsey hated leaving Truman and Nellie but said she felt better knowing she was leaving them with a trustworthy replacement.

During Jo's Skype interview with Baxter James, he'd spent *maybe* five minutes asking questions about her. He hadn't even bothered asking if she had any childcare experience. Instead, he'd spent most of the time asking about her favorite movies. Interesting people she would be working for.

They reached a brilliantly white, perfectly clean BMW, where Fitz stowed her suitcase while she took the passenger seat. She ran a hand over the plush leather seat, feeling overwhelmed by the luxury—a far cry from her 1990 Toyota Corolla with rust holes all over the back bumper.

Fitz backed out of the parking spot and slipped into the

SHANNON GUYMON

traffic then headed away from the airport. "So," he said as if
he was trying to fill the awkward silence. "Bax said you're
from Colorado. What part?"

Jo was so used to silence that she'd forgotten how it
made other people uncomfortable. "Colorado Springs. And
uh . . . what about you? Are you from here?" Was that the
appropriate response?

Fitz smiled, and she relaxed a little.

See? I can do this. She could talk to a good-looking
stranger as he drove her around in a BMW. *Yeah, no big
deal.*

"I'm a native Californian. Grew up in Culver City.
You'll love it here. Plenty of sun, beautiful beaches, and
enough fun to fill a lifetime."

Jo nodded and looked out the window as she felt a wave
of homesickness climb up her stomach and lodge in her
throat. *I don't want to be here.* She wanted to be at home with
her books, her dog Tinker, her best friend Sadie . . .

And Brian. She pushed the painful thoughts away and
cleared her throat, then turned toward Fitz and the
conversation he was attempting. She was here, and she had
to look to the future.

"You make California sound perfect. Tell me more
about yourself," she said, falling back on her go-to line when
she realized she had nothing to say. "You're a native. What
else?" Getting people to talk about themselves was much
easier than actually talking. Plus, it meant she got to sit back,
relax and listen. Win-win.

Fitz shrugged and zipped over two lanes of traffic. She
grabbed her heart and gasped as they came within a foot of
hitting another car.

"I'm just a regular guy," Fitz said casually. "I work for
the Jameses during the day as a driver and go to school a few

250

nights during the week. They pay well, and they're flexible with my schedule, so I'm lucky. I even get to see my dad and two younger brothers who still live in Culver."

Jo looked at him in confusion. "Wait, so you're *not* a model?" she asked doubtfully.

He grinned back. "You thought I was a model?" He sounded delighted.

She blushed, wishing heartily she hadn't blurted that out. Yet she couldn't help but ask. "You're not?"

Fitz laughed, and she glanced over, enjoying the deep, rich sound as it filled the car. "Flattering, but no, I told you— I'm going to school to be a civil engineer. What about you? Are you a career nanny?"

Jo let out a long breath and pressed her hands to her hot face. *Talk. Right. I can be normal.*

"I'm probably the farthest thing from a career nanny. I haven't even babysat anyone in at least seven years. I have a degree in art. I've been trying to get a job as a graphic artist, but with the economy and everything, it's a tough field to break into." She automatically ground her teeth a little in frustration.

Fitz smiled with commiseration. "The movie studios are always hiring good artists. After you're done being a nanny, you may decide you want to stick around." He zoomed ahead then slipped between two cars with inches to spare, making her squeal and cover her face. She prepared for impact with the semi beside them.

"*Relax.* I take it this is your first time in California?"

Jo slowly lowered her hands as she gasped for air and stared at the seemingly millions of cars around them. "Yes, and I want to see the ocean before I die."

Fitz laughed and turned up the radio. "We've got about a half hour to Santa Monica. Why don't you take a little nap?

The time will go by faster, and you won't have to scream every few minutes."

She glared at Fitz but decided to do as suggested since she'd rather have her eyes closed than stare death in the face. She covered her eyes with her arm and tried to get her breathing under control. The next thing she knew, she was being gently shaken awake.

"Hey, sleepyhead, we're here. Home, sweet home," he said as he pointed to the window.

Jo sat up, rubbing her eyes as she stared at the sprawling Mediterranean-style home. Fitz jumped out as she continued to stare at the huge house surrounded by sculpted bushes and bright flowerbeds with gorgeous palm trees that stood as tropical guards. She pushed the door open and got out, looking down at her black skinny jeans and vintage t-shirt that said *Frankie Says Relax* and the leather bracelets stacked up her left arm. She hoped the Jameses didn't have a dress code.

"Tru and Nellie are excited to meet you." Fitz got her suitcase and gestured toward the door. "Come on," he said and walked toward the front door.

She cleared her throat nervously. Meeting the kids. *Easy, peasy.*

Fitz opened the door. She walked into the large entry and felt her mouth hanging open. Whoever designed this house had gone for big and bold. Everywhere she turned, there were bright splashes of reds and yellows with creams and bright blues. Warmth, light and color.

"*Wow,*" she whispered. She'd be living in *this* house? For the last nine years, ever since her dad had left them to live in Florida with his secretary, home had been a condo shared with her mom.

"You'll get used to it," Fitz whispered. He took her by

the elbow and ushered her through the hallway into the family room with a spacious kitchen off to the right and an even more elaborate dining room, with the biggest chandelier she'd ever seen, to the left.

Jo swallowed another wave of nerves as she heard the sounds of bickering children.

"*Shut up, Nellie. It's my turn.*"

Jo followed the sound of the voices to a small room off the side of the family room, which looked like a small theater, with a large screen on one wall and six large, red recliners. A boy and a younger girl sat together next to each other, and they did not look happy. The boy wore a scowl, and the girl had tears and a pout going strong.

"Typical," Fitz whispered. "They fight constantly over whose turn it is to play Minecraft. It gets rather bloody sometimes. He's eleven and she's seven, so he feels it's his right to hog the game."

Jo frowned. "Well, that's about to change." She walked forward, clearing her throat. The two blond children jumped and turned around, looking surprised and wary at the same time. "You must be Truman and Nellie. I'm Jo, your new nanny."

Truman wore tan pants and a white polo shirt. Nellie had on blue pants and a red polo. Typical school uniforms. Private school kids. She knew them on sight.

"You don't look anything like Lindsey," Truman said accusingly.

Jo laughed a little. It was true; she didn't look anything like her cousin, who was tall and curvy, loud and happy and made friends easily. Jo was medium height, on the thin side, and more into books than people. These kids were in for a shock.

"You're right," she said, holding her arms out to her sides. "I'm not like Lindsey. Is that okay?"

Nellie stepped forward, revealing painfully tight ponytails. Jo winced. The poor girl looked as if someone had yanked every hair into place and glued it into submission.

"Do you give hugs like Lindsey?" Nellie asked, so softly that Jo had to lean forward to hear.

Hugs? No one had said anything about hugs. But at the yearning in Nellie's voice, Jo decided that she did indeed give hugs. "I absolutely do. Free hugs for everyone," she said with a nervous smile.

Truman narrowed his eyes suspiciously not buying it. *Smart kid.* Her mom had given Jo a brief hug that morning, but that was an anomaly. Jo hadn't hugged or cuddled that much with her ex-boyfriend either, though they'd graduated to holding hands in public. Hugs had never been her thing.

"When is Lindsey coming back?" Truman asked as his shoulders slumped.

Fitz raised his eyebrows as he stepped toward Truman, putting a gentle hand on his shoulder. "Dude, be nice. Give her a chance. Okay?"

Truman looked up into Fitz's face and appeared to be close to tears. "But I miss Lindsey," he whispered, then leaned his head against Fitz's side as he put an arm around the boy's shoulders.

The moment made Jo's heart melt. Truman obviously loved Lindsey; losing her must have been hard.

Nellie stepped forward and put her hands on her hips. "I'll give you a chance. What's your name again?"

Jo cleared her throat to answer, but Fitz beat her to it. "Jolie."

Nellie crinkled her nose. "What kind of name is *Jolie*?"

Fitz looked at Jo. "It means *pretty* in French. Don't you think she's pretty?"

Nellie smiled sweetly. "Yes. She has a fairy face."

Jo blushed. *A fairy face?*

Truman glared at her. "I think she has a *dwarf* face," he muttered.

Fitz narrowed his eyes warningly at Truman then turned to Jo. "I'll take your suitcase upstairs. The children have an hour of free time while you get settled. Then I'll give you their schedule so you can get familiar with it and look it over."

Jo nodded and glanced back at Truman. "I'd like for you to call me Jo. And you're right; I'm half-dwarf. That's why your dad hired me. He knew you guys needed a nanny who knows how to throw an ax."

Truman's eyes widened with interest, and Nellie squealed in delighted surprise. Jo grinned at their reactions as she followed Fitz up a monstrous staircase then along an even longer hallway.

"You're down here with me. The family's rooms are on the other side of the house." Fitz opened the door to a room and walked in, leaving her to follow. She walked in and took a moment to stare. The floor looked like painted concrete with swirls of different shades of purple and lavender. The room had a balanced and streamlined feel, although the bed looked comfortable, with a bright comforter with circles of pale lavender, and it was topped with bright purple throw pillows. One wall was covered with stacks of painted boxes. Some had pictures inside, others had vases.

I could use a few of them for my books, she thought, and smiled.

"Will it do?" Fitz asked. He looked at her with a half-smile, which did funny things to her stomach.

Jo blushed as she slipped her purse off her shoulder and tossed it on the bed. "It will do," she said softly, walking over to the large window which looked out onto the backyard. She had to blink twice at the luxurious pool and hot tub. She felt Fitz move to stand beside her. She was suddenly aware of his body—even the heat from his arm.

"You're welcome to use the pool whenever you want. The kids are great swimmers, so they spend a couple hours down there every day. I hope you brought a swimsuit."

Jo cringed, thinking of her boring, black tankini. "I did. Thanks for picking me up and showing me around. I appreciate it."

Fitz handed her a piece of paper. "Your instructions. Lila and Bax won't be home until late tonight, so you're in charge of dinner. If you have any questions, text me. My number's on the list. I'll be out running errands for Bax, but if you need anything, I'm just a call away. And if you need me to take you guys anywhere tomorrow, let me know."

Jo nodded, grateful to have someone to turn to if she needed help. Fitz looked at her intently. "Nellie's right. You do have a fairy face. Your mother was right to name you Jolie." He gave her a warm smile before turning and walking out.

Jo was surprised that someone as good looking as he was would say something like that to her. She hurried to the mirror over the desk and studied her face. She ran her hands over her cheeks and smiled as a trickle of warmth filled her heart.

Pretty?

She'd never thought so, but if Fitz thought she was pretty, maybe she could be. Today was turning out to be surprisingly good.

Two

Jo walked downstairs an hour later to find the kids eating ice cream and watching *Criminal Minds* on a small TV in the kitchen. A gruesome scene came to view just as she turned the TV off, wincing.

"*Wow.* Okay, we'll have to talk about appropriate shows for your age. That's not one of them." Hopefully Nellie wouldn't have nightmares.

Truman rolled his eyes. "We can do whatever we want, including watch whatever shows we want."

Jo took a deep breath and let it out slowly. *Be the nanny.*

"Actually, your father said that *I* am in charge. What I say goes, and I say that this summer, we're cutting down on the tech and going to explore."

Truman looked intrigued. "School's out in two days. What do you mean, we're going to explore?"

"Fitz says he'll drive us wherever we want to go, so I say we go *everywhere*—some national parks are nearby, so we can go camping." She let her imagination run free and went on. "At the beach, we can build sandcastles and learn to surf. We can go to the Getty Museum. We can do *anything*. Each of us can pick a few things to do. Sound good?"

Nellie smiled and clapped. "We're going on fieldtrips every day?"

Jo grinned. "We're going to *live*, Nellie. And there's more to life than sitting in a beautiful home and staring at different screens all day." She heard a sigh and turned to look at the little boy. "What do you think, Truman?"

"Everybody calls me Tru . . . and I guess it sounds okay." He didn't sound excited at all.

Jo smiled and ruffled his pale-blond hair. "Good enough. I wonder what we should have for dinner." She walked over to the subzero fridge and opened the door. Inside, she found everything she could have ever imagined asking for.

"Hummus *and* pesto," she said looking at all of the different, colorful jars. "You guys have a very elegant diet."

Nellie walked over and peeked under her arm. "Lindsey always made us macaroni and cheese. She didn't like to cook."

Frowning, Jo remembered her cousin's addiction to Kraft Macaroni and Cheese and shut the door. *Yuck.* "Let's take a field trip to a farmer's market this week to pick up some fresh fruit and vegetables. I think you'll like them as much as macaroni and cheese."

"I doubt it." Tru pushed his bowl away and leaned his chin on his arm. "Is Lindsey really not coming back? *Ever?*"

Jo felt her heart ache for the boy and walked over, putting a hand on his thin shoulder. "Now that she's married, she goes wherever her husband goes. I'm sure she'll come back for a visit, though."

Truman's face fell, and he looked at the counter, saying nothing. Nellie nudged Jo's arm. "He needs a hug," she whispered loudly.

Jo bit her lip and glanced at the miserable boy. He hadn't denied his sister's suggestion. Maybe he did want a hug. She leaned over and put her arms around Truman then laid her head against his. Within seconds, she felt his little shoulders begin to shake as he began crying. She sighed, pulled him more firmly against her, and rubbed his back.

"I hate it when life lets us down," she said. "It hurts when people we love walk out as if our whole life didn't revolve around them." She closed her eyes as emotion welled up inside her. A moment later, she felt his two small arms wrap around her waist. She fell in love with the cranky little boy and knew she'd do anything to bring his smile back.

"If someone's handing out hugs," a voice across the room said, "then I want one too."

Jo whipped around as Truman's arms fell away. A tall, good-looking man leaned in the doorway, staring at her curiously. She blinked in surprise, not recognizing him. She'd Skyped with Baxter James, but this man was much too young. She looked at Truman questioningly.

"Hi, Haiden," Truman said and wiped his eyes quickly on his sleeve.

"Well, what a tender moment," Haiden said, walking into the kitchen and smiling brightly at the children before looking back at her.

As he walked closer and closer, Jo cleared her throat nervously. She couldn't remember anyone mentioning a man named Haiden.

"I'm Lila's brother," he said, answering her unspoken question. "And you must be the nanny." His eyes narrowed as he looked her up and down. "You're not what I expected."

259

Jo laughed nervously and stepped back from Haiden, who was now standing very close. "What were you expecting?"

The man shrugged and crossed his arms over his chest, making his tanned biceps bulge. She might have been mistaken about Fitz's job description, but this guy *had* to be a model or an actor. She'd bet all of her books on it.

"I guess I expected someone like Lindsey—soft and cuddly. You're all angles and edges. But maybe you're still cuddly?" He raised his eyebrows suggestively.

Jo blinked in surprise and then snorted. *He has to be joking.* No guy like him would ever come on to her. "You're funny," she said and held out her hand. "I'm Jo. Nice to meet you, Haiden."

His eyes widened as a look of confusion came over his face. He recovered quickly, though, and smiled, showing very white, perfect teeth, which went nicely with his big, blue eyes, square jaw and blond hair. "Well, I'm sure Lindsey told you all about me," he said, giving her a deep look. "I'm one of the up-and-coming stars of *Beverly Hills Round-up.* It's a new drama on the WB. A critic said I was the best thing about the show." His face glowed.

Jo glanced at Nellie, unsure how to respond.

Nellie sighed and leaned her elbows on the counter. "Can we go swimming, Jo? I'm bored."

Saved from having to respond to Haiden, Jo smiled. "Good idea." She turned to Haiden. "Um, your sister and Bax aren't here, but I'll let them know you stopped by."

Haiden walked over and opened the fridge. "No worries. I live here," he said with a wink—and a leer.

Jo shuddered, nodded politely, and ushered the kids out of the kitchen, relieved to be escaping. She felt a pressure on her hand—Truman slipping his into hers—and smiled. She walked upstairs with the children and had them show her their rooms. While they were changing, she hurried to her room and slipped on her bathing suit then met them at the pool.

"This is nothing like my rec center," she whispered, staring at the natural boulders and rocks surrounding the pool. It looked like a naturally occurring pond in the middle of Santa Monica. Some of the stones were smooth and made a perfect waterslide into the deep, royal-blue water.

She grinned as the two children jumped in the pool, laughing and splashing. She dove in and joined them, starting a game of tag that lasted over an hour. When she glanced at the clock hanging on the side of the pool house, she was shocked to see how much time they'd spent in the water.

"Time to make tacos!" she yelled, and vaulted out of the pool. She stood up, smiling but then gasped as someone held out a towel. "Mr. James. Hello," she said, quickly wrapping the large towel around herself as she stared up at the tall, fit man with shaggy brown hair, an oversized nose and big smile.

Baxter smiled and waved at his children. "You're a natural with the kids. I knew you had to be when you said your favorite series was *Lord of the Rings*. Lila will be pleased." He sounded relieved.

Jo slicked her hair back from her face then hurried to hand towels to the two children, who were throwing their wet bodies against their father as he laughed and hugged them.

"I'm only home for a few minutes to change," he told Jo. "I'm meeting Lila and some friends for dinner."

"We're getting ready to have tacos," Jo said, wishing her first meeting with Baxter hadn't been in her swimsuit.

Baxter grinned. "That sounds pretty good. Go ahead and take the kids to a movie tonight or something too. Have some fun." He pulled out a credit card and handed it to her.

She took the card and looked down, blinking in surprise at reading her name on it. "Wait . . . *what?*"

Baxter shrugged and picked up Nellie in his arms, kissing her wet cheek as she laughed. "It's for taking the kids out to eat, to the movies and for whatever else you want to do. Have fun tonight," he said again and touched Truman on the shoulder before striding away.

Jo watched the look of yearning on Truman's face before resignation took over, and she realized that being these kids' nanny would be more important than she'd realized. Truman and Nellie needed love and attention. And she knew what it was like to wish for a father's attention. What it was like to have a mother so busy working that she never had time for you.

I may be a better artist than a nanny, but I'll do my best.

"Okay, then. Whoever can eat the most tacos gets to pick the movie."

The kids took off running, which made her laugh.

She spent the night getting to know the children, who turned out to be sweethearts, just as Lindsey had promised. Later, when she tucked the kids into bed, she ran a hand over their wispy blond hair and felt her heartstrings reaching out and wrapping around the little boy and girl.

The moment of vulnerability made her eyebrows draw together. Falling in love with these kids would be so easy.

But for her, love always ended in heartbreak.

Three

*a*t eight a.m. sharp, Jo walked into the kitchen, per her instructions. She scanned the contents of the fridge and decided on something basic for breakfast: scrambled eggs with toast. Ten minutes later, Tru and Nellie walked in looking sleepy.

"Tomorrow's the last day of school," Nellie said, "but no one shows up for that, so we get to have a party in class today." She jumped on a stool and pulled over a plate of eggs and toast.

Tru didn't look very excited about the eggs Jo pushed in front of him. "No Toaster Strudel?"

Jo rolled her eyes. "Not even I would eat those, buddy, and I'm pretty adventurous. Look, I sprinkled cheese on top of the eggs. Give it a try."

She watched as the kids each took a bite, and then she sighed in relief as they both inhaled the rest.

"Hey, that was pretty good," Tru said.

Nellie daintily patted her lips with a napkin. "Yummy. Will you do my hair before Fitz takes us to school?"

Jo looked at the mess of fine hair snarled by a night of tossing and turning and bit her lip. "Who usually does your hair?"

Nellie frowned. "Sometimes Marta, sometimes Mom. *Please?*"

They ran upstairs to Jo's bathroom, where she used a brush to get all the tangles out. "How about a French braid?" she suggested.

Nellie was too busy looking through Jo's makeup and just shrugged, so Jo quickly braided the hair, keeping it loose so the poor kid didn't get a headache. She smiled at the end result and spritzed it with hairspray.

"What do you think?"

She thought Nellie looked like an angel. The little girl looked up at the mirror and tilted her head. "It doesn't hurt! I love it." She turned around, giving Jo a quick hug before running out to grab her backpack from her room. Jo rushed down the stairs just as Fitz opened the front door, stepped in, and took off his sunglasses, revealing his gorgeous brown eyes.

"Ready to go, my little captains of learning?" He bent down and picked Nellie up, only to throw her into the air. Nellie squealed in delight.

Truman looked on with a wistful expression, probably wishing he was still little enough to be thrown in the air. Fitz gave him knuckles and a light punch on the shoulder, which apparently made up for it, as Tru's face lit up.

"Well, don't you look beautiful today," Fitz said to Nellie. "Who did your hair?" But he was looking up at Jo.

Nellie turned and pointed. "She did. Didn't pull my hair even once."

"Sounds like a keeper," Fitz said, smiling slowly. For some reason, the sight made her blush. "I'll take the kids to school, and then I'll come back to run Bax and Lila into the city, but after that, I'll be here if you need a ride anywhere. The kids won't be home from school until four, so you'll have some free time."

Jo walked the rest of the way down the stairs. "I think I may want to head to the beach then. Thanks."

"Lindsey always gave us goodbye hugs in the morning," Nellie said in a loud whisper. Truman and Fitz turned and looked at her expectantly.

Ready for the moment, Jo bent over and hugged Nellie first and then Truman, and was surprised by how strong his little arms were. "Have a good day today," she said after straightening and the children walked out the front door.

Fitz paused before leaving and looked back at her. "They don't have much," he said quietly. His eyes looked sad and serious as he added, "I hope they have you." He turned and walked out too, closing the door behind himself.

He hopes they have me. When she'd accepted the job, she'd seen it only as a temporary solution to her money problems. But already on her second day, she was beginning to feel emotionally attached to her charges. Walking away from them wouldn't be easy when summer was over.

She went back to the kitchen, where she cleaned up the breakfast dishes as she let her dreams of being an artist float through her mind. She compared getting her dream job to caring for Tru and Nellie and wondered what she'd choose if she'd had the choice.

"Oh, right. Bax hired a new nanny," came a woman's voice.

Jo turned around to see a tall, slim redhead standing in the doorway, staring at her with no hint of a smile or welcome. The woman—Lila—wore a long, white, silk robe and looked coldly beautiful.

"I'm Jo. You just missed Tru and Nellie," she said, feeling her heart speed up nervously as Lila walked toward her with a slight frown. She came close enough that Jo could make out fine lines around her eyes and dark circles from staying up too late.

"Well, I hope you're an improvement over Lindsey. I always thought she was silly. The kids were always laughing and being childish with her. Listening to it all gave me a headache. I hope *you'll* keep the children under better control. This summer I'll be busy with a new project for the head of Universal. He wants his girlfriend's beach house redone, so that has to be my focus right now. Just keep the kids busy and out of my hair when I'm home. Got it?" She looked Jo up and down critically.

"Got it," she said softly and went back to cleaning the kitchen.

How sad that the kids' mother didn't want to be bothered by her own children. Jo glanced down at her own clothes—striped leggings, a short jeans skirt and a simple v-neck tee. She'd tried to dress up a little but didn't know if it had worked.

She watched out of the corner of her eye as Lila took a carton from the fridge and poured gloppy, green liquid into a tall glass before closing her eyes and drinking it with a grimace. She left the glass on the counter and walked out without another word.

"*Hola.*"

Jo turned around to see a cute Hispanic woman in her thirties smiling curiously at her.

"You are new nanny. I'm Marta. I clean, you take care of kids," she said briskly, then began wiping down the counter Jo had been about to clean.

She put down the rag. "Thanks, Marta. It's nice to meet you." She hadn't had a chance to eat breakfast herself, so she glanced through the fridge then grabbed a handful of strawberries and a couple of eggs. Marta chattered as Jo puttered around, getting a pot for the eggs and a plate for the strawberries.

"Mr. James is nice man," Marta said. "Good man. Busy man, but good man. Loves babies. Mrs. James?" She looked around quickly, tilting her ear to listen for the sound of Lila's footsteps, then lowered her voice. "*Mean.* Watch out."

Jo noted the information and was grateful for a rundown of her employers.

Marta pointed at her with a bottle of Windex. "She fire you if she don't like you. She fire you if you prettier than her. She don't like to hear kids. You understand?"

"No worries about my being prettier." Jo smiled. "She's beautiful."

Marta pursed her lips and rolled her eyes. "Botox," she whispered. "You be careful. You pretty girl. If Mr. James notice, you're gone."

Eyes bugging out, Jo said, "Did Mr. James and a previous nanny . . ."

"No, Mr. James is good man." Marta paused in her energetic scrubbing of the kitchen window and frowned, shaking her head. "But once, he told a nanny she would look great on camera. Mrs. James fire her next day. You be careful. You have the same look."

Jo choked on a strawberry. Her appearance was so ordinary that Marta's suggestion was ridiculous. "You must be joking."

"You have the high cheekbones and big eyes." Marta shrugged. "I hear Mr. James talk on the phone about it all the time. He bring up screen test, *say no.*"

Laughing, Jo put two eggs in the pot then turned the heat to high. She wouldn't hold her breath. "What about, um . . . Fitz? Is he a good guy?" She hoped her voice sounded casual, knowing it was anything but a casual question.

Marta winked at her and grabbed a broom then went after the crumbs under the table and chairs. "Fitz? Good kid. Smart. He treat me with respect. Haiden? *He's* . . ." Marta straightened all of a sudden and looked over her shoulder as Haiden himself walked in, yawning loudly and stretching.

"Ah, perfect. I'm starving," Haiden said to Jo. "Sweetheart, make me an omelet with spinach, a little feta and those Portobello mushrooms." He walked over to the table, collapsing in a chair as he pulled a laptop toward him.

Marta raised an eyebrow and looked at Jo pointedly. "*Spoiled*," she mouthed, then turned her back on Haiden and went back to sweeping.

Jo looked unhappily at Haiden, not liking the way he'd just ordered her around. Well, she *was* hired help, but her list of duties didn't list cooking for Haiden.

"I'll be happy to throw a couple more into the pot if you want hardboiled eggs. And there are some more strawberries in the fridge if you want some of those, but I wasn't planning on cooking omelets this morning." She offered a polite smile as she walked to the fridge and took out the almond milk. She looked at the container and read the back. Milk made out of nuts? While in California, she would be open to new experiences. Even almond milk. She poured herself a cup then turned around to see Haiden looking impatiently at her.

"Lindsey always cooked for me. It's part of the job, angel. You really need to think about keeping me happy." He wore a smile, but his eyes looked at her calculatingly.

Jo shrugged. "Sorry, not in my job description. But an omelet is very easy to make yourself. Beat some eggs, pour them in a pan. Flip them when they're solid and add in all of the stuff you want."

Haiden narrowed his eyes at her and stood slowly. "You're seriously not going to make me breakfast?"

She motioned towards the boiling water. "I told you, I'm happy to add a couple of eggs to the pot, since that's what I'm having, but no, I'm not a short order cook. Sorry," she said, not feeling all that sorry.

He stared at her, his gaze turning hard before he walked out without another word.

The maid waited five minutes and then laughed. "That was *awesome*." She walked over and patted Jo on the back. "Stupid, but awesome. He's spoiled baby. He won't like you now."

Jo shrugged. "Anyone over the age of three who is still a spoiled baby needs to grow up." She plopped a strawberry in her mouth.

She spent the rest of the morning emailing her mom and Sadie then reading before Fitz returned to drive her to the beach. When they got there, she was surprised when he brought a towel and pulled off his shirt then lay on his stomach beside her. He grabbed a large text book out of his backpack and began reading.

She grabbed her book, the latest Cassandra Clare, and tried to ignore the fact that she was lying on a beach next to a gorgeous man. She did what Sadie would be screaming at her to do if she were here—she closed her eyes and tried to take it all in.

Live in the moment. That's what her best friend always said.

Jo smiled and opened her eyes, putting her book down as she stared at the ocean. She'd never seen it before. She took in a deep breath and enjoyed the salty scent and breeze.

She watched gorgeous people walking past in skimpy bikinis and knew she stuck out like a sore thumb here with her pale, thin legs. She didn't exactly fit in here.

"You're staring at the water like it's going to bite you. Why don't you try it out?"

She glanced at Fitz who now lay on his side, shading his face with one hand as he looked at her. She stared at his mouth for a moment before dragging her eyes away. "I saw something last summer called Shark Week, and there are these things called *sharks*."

That's when Fitz began laughing. He stood up and held out a hand to her. "Come on. I'll protect you from the sharks. You haven't lived until you've swum in the Pacific Ocean."

Jo took his strong, warm hand and stood, pulling her tankini top down over her pale stomach and licking her lips nervously. As he began pulling her toward the water, she said, "One guy got away from a shark by punching it in the eye. So if one attacks me, go for the eyes okay?"

Fitz laughed again as he walked her right into the ocean. She smiled at the coolness of the water and the sensation of wet sand between her toes.

"More people are killed by cows every year than sharks," Fitz said. "We'll body surf. You'll love it." And he began swimming out toward the waves.

Jo was a good swimmer and followed closely behind. She only squealed a little when a piece of seaweed got stuck between her toes. She lifted her head out of the water and stood up; the water was just below her shoulder blades.

"Here comes a wave!" Fitz yelled and dove toward the beach. She followed as a wave slipped over her head and sent her flying through the water. She regained her footing, sputtering, then laughed with joy. Fitz grinned back.

"*Again*," he said and pulled farther out.

They spent the next two hours body surfing, then stopped at a local sushi place where Fitz knew the owners.

"This was my mom's favorite place to eat," Fitz said, staring at a picture of the Japanese coast as they waited for their food.

Jo noticed pain in Fitz's eyes and wondered at it. "*Was?* Has she found a new place she likes better?"

Fitz lowered his head for a moment before answering. "Nah, not unless they serve sushi in heaven. She died a long time ago."

They sat outside under the shade of a palm tree and ate California rolls while Fitz told her about losing his mother to diabetes and what it was like being raised by a single father, who was loving but strict too. When Fitz stopped talking, she realized her hand rested on his arm.

"I'm so sorry, Fitz. Losing people is the worst," she whispered, trying not to cry at the thought of three boys and a father all losing the woman they loved more than anyone. "I lost a father, but to a secretary, not a disease."

Fitz's brow furrowed as he reached over and grabbed her hand. "Loss is still loss. I'm sorry."

She looked up and smiled. Fitz smiled back, leaning in as if he was going to kiss her. A car honked loudly, and the moment was lost.

"Well, we'd better get you back," he said. "The kids will be home from school soon. During this last week without a nanny, they sometimes came home to no one."

Jo followed him to the car, then slid in and yelped at the burning leather on her legs. "I think the back of my legs just melted. And I know what it's like to come home to no one. Being the daughter of a single mom who works a lot was lonely sometimes."

Fitz pulled into traffic. "Well, with Bax and Lila busy all

271

SHANNON GUYMON

the time, Nellie and Tru are lonelier than they should be. We're all relieved you're here. The kids really like you."

As she slipped her sunglasses on, she thought she heard him murmur, "So do I."

Jo stared at Fitz. "You're crazy." Her voice sounded squeaky.

"Don't look at me like I'm a shark." Fitz grinned and glanced at her. "I'm just an engineering student by night and a driver who fights crime on the side. No big deal."

Jo burst out laughing. "Santa Monica's Batman, huh?"

Fitz shook his head and slowed at a stoplight. "I see myself more as the Spider-Man type. But yeah, basically."

She studied Fitz's profile, enjoying their easy banter. They talked about their favorite movies until they arrived back at the house. They both got out of the car, lingering as if they didn't want their time together to end. "You should have dinner with us later," she said nervously, wishing she didn't feel like she was asking him out on a date.

His face lit up. "I'd like that. I was told many times this morning that your tacos are better than Taco Bell's. What are you having?"

Jo raised her hands in the air helplessly. "I have no idea."

Fitz walked up to the front door and opened it for her. "Then I'm there."

They walked in, and found Lila standing in the hallway with Haiden, whose eyes were bright with anticipation. Lila wore a cream-colored suit, while her long, red hair was swept up in an elegant twist. As calm and serene as Lila looked, Jo was warned by the anger in her eyes that something was up.

Lila whirled on Jo. "Jolie, is it true that you refused to make Haiden breakfast this morning?" she asked sounding doubtful as if she couldn't believe it.

272

Clearing her throat and straightening her shoulders, Jo noted Haiden's amused smile. "I offered to make him what I was having, but he didn't want that. I was never told I was supposed to cook for your younger brother." She spoke stiffly, embarrassed that Fitz was witnessing this.

"Well then, let's officially add cooking for Haiden to your list of duties." Lila walked over and pointed a finger in her face. "It doesn't matter if it's me, Baxter or Haiden. If we tell you to do something, *you do it.* I don't like seeing my little brother upset. If Haiden wants an omelet, *then make him an omelet.* I'm sure Bax is paying you enough to take ten minutes out of your day to help my brother." Her eyes narrowed threateningly.

Jo wanted to die of mortification as she looked at Haiden, who was whistling silently, mocking her with his powerful arms crossed over his chest. "Understood." She opened her mouth to quit right there but then closed her lips at the image of Tru hugging her yesterday as he cried. She'd keep her mouth shut for them.

For now.

Lila nodded, then walked to the door. "Fitz, I need a ride to the Upper West to meet Melissa for lunch. Haiden wants a ride into L.A. Let's go." And she walked out.

Haiden sauntered past Jo, stopping to touch a lock of her still-damp hair. "Now that you know how things work around here, I think you and I will be good friends," he said silkily, before disappearing outside into the bright California sun.

She turned around and stared after Lila and Haiden as Fitz walked over and put a hand on her shoulder. "He's pretty harmless, but if you want me to speak to Bax about him, I will. I don't want you to feel uncomfortable," he said with a hint of steel in his voice.

"I can handle him," she said, trying to smile. "He's just a spoiled brat. Lila is terrifying, though."

He sighed and ran a hand through his hair, making it stand up then fall perfectly into place. "That's mostly because she's trying too hard, and the stress of always being the best makes her miserable. I'll see you tonight." With that, he hurried after Lila and Haiden.

A pall was now on the day. She ran over everything that had happened, over and over, worrying over it like she would a bothersome hangnail.

Her conclusion: Keep her mouth shut and do what she was told to do. Truman and Nellie deserved someone who cared about them, and she did.

Who knew who Baxter James would hire if she left.

Four

LIVING LIFE

he next week passed by quickly since the kids were
out of school, and Jo made good on her plans to
take them on adventures every day. She took them
to museums and interesting historical sites. Her favorite
times were at the beach, just relaxing, the kids just being
kids, building sandcastles, and body surfing.

Of course, having Fitz with them almost every day,
when he wasn't busy driving Bax or Lila around, made the
days even better. She didn't dwell on why that was; it would
have been silly to even think about liking Fitz. He was too
different from her.

He was confident and well-spoken where she was an
introvert who had a hard time getting her lips to work right.
He was smart and ambitious, while she couldn't even get a
job in her major. Add the facts that he was flat-out gorgeous
and she was so average, and you had yourself a nonexistent
relationship. Or as her friend Sadie put it, *a fantasy.*

She watched Fitz play in the water with Tru and Nellie while she pretended to read a book. She watched the way his muscles moved under his tanned skin and sighed. He was kind to her. He was polite, and he was sweet, but that didn't mean he was attracted to her.

Not like the way I'm attracted to him, that's for sure, she thought. So what if he'd told her she was pretty? That was just Fitz's way of trying to be nice to a socially awkward nanny. He was being charitable, that was all.

She closed her eyes and allowed herself one little daydream of herself and Fitz, *together*, holding hands as they walked along the beach at sunset. He'd stop and put his hand on her face, looking deep into her eyes before he leaned down and kissed her. She grinned at the picture, and then jumped at her ring tone.

She grabbed her phone and stared in surprise. *Brian*?

"Hi, Jo. I just found out you moved to California. What's going on?" he asked, getting straight to the point, as usual.

Jo closed her eyes and pinched the bridge of her nose. It had killed her when Brian walked away from her. Worse, he'd chosen a new girlfriend seconds after dumping her. One who knew how to look and talk at parties. One who knew how to not embarrass him in front of the partners at his law firm.

"I'm great, Bri. How are you?" she asked faintly.

"Worried about you. You up and move to California? Just because you and I didn't work out doesn't mean you have to run away. Look, I feel bad about how things ended between us. Come back home, Jo. We'll talk." His voice was kind and soft.

Jo's spine straightened. "I didn't move to California because I was running away from you or anything else. I came here for a job. I'm working for one of Hollywood's top producers." Her voice had become as frosty as Lila James's.

Brian laughed. "Yeah, working as a *babysitter*. You're too talented to be watching somebody's brats. I may be able to help you find a job. My dad just opened an account with a new advertising firm, and he said he'd put in a good word for you. Come home, Jo. We can work it out."

She stifled a groan and looked up in time to see Fitz grab Truman and throw him in the water. Nellie clapped her hands and reached for the same treatment.

"There's nothing to talk about," she told Brian. "I don't fit your new image. I can't help you impress your bosses. I don't know how to make small talk at parties or fit in with your friends." Odd that bringing up the past wasn't bringing the usual rush of pain. "None of that has changed."

Brian sighed before answering. "You're right. When I left you for Janelle, I was shallow and thinking of my career. Things haven't worked out between us. She's so busy with her own career that she doesn't listen to me like you do. She cares only about herself." He was starting to sound irritated.

She rolled her eyes and stood up. "Yeah, it's rotten when someone you care about thinks only of themselves," she said dryly. "Look, I'm working right now. Let's talk later, okay?" She wanted to join the others in the water.

He paused. "I thought you'd want to get back together."

Jo blinked in surprise and stared at her phone for a second before answering. "I admit that the first month was hard for me, but I can see our relationship clearly now—so *no*. I want someone who is madly in love with me, not making do. Good luck with everything, okay?" She disconnected, put her phone in her shoe, and ran across the sand. She dove into the water and came up beside Fitz.

He grabbed her, and she found herself thrown in the

water. She burst through the surface, grinning and laughing as Tru and Nellie's arms wrapped around her, taking her back down into the waves. No, she'd never go back to Brian. Not where she wasn't appreciated and loved. Life was too short to be used and tolerated for being a good sounding board and listening to his every last, little thought.

Life is to be lived, she thought again, then dove for Fitz's legs, bringing him down as Nellie and Tru yelled with happiness. And maybe, really living life meant finding out what it meant to be truly loved.

She hoped so.

Five

STARLIGHT KISSES

"These pancakes taste like cardboard. Make me something else," Haiden said, sounding bored as he pushed his plate away and looked at her with a cruel smile.

Jo bit her lip so she wouldn't tell him exactly what she thought of him. "What would you like instead?" she asked tonelessly as she stared at the stack of perfect pancakes she'd spent fifteen minutes making him.

He yawned and scratched his armpit. "Hmm, I'm trying to be healthier. Make me a smoothie and chop up all that fresh fruit into it."

With a sigh, Jo sighed and turned around to open the fridge. Chopping everything would take another fifteen minutes. Fifteen minutes she'd have to spend with Haiden as he watched her every move.

Marta walked in, began dusting the cabinets, and gave

her a sympathetic look. "Jerk," she whispered softly as she walked by. Jo nodded her head in total agreement.

"Good morning."

Jo turned around to see Baxter standing in the doorway, looking at everyone curiously.

"Hi, Mr. James," Jo said. "Haiden wants a smoothie this morning. Can I make you one too?"

Baxter studied Haiden, unsmilingly, who was picking at his fingernail and ignoring her. "Jo, why in the world are you making Haiden a smoothie?" he asked, walking over and sitting down at the table.

Jo smiled sweetly at Haiden and motioned toward the large stack of pancakes still sitting in the middle of the table. "Because he said my pancakes taste like cardboard. And since your wife told me I have to do whatever Haiden says . . ." She sent a cold look at Haiden, who was trying to look innocent. He couldn't have been that great of an actor, because he wasn't pulling it off at all.

Baxter picked up a pancake from the pile and took a bite. "These taste wonderful." He turned to Haiden. "Did they cancel your show? Is that why you're sitting here, doing nothing while Jo cooks for you?" His voice was no longer nice and warm sounding.

"We have the week off," Haiden said with a shrug. "And if you think those pancakes taste good, you're crazy."

Bax glanced at her apologetically. "I didn't hire Jo to cook for you. I hired her to watch my children. Jo, where are Nellie and Truman?"

She sighed. "They're playing video games while they wait for me to finish cooking for Haiden. We have plans to see the Redwood National Park today."

Baxter's eyes narrowed at Haiden, and he shook his head. "Go ahead, Jo. If Haiden is hungry, he can eat the pancakes. Oh, and from now on? You *don't* cook for him."

Marta straightened from the dishwasher and grinned at her, but Jo swallowed nervously at the glare Haiden shot at her over Baxter's shoulder. "Um, Mrs. James was adamant that I do whatever Haiden told me to do. I don't want to cause any trouble." Yet she knew absolutely that she'd just caused trouble.

Baxter smiled at her. "Lila and I will talk about your duties. Have fun today, and be sure and bring me back a t-shirt."

"Okay, you have a good day, Mr. James," Jo said, relaxing.

He nodded and turned back to Haiden, whose face was now red. She hurried out of the room, collected Truman and Nellie, and rushed them outside, where Fitz was washing the car.

"It's a go!" she shouted and opened the car door for the kids. "Buckle up," she instructed, then shut the door with a grin.

As they drove, she told Fitz everything that had happened while the kids watched a movie.

Fitz blew out a breath and looked at her worriedly. "He could get you fired. Lila spoils him. She supports him—forces Baxter to get him jobs and turns her head whenever he acts like an idiot. Or like in your case, she backs him up because she thinks that's what love means."

Jo glanced at Fitz and noted his dark expression. He really was worried about her.

"That's kind of messed up. Why does she put up with him?"

Fitz shrugged and glanced in the rearview mirror at the kids. "Lila's mom was an alcoholic, and she practically raised Haiden. Everything she does is to erase their past and what they dealt with growing up. Too bad she's so busy making sure her image is perfect and that Haiden has the best of everything. She's completely overlooking the fact that she has a great husband and two amazing kids."

Jo's heart hurt for Lila, and even for Haiden a little, as she understood better the emotional dynamics of the household. "That's so sad," she said, feeling grateful for her mom and her imperfect childhood.

"These kids need you. If you get sacked, who knows who Bax will bring home next? Probably some homeless person he had a great conversation with about Meryl Streep," Fitz said with a dry laugh.

Fitz had a point. "I got hired because I like *The Lord of the Rings*."

"I was hired because of my love of all things *Star Wars*. But seriously, watch your back. Haiden may look like every woman's dream come true, but he's just a little junior-high bully." He looked at her with worry in his eyes.

Jo ran her hand through her hair as she considered the ramifications. "I'm aware. And he's *not* every woman's dream come true." She couldn't help but stare at Fitz's profile.

He came to a stoplight and looked over at her. "Oh, yeah? What's your dream guy like?"

Jo knew she was turning red in the face. She'd never been good at flirting. *Should I try?*

"*Hmm*, my dream guy?" she said as she continued to blush. "He's smart. Gorgeous. He's sweet to children and easy to talk to." She wished that her first love had been Fitz instead of Brian.

Fitz looked back at her and reached over and took her hand. "Want to know what my dream girl is like?"

Jo stared at Fitz's large, tan hand covering hers and swallowed. "Yes," she whispered.

He ran a thumb over the back of her hand as he continued to drive. "*You.*"

She looked up in shock as Fitz kissed the back of her hand lightly, and she felt every butterfly in the state of California jump around in her stomach. She tilted her head back and laughed. Not because it was funny. But because sometimes life was so sweet, there was no other way to express joy.

She was Fitz's dream girl? She hoped he never woke up.

They spent the day exploring the forest and picking out the best t-shirts before having lunch at a local diner. By the time they got home, it was dark, and the kids were asleep in the backseat. She was grateful when Fitz helped her to carry the children inside and put them to bed.

"Care to gaze at the stars with me?" Fitz asked, taking her hand in his as they walked downstairs.

Jo melted into his dark eyes and felt a moment of wonder. Gazing at the stars with a gorgeous man was not an experience she was used to. She reminded herself to email Lindsey and thank her again for this job. Coming to California was the best decision she'd ever made. "I'd *love* to."

She followed him out to the back patio, where they climbed onto the highest boulder by the pool and lay back, cradling their heads in their hands. Fitz pointed out all of the stars he could remember, and she told him the Greek myths that went with the constellations.

"So Aphrodite turned Adonis's blood into flowers *after* he was killed by a wild boar? *Weird,*" Fitz said and turned on his side to play with her hair.

She smiled up at the sky. "She couldn't stand to lose him. She loved him too much and wanted to have at least something to remember him by. I think it's beautiful."

Fitz snorted. "I'd rather have a kiss to remember someone by," he said, then wasted no time as he leaned down and touched his lips to hers.

A tremor moved through her body as he continued to kiss her lightly. She turned her head and kissed him at a different angle, and suddenly the kiss changed from light and playful to something else entirely.

He pulled back a few moments later and stared at her, his shadowed eyes gleaming as he caressed her cheek. "Kissing is like drinking salted water. You drink, and your thirst increases."

Jo sighed lightly as she ran her fingers through his thick, silky hair. "Did you just make that up?"

Fitz grinned. "Ancient Chinese proverb, but I agree with it. Now that I've kissed you, all I want to do is kiss you again."

Jo laughed and sat up, gazing at the starry sky. As far as first kisses went, it had been perfect. "You're so different from all of the other guys I've known. You're so sweet and gentle."

Fitz sat up too and put his arm around her shoulders. "It sounds like you've had a bad experience with men."

She sighed and looked away. "My last boyfriend broke up with me because I was shy at parties and didn't know how to talk with his boss. He called me today and wants me back." Her voice had dropped off. She could feel Fitz stiffen beside her as she looked up at him. "I'm not going back."

Fitz let out a sigh as if he was relieved. "Just so you know, I hate parties." And he began kissing her again. Jo softened against him as his arms tightened around her, pulling her closer and closer.

As the night grew darker, Jo realized two things. She'd never really been in love before. And she was on the edge of knowing exactly what it meant.

Six

PAYBACK

Jo sang to herself as she made the kids breakfast—an apple crisp with honey and walnuts. It would be delicious but healthy, too. She took the casserole dish out of the oven and smiled at the fragrant steam.

"Perfect," she murmured and set it on the stove then heard someone clearing their throat. A shiver of dread slipped down her spine as she turned around to see Lila staring at her unhappily.

"Care for some apple crisp?" Jo asked lightly. She took off the oven mitts and held them before her like a shield.

Lila glanced at the dish then walked over and took in a deep breath. "It does smell good."

"And it's very healthy," Jo added quickly, walking over to grab a plate and a fork. She dished up a small square and handed it to Lila, who looked at Jo like she was handing her a snake.

285

Lila took the small plate but held it suspiciously. "That has carbs," she said. "I'm not allowed to eat carbs."

Jo raised an eyebrow. "Who says? It has complex carbohydrates, which your body needs for energy. Plus, it has protein from the nuts. Come on, just a little taste."

With the spoon, Lila put a sliver of the crisp into her mouth and closed her eyes as she savored the flavors. "This is *divine*," she whispered. But then she shook her head, opening her eyes and looking sad and lost for a moment. "My mom used to make apple crisp like this before she . . . well, before she got sick."

Maybe Truman and Nellie weren't the only ones who needed a hug.

Lila put the plate down and motioned to the table. "I want to talk to you about what happened yesterday with Haiden."

Jo walked over and sat down next to Lila, bracing for whatever was coming.

"He says that you made him look bad in front of Baxter yesterday. He also says that you've been disrespectful to him. I can't allow that." Lila sounded tired.

Haiden had certainly twisted the facts to suit his purposes. "Well, I'm sure that if you talk to your husband, he can tell you what happened yesterday," she said, feeling shaken as the thought of being fired entered her mind. "He was there."

Lila sighed and massaged her forehead. "I already did, but he said what he always says—that Haiden is spoiled and immature. *Which isn't true at all.*" She looked at Jo fiercely, as if daring her to argue.

Jo remained silent as she waited for the words, *you're fired* to fill the room.

"But the kids seem to like you, and you've kept them out of my hair, so we'll call this a warning."

Jo felt relief so acute, her hands began to shake and so she clasped her hands in her lap.

"I'll admit that Haiden can be demanding," Lila continued, unaware of the effect her words had had on Jo. "But he has a good heart and means well. He was just hungry." Lila gave a brittle laugh. Her tone shifted to one of veiled anger. "And I hate the idea of him going hungry."

Jo bit her lip, hesitant to speak, but knowing she had to. "Mr. James told me specifically not to cook for Haiden anymore. He said that it's not what I was hired to do, and that I'm only supposed to look after the children—that's it." Trembling slightly after speaking so boldly, she added a bit more quietly, "If Haiden is hungry or needs something, shouldn't he be able to take care of himself?"

"Yes. *And no.*" Lila sighed and shook her head. "I don't know. But I can't handle the stress of Haiden coming to me all the time, unhappy about what you're doing or not doing. You'd better either get along with my brother, *or* . . . or you're gone. Understood?" She stood up, not waiting for an answer as she walked out of the kitchen.

Jo sat there, feeling as if she'd been punched in the stomach. She'd been expecting the words, but hearing them was a different matter altogether.

Should I go to Baxter? No. Even if he'd stick up for her again, if Lila said the nanny was gone, she was gone. The thought of leaving the kids now made Jo want to cry. If she needed to make pancakes and smoothies for the little man in order to stay, then that's what she'd do. Who cared about pride when children were depending on her?

She put on a smile as Tru and Nellie ran into the kitchen, smiling and laughing as they rushed to the stove and smelled the apple crisp. She felt her heart ease at their simple joy in something new and delicious. She served them and even smiled as Haiden walked in with a complacent expression, as if he already knew he'd gotten his way. Before he could say anything, she dished up a large portion and handed it to him.

The next month settled into a pattern. She and the kids spent a couple of days a week driving out to far destinations and exploring all kinds of fun things to do in California. The rest of the week, they spent at the beach or relaxed at home by the pool. She made it a point to take the children to the library at least once a week, and she introduced them to her favorite books, starting with Robin McKinley's *The Blue Sword*. Slowly but surely, she was weaning them from the video games that had been such a big part of their lives. Truman could now be found reading Rick Riordan on a couch with his feet up, and Nellie was now obsessed with *The Magic Treehouse*; she zipped through five books in a matter of weeks.

Baxter was thrilled with everything they were doing and insisted that Jo take pictures of the kids and text them to him throughout the week. He always promised to come along on their next adventure, but something always came up, and he backed out last minute.

As she lay on a chaise lounge next to the pool and watched the kids swim, Baxter texted her to have the kids ready that night to walk the red carpet for a friend's movie premier, she jumped up and down in excitement. *Finally*, the kids would get to spend time with their dad. Her phone beeped, and she glanced down at it.

You're coming too. I'll watch the movie with you guys, but I'll have to stay for the after party. Have Fitz drop you off. Wear something nice.

Jo thought of her clothes and groaned. She glanced at her jeans and her nicest t-shirt as she texted back.

Do jeans count? LOL. She added a smiley face emoji and sent the text. She was embarrassed she that didn't have anything nicer.

Within seconds, she had a reply. *Take the credit card and run to Stella's Boutique. I'm friends with the owner. I'll text her to say you're on your way. Don't worry about the price. If people take pictures of my family, I want everyone to look their best.*

A smile slowly broke across her face. *His family?* She closed her eyes and wished for a moment that she really were. Then she quickly texted Fitz about the situation. He replied with an offer to take the kids to lunch while she shopped.

Two hours later, she had a shopping bag with the most gorgeous dress she'd ever seen. She chose a plum-colored, sheath dress with matching shoes and earrings.

She felt guilty taking up so much of Fitz's time as he drove her all over L.A., but there was still one problem—her makeup. Back in the car, she mentioned her worries to Fitz, so he drove her to the mall, where he introduced her to his cousin Charlotte—a tall, gorgeous woman with long, black hair and bright-red lipstick. When she finished with Jo's makeup, she couldn't recognize herself. She looked so glamorous. She looked amazing.

I look pretty.

She had no idea what to do with her hair, though. She usually wore it in a ponytail. "Charlotte told me to go down the street to her friend who does hair, but we don't have enough time," she said, pulling the mirror down in the car to study her hair.

"It's beautiful the way it is," Fitz said.

Jo blushed and held the door open for Truman and Nellie. "I would hate to embarrass Bax."

Fitz snorted and shut the door behind them. "You won't embarrass him; you're gorgeous. People will probably be wondering who the smokin' hot girl is."

Jo laughed and turned to walk upstairs and came face to face with Haiden. "Hello," she said coolly, and tried to move around him.

He blocked her way though, making her step back. "Where have you been all day?" he asked. "I had to make myself a sandwich for lunch."

She concentrated on not rolling her eyes as she glanced at Fitz and noted his faint sneer. "I had to do a little shopping. We're going to a premier tonight with Baxter." Again she tried to pass him.

Again Haiden moved in front of her. "He didn't mention a premier to me," he said, sounding insulted.

She sighed loudly in frustration. Fitz handed her the sack and pushed her up the stairs, past Haiden, smiling politely at him. "I think it's a kid movie. A new star like you wouldn't be caught dead at a kid's movie premier. No worries."

Haiden continued to scowl; as she climbed the staircase, she could feel his eyes on her back. "But why is *she* going?" he asked, sounding jealous.

She didn't wait to hear Fitz's explanation, instead hurrying to the children's' rooms. She went through their closets, marveling that Truman had his own tuxedo and Nellie had more than six formal dresses. Being the children of a movie exec had its perks. She pulled out clothes for them and instructed them to take showers. She checked her watch; she still had enough time to get herself ready and curl Nellie's hair. Hopefully Lila would be pleased when she saw how cute her kids looked.

When she walked down the stairs wearing her dress the

cool slide of the silk made her feel like she belonged in this house, and in this life. Nellie clapped, but Fitz stood at the base, staring at her with his mouth hanging open. She had to stop and grin at that.

Truman smiled sweetly at her. "I guess Nellie's right. You do look like a fairy," he said shyly.

Jo walked over and hugged him. "You are a charmer, Truman James."

Fitz walked over and touched her shoulder. "You'll fit right in on the red carpet. You're stunning."

Jo looked away shyly, not knowing how to handle such a compliment gracefully. Probably because she'd never had any practice at it.

Time to change the subject.

"Is Lila coming?"

Fitz shrugged and opened the front door for them. "She usually doesn't. We'd better get going. Traffic is going to be brutal."

Jo shook her head ushered the kids into the BMW. When she looked back at the house, Haiden stared at them from his bedroom window, and Jo felt a shiver as their eyes met and felt a wave of hostility aimed at her. She shook it off, though, determined to enjoy her first premier.

When they arrived, Baxter was waiting for them. Nellie and Truman flew out of the car and were immediately enveloped in a warm hug from their dad. Jo looked around at all the A-list actors and models walking around and felt like shrinking back into the car. But with Baxter's hand firmly on her back, she was propelled with Truman and Nellie onto the red carpet. She waved goodbye to Fitz as he drove off wishing he could be standing there with her. The constant flash of the cameras was overwhelming at first, but Nellie and Truman confidently held up their chins like pros and posed for the cameras. Jo took a deep breath and followed their example.

She comforted herself with the knowledge that she was a nobody. None of these people cared about who she was. She walked with the children, stopping when Baxter stopped, moving on when he moved. Sometimes the reporters had questions for Baxter, and he pulled Truman and Nellie in front of him. She pretended she was at the beach and tried to smile serenely.

This is no big deal.

"And who's this gorgeous creature, Baxter?"

She felt Baxter's hand on her arm, and her head swiveled in surprise as he pulled her forward to stand next to him and the children. Baxter smiled and winked at her. "This divine creature is Jolie Barrett, an up-and-coming artist and close family friend. I'm working up the courage to ask her to be in my next project." He grinned as a million cameras suddenly exploded.

She guessed his explanation was Hollywood speak for *this is my new nanny.* She concentrated on keeping her smile in place but squirmed inside.

Moments later, they were safely inside the theater, and Baxter disappeared to speak to some friends. One of the countless people working the event ushered them to their seats, and she spent the next fifteen minutes until the movie started listening to Truman and Nellie point out all of the celebrities they knew. The list was long and intimidating.

When the movie started, Baxter showed up and sat next to her, handing her and the kids large tubs of popcorn and packs of red vines. Jo sat back and enjoyed the movie about a teddy bear brought to life and an evil woman who wanted to stuff him. Jo glanced at the children a few times, watching the joy on their faces and wishing she could bottle the moment to remember forever.

Afterwards, Fitz showed up and ushered them outside to their waiting car. When they got home, she put the kids to bed, then spent ten minutes washing her face before putting on shorts and t-shirt. She met Fitz in the kitchen, and they spent the next two hours talking and laughing about the evening.

But the best part was the kissing by the pool, which followed the talking.

"You must have kissed a thousand women to be so good at this," Jo said, leaning back.

Fitz grinned and shook his head. "*Nah.* It's just different when you kiss a woman you care about." He lowered his voice. "It means more."

She gazed at him silently, trying to decode what he'd said. *He cares about me?*

He put his arm around her shoulders, and they stayed like that for a while before she yawned and he insisted she go to bed.

She woke up the next day fully expecting to take the kids to the Santa Monica Pier. She wanted the kids to feel a live starfish at the little aquarium. She floated down the stairs, smiling as she wondered what to make them for breakfast.

"There she is."

Jo's head whipped up as she reached the bottom step. Haiden and Lila looked at her with twin glares.

"Uh, *hi*," she said, voice sounding squeaky as she moved farther into the foyer.

"I suspected something was going on, but to have this thrown in my face is too much," Lila said, studying the nanny as if she were a disease on a petri dish.

Jo looked from Lila to Haiden and back again. Haiden grinned maliciously at her. "*What's* going on?"

Lila held an iPad out to her. Jo took it and stared at a picture of herself, Nellie, Truman, and Baxter—who had his hand on her shoulder as he grinned at her as she smiled confidently at the camera.

I looked pretty good.

Then she read the caption.

Baxter James's new mistress displayed for the whole world to see, shamelessly flaunted in front of the world and his children as his aging wife stays at home, forgotten and ignored.

Jo's mouth fell open. She gaped at the picture in horror. "*No.*" She pushed the iPad back at Lila. "That's a lie," she croaked. "I went to be with the kids, so Bax could talk to everyone. I would *never . . .*"

Haiden sneered as he put his arm around Lila's shoulders. "Told you something was going on between them. The way he always stuck up for her was a huge clue."

A wave of anger built up inside Jo's chest. "*Shut up,* Haiden," she snapped before turning back to Lila. "I am *not* having an affair with Bax. I would never do that to you, and I would never do that to *myself.*" In spite of her firm voice, her heart raced.

Lila closed her eyes and shook her head. "Pack your things, and get out of my house." She spoke softly before she turned and walked away.

Haiden eyed Jo with scorn. "Maybe you should have been nicer to me when you had the chance." And he walked away.

Jo stared after them as her world spun out of control. *I've been fired for having an affair with my boss?* This could not be happening to her. She turned to escape up the stairs but bumped into Nellie and Truman, who were staring at her with haunted eyes.

She realized they must have heard everything and felt horrified.

"You're leaving us because you love our dad?" Truman's voice sounded faint.

"No." Jo shook her head and collapsed to her knees. She grabbed the kids in a hug and began crying. "*No.* Someone made up that lie, but your mom believes it. I love you both too much to ever hurt you that way."

She headed to her room, and the kids followed. But she needed a moment alone, so she went to the bathroom and shut the door. She sat on the toilet lid for five minutes and sobbed her heart out. She leaned her head against her hands, feeling the weight of the situation crash upon her.

When she finally opened the bathroom door, she found Tru and Nellie talking quietly on her bed. She gave them a watery smile and began packing.

"I was texting my dad while you were crying in the bathroom," Truman said. "He told me to tell you not to leave. He wants you stay here with us." His eyes were calm and hopeful.

Nellie nodded in agreement and she put her hand in her brother's. "You love us. You can't leave," she said, her chin quivering pitifully.

Jo's shoulders sagged. She grabbed the kids in a big hug, taking more comfort from them than she was giving, she was sure. She pulled and wiped her eyes, then had to grab some tissue to blow her nose.

"Okay, we'll wait for your dad," she said, running a hand over Tru's bright-blond hair.

Five minutes later, a banging sounded on the bedroom door, and Truman looked at her worriedly as he jumped off her bed and stomped over, ripping the door open. His shoulders relaxed before he flung himself into Fitz's arms.

"They're trying to get rid of Jo," Tru said, his voice trembling.

Jo looked at Fitz in misery; he returned the look with dark, worried eyes. "Haiden has informed me that I'm to escort you out of the house and drop you off at the airport."

She nodded. Tru and Nellie began talking over each other as Fitz turned and shut the door before sitting on the bed beside Nellie. Tru took charge and explained his dad's instructions. Fitz looked relieved and reached over to hug Tru. "You did everything right, buddy. Way to go."

The sound of a car engine drew everyone to the window. They watched as Baxter jumped out of his Jaguar, his face grim. Fitz reached back for her hand, and she melted into the comfort of his side.

"I'm going to go see what's going on," Truman announced, and walked to the door.

Fitz shook his head quickly and jumped in front of the child. "That might not be an appropriate conversation for you to hear. *I'll* go see what's going on." And he disappeared out the door.

Twenty minutes later, someone came through the door. They looked up to see not Fitz, but Baxter walking in. Although his smile was real, his eyes were tired. "Mommy is leaving for a much-needed vacation at her favorite spa. And Fitz is helping Uncle Haiden move out right now, so I'm taking everyone out for breakfast. Sound good?"

Nellie reached for her dad's hand. "Does Jo still have to leave?"

"*No.* Jo never has to leave." Baxter turned and looked at her with embarrassment in his eyes. "She can stay with us as long as she wants to."

Truman walked over and slipped his hand into hers. "Then she's never leaving. She loves us." His voice sounded relieved and strong. "And we love her."

Her face slowly lifted into a smile. She knelt beside Tru and wrapped her arms around him, leaning her head against his. "I *do* love you," she whispered. Nellie's arms wrapped around her from behind.

Baxter nodded. "The first time I saw you on Skype, I knew that you had love in your heart to give. Nellie and Tru need you, Jo. I know this whole situation is embarrassing and stupid, but I promise to make it up to you." His voice turned sad and tired as he added, "Please, don't leave them."

Jo saw anxiousness in Baxter's eyes. "I always wanted to be an artist because I love beauty. I never realized that loving children was the most beautiful thing I could do."

"Well said." Baxter smiled and held his hand out for Tru. "Now, how about some pancakes?"

Truman grinned, grabbing his dad's hand and looking up into his face as if his father could solve any problem in the world. "I vote donuts."

Nellie laughed and jumped into her dad's arms. "Donuts, donuts, donuts!"

Jo laughed and stood, wiping a few stray tears off her cheeks. "I vote donuts too," she said as Baxter grinned and opened the door for them.

That night, as she sat by the pool with Fitz, he told her everything. How Baxter had been alerted by one of his assistants earlier that morning about what TMZ was about to publish. How Baxter was able to use some leverage to find out who the source was—Haiden.

Baxter offered TMZ prime interviews with a few of his famous friends if they printed a retraction that afternoon. He'd been in the middle of negotiations when he'd gotten the texts from Truman and hurried home.

Fitz described the resulting yelling match between Haiden, Bax, and Lila; it sounded brutal.

SHANNON GUYMON

"Haiden will do anything to manipulate his sister so that she depends on him emotionally. He wasn't only trying to get her to turn on you, but on her own husband as well. When Baxter showed Lila proof that Haiden had lied about the affair, she slapped her brother and collapsed on the floor. I think you'll be relieved to know that Haiden won't be back."

"I still don't get it," Jo said, shaking her head. "He took one look at me and decided to hate me. *Why?*"

Fitz shrugged as he stared up at the stars. "He's a twisted guy raised by an overprotective sister and an alcoholic mother. He knows how to manipulate, and he knows how to survive. He could see how much the kids liked you and that Baxter approved of you. He didn't like what that meant for his position here. I say good riddance."

Even so, Jo couldn't help feeling unsettled. "And when Lila gets back and finds me still here? What then?"

Fitz looked at her and grabbed her hand. "She knows you love the kids. Now that her brother is gone, she'll be fine. Listening to him was messing with her head. She can be tough but when it comes down to it, she just wants a good life for her family."

She looked down at her fingers linked with his. "I can understand that."

He put his arm around her. "Speaking of families, I think it's way past time you meet mine."

"You want me to meet your dad and brothers?" Jo blinked in shock.

Fitz pulled back, surprised. "Of course. I want them to meet the girl I've fallen in love with."

Love? Jo stood up suddenly and ran her hands through her hair as she paced the rock courtyard. She turned and stared at him.

298

"You *love* me," she stated, although even she heard a question somewhere in her voice.

Fitz stood and walked over, grabbing her hands and looking into her eyes as he pulled her closer. "This morning when I was told to take you to the airport, I realized I might never see you again. I can't imagine my life without you. If I couldn't see you every day . . . I think I'd shrivel up and blow away. Jo, I need you. As much as Tru and Nellie need you, I think I need you more."

Jo stared at him, wanting desperately to believe him. "But what if I *had* left?"

He put his hands on her arms, bringing their faces closer. "I would have quit and followed you. Don't you feel it, Jo? Can't you feel what's between us?" His voice soft and warm.

Her hands began to shake. "I do," she whispered, "but I wasn't sure if I could trust what I was feeling. We're so different, Fitz. How can we know it's real?"

Fitz cupped her face in his large hands and touched his nose to hers. "Because I was always meant to find you and love you. Our souls are connected on the most basic level there is. Because we *belong* together."

She closed her eyes and lifted her face to the starlight, her heart expanding with pure joy. "And to think I didn't even want to come to California."

Fitz grinned and wrapped his arms around her. "And?"

Jo lifted her lips to his. "And I love you too," she whispered before she lifted her hands to cradle his face. The kiss was so sweet and melting that she knew for certain she wanted to kiss Fitz for the rest of her life.

He pulled back, his eyes soft and intense. "Then promise to stay."

She leaned her head against his heart as the warm California breeze caressed her neck. She sighed happily.

"I promise," she said and made a cross over Fitz's heart.

ABOUT SHANNON GUYMON

    I live in Utah with my six children and I'm the author of thirty-three books so far. I write YA Paranormal Romance under my pen name, Katie Lee O'Guinn. I enjoy the outdoors, reading and being with my children. I'm also a supporter of the Elizabeth Smart Foundation. For more info on her cause, please go to: ElizabethSmartFoundation.org

    As you've probably already guessed, I'm a huge believer in happy endings. Scarlett really should have been happy with Rhett and it's a darn shame Leo and Kate didn't float safely into New York on the Titanic. Don't even get me started on Romeo and Juliet. To find out the latest on my books, check out my blog at ShannonGuymon.blogspot.com or KatieLeeOGuinn.blogspot.com. You can purchase all of my books on Amazon.

A Place to Call Home

Sarah M. Eden

OTHER WORKS BY SARAH M. EDEN

Seeking Persephone
Courting Miss Lancaster
The Kiss of a Stranger
Friends and Foes
An Unlikely Match
Drops of Gold
Glimmer of Hope
As You Are
Longing for Home
Hope Springs
The Sheriffs of Savage Wells
For Elise

One

ost people believe the three most important words in real estate to be *location, location, location*. Ada Canton knew better, and she had four years as the top Realtor in her area to prove it.

Her three crucial words? *Home, sweet home.*

Even if she was helping a client find a vacation home, it was still a *home*. The key lay in discovering what meant *home* to each client.

She looked over the requirements that her newest client, Craig Adamson, had provided. They included the usual emotionless list buyers came up with first: *Condo or Townhome. 2+ bedrooms. 2+ baths. Backyard.* His price range would work, provided he wasn't looking for a beachfront or ocean view.

She had enough to get started. After all, the first day out wasn't about *finding* a perfect match; it was about discovering what would *make* a match perfect.

"Ada." The receptionist, Shantice, peeked inside the office, the many strands of her bright yellow earrings clanking about. "Your ten o'clock is here."

"Thanks." Ada closed her laptop. "Any insights?"

Shantice leaned against the doorframe. She spun her bangle around her wrist. "Late thirties, I'd guess."

More likely to have reasonable expectations.

"Sharp dresser, but nothing designer."

Looking for quality but probably not a lot of wiggle room in the budget.

"He took a call from someone with a missing homework assignment that turned out to be in their backpack."

Second bedroom is for his kid. As is the backyard, probably. She mentally crossed one location off her list; the schools weren't great in that area.

"Anything else?"

"He's hot." Shantice always brought Ada a report on new clients, but she'd never included *that* type of information.

"Why is it important for me, as his Realtor, to know that?"

"It's not important . . . as his *Realtor*." She cocked her head to one side, eying Ada scoldingly. "It's important for you as a woman who hasn't had a steady relationship in two years or a date in at least a month. I'm telling you, he's smokin'."

"My last boyfriend was hot," Ada said, pulling her handbag off its hook near the door. "And a jerk. Being 'smokin' isn't enough."

"Maybe this guy's different."

"Maybe." Ada made sure she had her phone. "But he's not here looking for a date; he's looking for a home."

Shantice gave her an exasperated look. "You won't even consider it?"

"I'm not bitter or against the idea of finding someone or anything like that," Ada said. "I'm just not falling all over myself looking for a guy."

"You were there for me when my life was falling apart," Shantice said. "I want to return the favor."

Ada shook her head. She didn't really think *her* life was falling apart. "If I do find someone interesting—especially if he isn't a total jerk—I'll give him a chance. I promise."

Shantice's gaze narrowed. "Promise you'll tell me if it happens?"

"Of course I will." They were best friends, after all. "You're the best."

"According to your business cards, *you* are the best."

Shantice had given her a hard time over that ever since Ada's new cards had arrived. But when a person's named the top in her profession several years in a row, that sort of thing ought to be mentioned. It wasn't as though she'd had it printed in an extra-large font or anything.

Ada slipped the tablet into her shoulder bag. "Time to go work my magic."

They turned the corner. Only one person sat in the sitting area—a guy, as Shantice had described, probably mid-thirties, dressed nicely but not overdone. And definitely good looking. Dark, wavy hair. A hint of stubble on his firm jaw. An absolutely tantalizing mouth.

It was a lot to realize about a person so quickly, but not noticing those things would have been impossible. Ada reminded herself that looks could be deceiving—she'd certainly learned that with her last few boyfriends—and crossed directly to him.

"Mr. Adamson?"

He set aside his magazine and stood, unfolding himself from the seat. The man was tall and slender without being lanky. And he smelled good too. She allowed herself only the smallest fraction of a moment to add those things to her list of reasons why Shantice had been completely right in her description.

Back to work, Ada.

She held out her hand for him to shake. "I'm Ada Canton. It's nice to finally meet you."

"You, too. And call me Craig." His handshake was firm without being painful. Too many of her male clients didn't know how to strike that balance.

"If you're ready, we can get started," she said.

He motioned for her to lead the way. Craig even held the door. *Nice guy.*

They stepped out into the bright early-summer day.

"The first property is a condo at the bottom of your price range." She slid on her sunglasses.

"Bottom of my price range? I like it already."

"Less expensive isn't always a better deal," she warned.

"Are you taking me to a slum?" *Nice and a sense of humor.*

"I specialize in slums." She adjusted her purse to hang more firmly on her shoulder. "And I have a lead on a cardboard box under the Vista Way overpass."

"Two bedrooms?" he asked.

"Of course." She clicked her car door remote. "Are you single?"

"We're jumping right to relationship status? You aren't even going to awkwardly ask if I want to get coffee or see a movie or something first?" Even his eyes smiled.

Focus, Ada.

"I just want to make sure there isn't someone else who ought to be part of the house search."

He laughed. "Ah. That's why you asked."

"Ah." She mimicked his tone.

"No one else," he said. "Just me and my son. Except for every other weekend, when he's with his mom." His words stopped abruptly. "I have no idea why I told you that last part."

"It's because of a magical power all Realtors have." She crossed to her car. "Next you'll be telling me your middle-school locker combination and who you voted for in the last election."

"And then my blood type?" he guessed, stopping at the car parked next to hers.

"That's not until the third or fourth property."

Man, he had a great laugh. And, man, did she need to focus.

He followed her to the condominium complex where she meant to begin. She slipped out of her car quickly so she could watch Craig as he eyed the less-than-pristine complex with its faded paint and patchy grass. It wasn't a dump—far from it—but it wasn't like new, either.

Craig looked unimpressed. So aesthetics *were* important to him. And property upkeep.

"Let's take a look," she suggested.

His reaction to the condo was what she'd figured it would be—nothing was glaringly wrong with the property, but nothing was particularly eye-catching about it either. Many Realtors started with a bang, presenting the best right away. Ada knew better. She'd learn far more this way.

Ada pulled out her tablet. "What do you dislike most about this place?"

He went through a long and telling list. He needed room for his son, a basketball court or at least a hoop, something nearer the beach, with a little pop but not necessarily pizazz. She scrolled through her list of possibilities for the day and quickly chose three. She'd learn more talking to him at those locations.

"What do you say we move up a little in the world?" she asked with a smile.

"Does this mean a no on the cardboard box?"

She slipped her tablet into her bag. "That's my big finale."

They spent two more hours looking at other locations. She took notes, watched him looking over the properties, and gained a better idea of what he was looking for. Through it all, they laughed a lot, and he spoke fondly of his son.

He didn't seem like a jerk, but she didn't plan on telling Shantice that. If she did, there'd be no end to the hints— subtle and not so subtle—that asking him out was the logical next step.

No, Ada would enjoy laughing and joking with him for the few days without worrying about anything beyond that. She hadn't given up entirely on finding love; she was simply unwilling to waste her time on guys who weren't worth it, or on guys who didn't think *she* was worth it, or on relationships that were doomed to fall apart.

Not again.

Two

"What did you think of her?"

Craig had been expecting that question from his sister-in-law all through dinner. "Half of the population is made up of *hers*. You'll have to be more specific."

He met his brother's laughing eyes. They both dropped their gazes to their plates.

Bianca wasn't amused. "Ada. What did you think of Ada?"

"Oh, that's who you were talking about." He held his hands up as he nodded, pretending she'd solved a big mystery for him.

She'd recommended Ada for his house search, but he'd suspected that she had more personal reasons for the suggestion. The woman had been trying to set him up ever since his divorce was final.

"How would you like me to rate my impression of her?"

Craig asked. "Perhaps on a scale of Gina the dog walker to Hailey the Nordstrom's makeup counter lady?" He'd been set up by her so many times.

"I remember Gina the dog walker." His brother laughed. Gina had been . . . interesting.

"Don't encourage him, Rob." Bianca shot her husband a warning glare. "He never gives anyone a chance, but Ada is amazing. Didn't you think so, Craig?"

He'd liked Ada, really. She was fun. "She's very good at her job. I think she'll be able to find exactly what I'm looking for."

"And what *are* you looking for?" Bianca's pitying tone was all too familiar. "I admit that Gina was a miscalculation on my part, but Hailey was great. You remember Teresa. She was . . . pretty great. If I just knew what you're looking for."

"I think *I* know his type." Rob leaned back in his chair, eyes narrowed, brow pulled low. "Someone quite a bit taller than he is. Skyscraper bangs are a must. The fewer teeth, the better."

Bianca threw a napkin at her husband. "The two of you are impossible."

Craig was immediately back to biting his smiling lips while staring intently at his plate. He loved it when his brother came around, meddling sister-in-law and all.

"What was wrong with Ada?" Bianca asked.

"When did I say anything was wrong with her?"

"Then you *did* like her." Bianca sounded way too excited.

"As much as anyone can like a real estate agent," he said somberly. He couldn't resist peeking at her expression—shocked, just as he'd hoped.

"You object to her profession? It's not like she's a bank robber or something."

Good ol' Rob jumped in. "She's also not a professional puppy rescuer. So, I'd say there's room for improvement."

"You're impossible." Bianca pushed her chair back from the table and stood. "I don't know why you're so opposed to dating."

"It's not that I don't want to. I don't feel the need to. So I'm not desperately clawing around for a girlfriend."

Bianca huffed. "There's nothing 'desperately clawing' about asking someone out if you think she's amazing."

"*You* said she was amazing," he reminded her.

"Don't you think she is? Or at least might be? You should see her again, Craig. You really should." Bianca really was too easy to string along.

"I'm seeing her Friday, actually. Jack will be at his mom's, so I have the evening free."

She clapped her hands in excitement. Craig didn't dare meet his brother's eyes.

"We're going to look at a couple more properties," Craig added casually.

"'Look at a couple of properties'?" Rob repeated. "Is that code for something? Dinner and a movie? Coffee and dessert?"

"Dog walking?" Craig tossed in.

"So it's not a date?" Bianca demanded, hands on her hips.

"She's my real estate agent. Nothing more."

Another of Bianca's signature huffs was cut off by the sound of the back door opening.

"Dad! I got ten!" Jack came running in, basketball under his arm. "I totally made ten shots in a row."

"Up top, little man!" Craig high-fived his son. "Layups or dunks?"

"Daaaaad." Jack always drew his name out long when he

thought Craig was being ridiculous. "I can't dunk on a regulation hoop. I'm only nine."

Bianca nudged Jack's untouched dinner plate closer to him. "Nine or not, you need to eat," Bianca insisted. "After we all sat down, you ran out of here so fast, you've hardly eaten anything."

"Yes, Aunt Bianca." Jack set his ball on the table and reached for a dinner roll.

"Jack," Craig warned.

"Sorry, Dad." He moved the ball to the floor. "There's only two weeks left of school," he said to no one in particular. "Then we're going to go to the beach to watch the seagulls attack tourists. It's gonna be awesome."

"Time well spent," Rob said.

Jack looked over at Craig. "Mom says I need a new swimsuit 'cause mine's too small." Breadcrumbs sprayed everywhere as he spoke. They'd need to work on table manners.

"Does she want you to have it before you go to her house this weekend?"

Jack grabbed another roll. "I don't know."

"I'll call her." He ruffled Jack's dark hair. "In the meantime, you need to get to your homework."

"I want to go shoot some more hoops," he protested.

"Two more weeks, and you can shoot hoops all summer long."

Jack complied, dragging himself, basketball under one arm as always, down the hall toward his room.

"How does he feel about the move?" Rob asked.

"He says that as long as there's a basketball court, he'll be happy." Craig fully intended to find one. He felt bad that his son would be losing his backyard hoop, but the landlord was raising their rent, so he no longer had enough reasons to put off buying his own place. "And he loves the pool at Carol's, so I'm looking for that too."

"Ada will find something perfect. She's fantastic."

"No. You said she's *amazing*," Rob corrected.

"Stop it." But Bianca laughed. She did have a good sense of humor. Craig and Rob simply knew how to push her buttons, and they enjoyed doing it. "After you 'look at a couple of places,' why don't you go get some coffee or something with Ada?"

"I don't like drinking coffee alone," Craig said.

"You wouldn't be alone." Bianca dropped her head into her hand. "You are hopeless."

"I don't know about that. Rob is more pathetic than I am, and he didn't end up as a lonely cat lady living in an abandoned attic. I figure my chances are pretty good."

Bianca rolled her eyes. "I don't know why I even try." She left the kitchen and dropped onto the couch in the living room, just out of earshot.

"She worries about you," Rob said confidentially. "You and Jack both."

"I know."

Rob finished his Coke. "Any chance you'll take this Realtor of Destiny out, or do I need to brace myself for another night of Bianca listing possible love interests for you while I'm trying to watch the eleven o'clock news?"

"You might want to get your news online." Craig stood, then grabbed his plate. "I'm done dating."

"But you haven't dated since the divorce. That's three years." Rob brought his plate to the sink, where Craig was rinsing his.

"And yet, I don't miss the dating scene." He did miss it a little, just not enough.

"Could be fun," Rob said.

"I'm an accountant. How much more fun could my life possibly get?"

"You—"

"Dude. Lay off."

Rob grinned. "Okay, but if Bianca asks, I grilled you, made a lot of good arguments, and convinced you to at least consider it."

Craig laughed and shook his head. "Got it."

"And one more thing—"

Craig muttered something a little colorful under his breath and braced himself.

"If Ada doesn't catch your interest, Bianca is going to try setting you up with her manicurist—she thinks Russia is the gridlock that clogs the freeway twice a day. And she laughs like a goat. All the time." Rob gave him a pointed look. "I had to fake appendicitis to get out of picking Bianca up from the salon last time."

"You had your appendix taken out when you were twelve."

"Which tells you how desperate I was—couldn't even come up with a realistic lie." Rob said. "If Ada the Realtor can hold an intelligent conversation, you ought to consider the coffee thing, at least. It'd get Bianca off your back and save you from Mademoiselle Goat Laugh."

"Very generous warning," Craig said.

"I'm a very generous person."

Craig eyed him dryly. "The fact that you regularly hung me out of our bedroom window by my ankles when we were kids argues otherwise."

"I didn't drop you, did I?"

"Brotherly love, right there." He slapped Rob on the back as they walked toward the living room. "I'll think about having coffee with Ada. Happy?"

"I don't really care," Rob said.

"But *I'm* happy," Bianca declared from the couch. "And I expect you to call me first thing Saturday to tell me how it went."

"Rob," Craig muttered.

"Yes?"

"You should have dropped me."

Three

"The second bedroom is a little smaller than the last one we looked at earlier this week, but it's bigger than the first condo."

Craig turned slowly, looking at the living room again. He liked this place. It had the amenities he wanted. Close to the beach. The backyard even had a basketball hoop. "This is in my price range?"

She'd already assured him of that, but maybe he'd misheard.

"Ten thousand below your budget."

"So what's wrong with it?" He didn't for a moment believe that Ada was showing him a dump in disguise. "Built over a cemetery? Pipes made out of old gum wrappers?"

"They skipped the paint and just covered the walls in pure lead."

"Ah." He nodded slowly. "Perfect."

"Good schools in this area."

She'd thought of everything. "You are really good at this. I'd expected to settle for something 'good enough.'"

"I don't do 'good enough.'" Her tone held enough laughter to take out any arrogance. "I also don't do 'impossible.' An agent I work with has the task right now of finding a 5-bed, 5-bath beachfront for under a million."

"Has he tried cutting out the middle man and just searching for a time machine?"

"Exactly."

Craig was finding that he had a weakness for confident, focused women.

He looked around one more time. "Jack would love all of this."

Her smile was soft, empathetic. "His room was your first, biggest concern. That told me you'd be where he'd be happiest. So that's what I looked for."

"I think you found it."

"Don't rush yourself," she answered. "This is a big decision. It's better to be right than fast."

She locked up, and they walked back to their cars. They'd met up at the condominium complex. He almost left things at that. He almost got in his car and drove off. Almost.

"This will probably end in humiliation and awkwardness, but—" His courage deserted him faster than cockroaches fleeing light. Still, he pushed on. "Jack is at his mom's, and, since I thought this would take a lot longer than it did, I have the rest of the evening to kill. Do you—would you be interested—" He wasn't usually so bad at this sort of thing. For some reason, Ada made him nervous. "Do you want to go get some coffee or something?"

Lame but to the point.

She didn't answer right away. Was that a good sign, or not? "Would this be a date?"

"Doesn't have to be." He'd kind of prefer that it wasn't, actually. "Just hanging out, having some coffee." Had his voice shook? It as if he was a teenager again.

"Pier View Coffee's not too far from here," she said.

That was a yes, wasn't it? He wished she sounded more confident. "Okay."

"Coffee. Hanging out." She swung her key ring around her finger. "Sure. If you're still interested."

"Pier View it is."

She held up a hand to halt him. "On one condition."

"Shoot."

"Shooting is not my condition." She managed to sound serious, though her eyes were laughing. "All I ask is that we not talk about real estate. It's the end of a long work week, and I am dying to not think about comps or floorplans or subdivisions."

He could appreciate that. He didn't want to talk about real estate either. "And I'm eager to forget all about ledgers, payroll, and expense reports."

"You're an accountant?"

"By day."

She leaned her forearms against the passenger side of his car, talking to him over it. "What are you by night, a superhero or something?"

"Is being awkward and boring a superpower? If it is, then *yes.*"

She tapped the top of his car. "See you at Pier View in a few minutes, Awkward Avenger."

"Not if I beat you there, Captain Realtor."

She stepped back. "I need a better superhero name than that."

"Last one there buys the other one coffee," he challenged.

"Deal." She hopped in her car without hesitation.

Craig was in his a second later. A second after that, he realized he wasn't entirely sure how to get to Pier View. Ada had already pulled out. He opened the maps app on his phone. While it searched, he sent Bianca a text.

Getting coffee with Ada.

He popped his cell into the holder on the dash. The map pulled up. The café was only a few minutes away. Ada would get there way before he did. That was embarrassing. Still, he'd intended to buy her coffee all along, so losing the bet wasn't a big deal.

Just as he turned the key, a text came through from Bianca.

Aaaaaaaaaaaaaaaaaaa!!!

He laughed. Poor Rob was likely being harangued with questions now. Served him right. Of course, Craig would be the one getting harangued by Bianca tomorrow.

When Craig arrived at the coffee shop, Ada's car was parked and empty. He found her inside the café, already seated and grinning at him.

"Looks like the coffee's on me," he said, sitting across the small table from her.

"I honestly thought the contest would be a little closer. Did you come by way of L.A.?"

"Was that the wrong route?" He scanned the menu hanging above the counter. "Let me know what you want. I'll go order."

While waiting in line, Craig took a moment to breathe. He didn't know why he was so nervous. He hadn't felt like this over a non-date date since high school. His confidence hadn't increased much by the time he'd paid for and picked up their coffees and headed back to where she was sitting. The Awkward Avenger, for sure.

"Here you go." He set her drink down and retook his seat. *Don't be a loser.* "I'm not allowed to talk about real estate, but I don't know anything else about you, so I'm kind of at a loss."

"Don't worry. Captain Realtor to the rescue." After a sip, she said, "How old is Jack?"

"Nine."

"Third grade?" Ada guessed.

"Just finishing. Looking forward to summer vacation."

She smiled and nodded. "As a kid I couldn't wait for school to be out. Days at the beach. Going to Disney."

"Jack's more of a Legoland kid." This was going better than he'd expected. But, then, talking about his son was always easy.

"I took my niece and nephew there a couple of weeks ago. Small price to pay for the title of Best Aunt in the World. Now don't tell anyone" —she leaned in close and lowered her voice—"but it wasn't as much torture as I kept telling them it was."

"Next time, take them to the beach to watch the seagulls harassing the tourists."

She nearly spit out her iced coffee. "You do that?"

"It's pretty hilarious, actually. Plus, after a while, Jack gets tired of it and builds a sandcastle or plays in the waves. I bring snacks and a cooler with drinks, and I get to spend the day at the beach."

She nodded her approval. "Win-win."

"What about you? Are you a beachcomber? Surfer? One of those people who goes to Disneyland every day?"

"I believe those are called *cast members.*" She was quick with a comeback. He liked that. "Though I did sell a house in Anaheim earlier this year, and—"

"Wait, wait. You promised not to bring up real estate."

She shook her head, smiling with amusement. "*You* promised not to bring it up."

"No. I promised to be boring and awkward. And" —he tugged both sides of his collar in a self-congratulatory way—"I'm expertly holding up my side of the agreement."

"Personally, I think you're failing miserably. I haven't been bored yet, and, other than having to wait for you to get here, nothing about this hanging-out-and-getting-coffee evening has been awkward."

He looked away to hide a surge of triumph. The Awkward Avenger was doing pretty good for himself.

"It's getting hot in here," Ada said. "Want to sit outside?"

"Good idea." The coffee shop was busy, and it was pretty warm. "What do you do for fun, then, if not the daily Disney thing?"

"I'm in a book club, which is, I realize, not very exciting."

He motioned for her to go out the door first. "What do you like to read?"

"Guess." She twitched an eyebrow in challenge, turning to look directly at him.

He narrowed his eyes, pretending to study her closely. "Monkey fiction?"

"Fiction about monkeys?"

"No. Fiction *written by* monkeys." As he took another sip of his coffee, he twitched his eyebrow just as she had a moment ago. "I hear it's the next big thing."

"You nailed it." She sat at the only empty outside table. "I spend every third Tuesday at the Monkey Fiction Book Club."

Half an hour must have passed while they chatted. They covered siblings, hobbies, which ice cream flavor was actually the best. Thanks to Bianca, Craig had been on a lot of first dates over the past few years. This non-date date was the least disastrous of any of them.

Ada was easy to talk to. She was funny and upbeat. For the first time since the divorce, he was honestly considering seeing someone a second time. He wasn't sure he'd actually follow through with it, but he was *thinking* about it.

Four

*a*da stood at the top of the beach access stairs, her beach bag over her shoulder, chair under her arm, and her phone, unfortunately, pressed to her ear. "I promise, Vincent, I will tell you if I hear about a miraculous beachfront for under a million. But I don't think one exists."

"I've got to find something," Vincent said. "The McEllens don't believe it's as impossible as I've told them. They're turning on me. I'm bringing George along for protection."

George wasn't even five-foot-six, so Ada didn't think Vincent actually thought he was in any danger.

"I'll be sure to offer a moving eulogy at your funeral," she said, "but only if you don't call me again. It's my day off."

"What Realtor gets to take a Saturday off?"

"One who got five incredible deals for clients this week," she said. "Like my business cards say, I'm the best."

"I hate you." Vincent said that a lot, but never meant it. "Have fun goofing off."

SARAH M. EDEN

"Have fun cowering behind George." She dropped her phone in her bag and took a deep breath of salty ocean air.

It *had* been a good week. She'd negotiated killer prices for clients, found an amazing new home stager to use, and signed a new client looking to spend a small fortune. The one downside: Craig hadn't called or texted except to discuss the townhouse he'd made an offer on. He'd seemed happy to get an even better deal than expected. He asked a few technical questions. Their interaction had all been very impersonal.

I guess our date really wasn't a date. And here she'd been, thinking it was the best first date she'd ever been on. She, doubting Ada that she was, had actually been hoping for a second one. She never hoped for a second date.

Her thoughts kept swirling as she took the stairs down to the beach. She and Craig had a lot in common. They talked easily, as if they'd known each other for years instead of days. But maybe he was like that with everyone.

"Ada!" Shantice had beat her to the beach. She waved Ada over.

Shantice always looked like she'd stepped off the cover of a fashion magazine, even at the beach. Her striped sunhat perfectly matched her red suit. Her sandals weren't the usual dollar store flip-flops everyone else wore. She could probably have given the Hollywood red carpet walkers a run for their money.

Ada, on the other hand, tended to buy the first suit that fit and added whatever accessories were most sensible.

"How's the water?" Ada asked.

"Too cold for me. But Devon and Ruff don't seem to mind."

Shantice's boyfriend and dog were playing fetch in the waves. They weren't alone. California's beaches filled up in June despite the water not being very warm yet. For her part,

326

Ada enjoyed just sitting on the beach, clearing her mind of work and worries.

They talked while she set up her chair next to Shantice's. They touched on everything from family issues to weekend plans to the latest movies. Conversations between them had come easily ever since they met at the agency. Ada had supported her through a terrible divorce. Shantice had been there for her when her mother died. They were as close as sisters.

Ada settled into her beach chair, ready for a relaxing morning.

"Okay, now, don't shoot me, but . . ." Shantice eyed her nervously.

"That doesn't bode well."

Shantice didn't move from her position lying out on the lounge-style beach chair. "I just want to know if you've heard anything from Craig."

"Not since you asked last night," she said dryly.

"Why are guys so stupid? You two hit it off, and he doesn't ask you out for real? That's lame."

Ada adjusted her sunhat to shade her face better. "In his defense, I could ask him just as easily."

"So why haven't you?"

Why haven't I? "Probably because I figured he'd say no. I got a strong he's-just-not-that-into-you vibe this week."

"But he asked you out," Shantice repeated for the hundredth time that week. "That sounds interested to me."

Ada shrugged. What could she say? She'd thought he was interested too.

"Maybe his divorce was nasty," Shantice said. "That makes dating seem like a disaster waiting to happen."

Could be.

"And you said he has a kid. That would make any guy—any decent guy anyway—more cautious."

"I wasn't looking to move in or take over his life. I was just hoping for a second date."

And yet, Shantice had a point. He had reason to be careful. But she'd also thought there had been a reason to talk to her about something other than his condo.

"Ada!" Shantice's whisper was almost frantic. "Ada, look. Look who's talking to Devon. Look!"

She knew that dark, wavy hair in an instant. *Craig.* How was this possible? Miles of beaches, millions of people, and Craig was standing right there, talking to Shantice's boyfriend. A boy—Jack, probably—was playing with Ruff.

"It's fate," Shantice whispered. She whistled, and Ruff came bounding over.

Ada was immediately on alert, sitting straight up in her chair. She didn't trust the scheming look in Shantice's eyes. "What are you doing?"

"Getting you a second date." Shantice waved the dog over more eagerly.

An instant after Ruff arrived, Jack did too. The dog's tail wagged excitedly.

"You can keep petting him if you want," Shantice said. "He likes you, I can tell."

"He's great," Jack declared, popping to his knees in the sand and going to town petting the dog and scratching behind his ears.

"His name's Ruff. I'm Shantice. This is my friend Ada."

"My dad knows someone named Ada," Jack said, not looking away from Ruff. "He told my aunt Bianca about her."

Shantice shot her wide-eyed look and an I-told-you-so nod. Ada didn't let herself get her hopes up. Bianca Adamson was a friend of a friend. She was the one who suggested that her brother-in-law hire Ada. Craig could have mentioned her as nothing more than his Realtor.

"I know your dad, actually," she told Jack. "I'm helping him buy his new house."

"Oh, then you're not Coffee Ada." Jack shrugged, looking a little disappointed.

"*Coffee Ada*," Shantice mouthed.

Ada's heart leaped around unexpectedly. She was usually pretty levelheaded. "I might be," she told Jack. "We did have coffee on Friday."

That brought the boy's gaze to her face at last. "Really?"

"Really."

Jack jumped to his feet. "Don't go anywhere, Ruff." Then he bolted toward the waves. "Dad! Dad!"

Ada couldn't hear what he said, but Jack pointed back at her as he spoke to his father. Almost as if in slow motion, Craig turned his head in her direction. Surprise registered on his face, followed by a slow, heart-melting smile.

"You are *so* getting a second date," Shantice said.

Ada couldn't take her eyes off Craig. "That smile. It's killer, isn't it?"

"Mm-hmm."

"And he's a genuinely good guy, which is even better. Smart. Funny. A great dad." It was little wonder she'd wanted a second date so badly. You didn't meet someone like that every day.

Craig, Jack, and Devon made their way over, Craig eying her with curiosity.

"Hi," she said when he was in earshot.

"Small world. What brings you out?"

She moved her sunglasses to the top of her head. "I thought I'd come watch the seagulls attack some tourists."

"Hey, Dad, that's what we do!" Jack had a nine-year-old's version of his dad's smile. In a few more years, he would break some hearts.

"Have you seen any attacks today?" she asked Jack.

"Nah. The seagulls are busy or something." His eyes kept darting to Ruff, who ran back and forth between Shantice and Devon.

Craig, however, was looking at her.

"Do you and Devon know each other?" she asked.

"We go to the same gym, though he's obviously getting more out of his membership." He patted his belly as if there were a big gut hiding under his close-fitting t-shirt rather than the trim stomach actually there.

She stroked her chin in an overdone show of contemplation. "I'm sure there's a protein shake for that."

Good grief, that smile!

Devon held a hand out to Shantice. "Come into the water, babe. It's not that cold, I swear."

The doubtful look she threw at him was almost comical.

Devon tried again. "If it's freezing, I'll get you a tea on the way home, okay?"

Shantice took his hand in one of hers, the other holding her hat against the stiff breeze, and let him pull her to her feet. Before walking out with Devon, she shot Craig a quick look. "You can use my chair. Then Ada won't have to crane her neck so far back to talk to you."

He took the offer, plopping next to Ada as though entirely comfortable around her. So he probably hadn't hated their coffee non-date. Why were guys so hard to figure out?

"How does Jack feel about switching schools?" she asked.

"He didn't throw a party or anything, but he seems okay with it. Jack's a resilient kid. He's had to be with everything that's happened."

Ada could appreciate that. "My folks split up when I was a little younger than he is. They never quit hating each other, and my brothers and I were always caught in the middle. We learned quickly how to negotiate any minefield." It had been a miserable way to grow up.

"That's why I try so hard to get along with my ex. It's not Jack's fault our marriage fell apart, and I don't want him to suffer for it any more than he has to." He shook his head, even laughed a little bit. "I don't know how you get me to spill so many things. I don't usually talk about myself so much."

She slid her sunglasses into place once more. "I'm telling you, it's a superpower."

His attention returned to Jack, who was laughing uproariously as he and Ruff chased each other. "Why do I get the feeling I'm going to have to buy a dog?"

"That's a dog's superpower."

Craig's laugh sounded very much like a deeper version of his son's. "Dogs get kids addicted. It's underhanded."

"Shantice and Ruff come here almost every Saturday morning. You're welcome to bring Jack if he ever needs a dog fix. I'm here, too, whenever I can get a Saturday morning off."

Did that sound pathetic? Could he tell she was hoping he'd start showing up here on Saturday mornings?

"This beach is closer to the new condo than our old place. I thought I'd let Jack get used to coming here."

They're going to be regulars. Ada held back a gleeful squeal. "There's a great hot dog joint a quick walk from here. If you two aren't in a hurry, I'd love to treat you both to some lunch. You did pay for coffee last time, after all."

Oh, man. That was definitely pathetic. It was embarrassing enough to not get asked out over the phone. To ask him out—sort of—in person only to have her invitation rejected would be humiliating.

"I think we could be talked into a couple of hot dogs." Craig didn't sound blown away by the idea, but he also didn't seem to have any real objection to it.

Ada took that as a tentative victory. A step forward, anyway. They sat there, soaking up the sun, chatting about a million different things, while Jack ran around with Ruff. Conversation had been easy between them from the very beginning. Didn't he see that? Wasn't he at all curious to find out if there could be something more between them than friendly banter?

As noon approached, his son said, "Hey, Jack! You hungry?"

"Starving." Jack dropped onto the towel near Craig's chair.

"Ada knows of a hot-dog place nearby. She's going to take us."

Jack flashed Ada a heart-tugging smile. "Awesome!"

Jack carried the conversation as they walked to get lunch. Ada heard all about his friends, his pet fish Francisco, his new swim trunks, and his new home. Though she was thoroughly familiar with the townhouse, she let Jack tell her everything he knew and thought about it. The boy was a charmer, for sure. He didn't stop talking until he took the first bite of his hot dog.

"I should have warned you that he likes to talk," Craig said under his voice.

She waved off the unspoken apology. "I'm used to it. My brothers were all the same way, and their kids are the same."

"Our new house has a pool," Jack tossed out between bites.

"That's great," Ada said. "Sounds like you're a swimmer."

Jack shrugged. He spoke, though he was still chewing. "I

usually swim at my mom's house. It's the only thing she likes to do with me."

In that moment, Ada's heart broke. *It's the only thing she likes to do with me.* She glanced at Craig. Tension tugged at his eyes and mouth, though he did a good job of hiding it.

"Your dad tells me you play basketball."

Jack lit up again. "I'm good."

Ada leaned a little closer to him. "So am I."

Jack's eyes grew wide. "Really?"

"Really. I played in high school and college."

"No way," the two Adamson men said in unison.

"Way."

"What position do you play?" Jack asked.

Craig hazarded a guess before she could answer. "Point guard."

"How'd you know?"

"It fits you." He wiped a bit of mustard off the corner of his mouth. "You're not super tall—no offense—but more than that, you're a strategist. You approach real estate the way a point guard approaches a game. It's all about taking stock of the situation, figuring out what people need even if they don't see it."

Ada was pretty sure she was blushing. That was the kind of compliment women wanted to get but seldom did: an acknowledgment of her strengths and abilities. Most of the time, all women heard about was their looks, as if that was their defining characteristic.

She looked at Jack. "What position do you like best?"

He sat up straighter. "I'm a power forward."

Ada loved the confidence and enthusiasm in that declaration. "Up top, dude." She held her hand up for a high-five and received an enthusiastic one. "What's your favorite shot?"

"Layup, but I'm not very good at it yet. Dad said I just have to keep practicing."

"I was never good at layups."

Jack gave her a *duh* look. "You *are* a point guard."

She and Craig laughed at that. She liked Jack. What a great kid.

"Do you play on a team?"

He finished off his hot dog. "The Gorillas."

"City league," Craig filled in.

"We have a game on Tuesday. You could come if you want." Jack sounded so hopeful. Did his mom ever come to his games? Maybe she lived too far away.

"What time is your game?" she asked.

Craig cut off Jack's response with a wave of his hand. "Ada, you don't have to."

"I like basketball," she assured him. "It'd be fun."

But he was shaking his head. "It's okay, really."

"But—"

"He doesn't need you to come."

That was too pointed to be misunderstood. It wasn't so much that Jack didn't need her there, but rather that Craig didn't want her there.

"Sorry," she said. "I didn't mean to—"

To like basketball. To be nice to your kid. To ask you on another non-date date.

"Sorry."

Jack's gaze darted from one of them to the other. She tried to smile, but it felt awkward. "They have good ice cream here. You want a cone?" she asked him. "If it's okay with your dad."

"Can I, Dad? Please?"

Craig sighed a little—not a good sign. "I guess it wouldn't hurt."

"Vanilla or chocolate?" she asked Jack.

"Vanilla," he answered firmly.

Ada jumped up from the table, grateful to leave them behind for a minute. She wasn't sure where things had gone wrong, but they definitely had. She hadn't been pushy or anything.

What did I do?

"Ada, wait up."

She slowed, but didn't look at him. A person could only be shot down so many times.

"Look, I—"

"Don't worry about it. I didn't mean to push myself where I'm not welcome. I like basketball, and youth league games are fun to watch. No big deal." She got in line for ice cream, still not looking at him.

"You and I—we just don't know each other very well." He'd apparently followed her all the way to the line.

"I know," she answered quickly. "No biggie."

"Jack's a friendly kid, and he welcomes people into his life without thinking. I don't want to see him get hurt."

She held her hands up in a show of frustration. "How could my going to a basketball game hurt him?"

He turned stone-faced. "People have walked out on him. I have spent years holding him together. I have reasons to be careful."

"There's a difference between being careful and not giving someone a chance."

"I've known you for two weeks," he said. "*Not* inviting you into my son's life is reasonably cautious."

He had a point. But it still stung.

"Next," the guy at the counter called.

Ada stepped up. "A vanilla cone, a chocolate cone, and—" She looked over at Craig. "What do you want?"

He did three-quarters of a double take. "You're still buying us ice cream?"

She rolled her eyes. He really did think she was a flake who broke promises on a whim. "Vanilla or chocolate?"

"Chocolate." The statement had the vaguest hint of a question behind it.

The rest of their non-date lunch date was every bit as awkward as he'd predicted their first one would be. Jack seemed oblivious, which was the only good thing Ada could say about the afternoon. The moment Jack finished his cone, Craig said they had to go.

Ada pretended the declaration didn't seem like a desperate attempt to escape. "I'll let you know if anything changes with your closing date," Ada said. "But as of yesterday, everything was on schedule."

"Sounds good."

No, it sounded . . . disappointing.

Five

"I can't believe you convinced me to do this," Craig told Bianca. They sat in his car outside a stranger's home, contemplating his next move.

"I've listened to you whine for almost a week about how you messed up with Ada," Bianca said. "You have to try to fix it."

"But at her book club? That's so—"

"Romantic," Bianca said. "Didn't you see *Jerry Maguire*?"

Wait, she was having him reenact a scene from a chick flick? Not a good sign. "Public humiliation is not my jam."

"Really? Because the story about the ice cream/hot dog fiasco says otherwise."

He lightly banged his head against the steering wheel. "I am so bad at this."

"Luckily, being really bad at talking to someone you're interested in is kind of endearing." Bianca twitched her head toward the house. "Go tell her what you've been telling me. Ada's reasonable, and, if Gina's right, she's totally into you. So go talk to her."

Gina was Ada and Bianca's mutual friend. He hoped Gina was a reliable source for gossip.

"You're telling me to man up," he said.

"Pretty much."

He squared his shoulders and opened the car door. "Don't steal my car while I'm gone."

The walk to the front door was one of the longest he'd ever made. This would either turn out to be a great idea or a huge mistake. He rang the doorbell and waited.

He and Ada hardly knew each other. Why, then, had he been unable to get her out of his mind? The business-like phone calls they'd had about the townhouse ever since the beach had been torture. He'd driven his brother and sister-in-law crazy by going on and on about Ada and the fallout in the ice-cream line. There was just something about her, and he needed to figure out what.

The door opened. Craig reminded himself of the need for this to happen. "Is Ada Canton here?" he asked the woman who'd answered.

"Yeah." She motioned him inside and around the corner to a living room. "Ada, someone's here to see you."

A dozen pairs of eyes focused on him, including Ada's deep-brown ones.

She stared a moment, not speaking, not moving. Her mouth hung the tiniest bit open. "Craig?"

"I don't want to interrupt, I just—Could we talk for a minute?"

"Yeah, sure." She crossed toward him. "Is something wrong?"

Everyone was still watching. "Outside, maybe?"

She agreed. He had a few more moments to try to decide what to say. They stopped on the front step. Ada watched him expectantly. Despite having rehearsed this moment over and over, his mind turned completely blank. He'd have to wing it.

"I—I'm kind of an idiot."

She didn't disagree.

"I've been thinking about how things went that afternoon at the beach, and I owe you an apology."

"I'm listening."

Time to explain what he didn't entirely understand himself. "Jack likes you. And understandably—you're a great person."

She smiled ruefully. "Thanks."

"I saw Jack getting hopeful, and I panicked." He still got a little panicked when he thought about it. "His mom walked out on us when he was four. She decided that being a wife and a mom wasn't really her thing. I have primary custody, and seeing him every other weekend is enough for her. But it's not enough for him. He hides it well, but I know it hurts."

And seeing that hurt every other Sunday when Carol brought Jack back home broke Craig's heart.

"I can see why you're cautious," Ada said.

"But you were right. A city-league basketball game isn't really the huge risk I made it out to be. And Jack was so disappointed." Sometimes Craig felt like a complete failure as a parent. Seeing Jack's face at Tuesday's game when he realized that Ada hadn't come qualified as one of those moments. Craig had been disappointed at not seeing her again too. "If I haven't completely pushed you away, I—well, there's a—Jack has a game on Tuesday, and it'd be great if you came."

He held his breath. That was about as on the line as he could lay it.

A smile spread slowly over her lips. "Tuesday would be great. I'm also free tomorrow night. I know Jack will be at his mom's. You know, in case you want to go do something."

Was she asking him out? He'd been hoping she'd simply listen to his apology. A date was more than he'd bargained for. Not that he was complaining. "Well, we've done coffee and hot dogs. I think the natural next step is a meal requiring utensils. Maybe a movie or something too."

"Sounds good." Her smile turned laughing. "Should we ask the book club what they think?" She motioned toward the front window.

The entire book club was watching them, faces pressed to the glass. Some of the ladies had to have been standing on furniture. One had her phone out, meaning Craig's awkward efforts were probably already on Twitter.

He waved at them, and the group scattered.

"So, pick you up at like six?" he said.

"I'll text you my address."

"Perfect." He didn't know if he was relieved or scared out of his mind. He didn't want to blow another chance to get to know her better. "See you tomorrow."

He, the Awkward Avenger, had a date.

The next evening, Craig pulled into a low-key condo community a little before six o'clock. Somehow he'd pictured Ada living in a flashy, high-end house, maybe on the beach. Yet the sensibleness of it fit her.

As he climbed the stairs, his heart leaped around a little. He hesitated a minute before knocking.

When she answered the door, she was on the phone. She waved him in and silently mouthed, "Sorry."

He wasn't upset at all. The extra minute to catch his

breath was welcome. The prospect of spending an entire evening with Ada had him tied in knots.

"I can get you two of your three requests, but not all of them," she said into the phone. "Finding that size of home in that neighborhood for that price just isn't possible."

She looked amazing, as always. Craig had always been a sucker for brunettes. But the way her blue sweater made her eyes look even bluer than usual pulled him in that much deeper. She was definitely out of his league.

"I'm a Realtor, not a fairy godmother," she said.

Craig bit back a laugh. She didn't put up with a lot of drama. He liked that about her. He liked it a lot.

She met Craig's gaze, then pointed to her phone and shook her head. Still talking to whoever was on the other line, she said, "Having an agent who fits you is almost as important as finding a property that suits you. So if you feel you'd rather work with someone else, I won't try to talk you out of it."

She was about to get fired by a client. From the look of things, she wasn't broken up about it.

"Best of luck to you. I hope your new agent is the miracle worker you are looking for. Okay. Bye." She clicked off her phone and slid it in her back pocket. "Why in the world do I do this for a living?"

"Because you're good at it."

She tipped him a half-smile. "I'm good at vacuuming, too, but you don't see me working as a janitor."

"You would hate being a janitor. But I've seen your face when you find someone the perfect home. You love that moment, admit it."

Her eyes instantly regained their sparkle. "Man, I love that moment. I'm helping someone shape the next few years of their lives, possibly the *rest* of their lives. Knowing I've been a part of making that future better . . . I love that."

SARAH M. EDEN

"I'd say that's your answer. Drama and shenanigans aside, that's why you do this for a living." He narrowed his eyes as if contemplating something more dastardly. "Of course, if you need me to go bust a couple of heads, I'd be happy to do it."

She reached out and took his hand. "I'm glad you're here. This day has been horrible."

"Italian food makes everything better," he said. "What do you say?"

"Sounds perfect." She grabbed her bag from its hook near the door and her keys from a bowl on a side table. "Ready when you are."

Outside her door, he slipped his hand around hers once more. A lot of time had passed since a woman had been affectionate with him. Her touch was magical in a way that had very little to do with his own loneliness. There was something about her.

"What do you think of my swanky digs?" Ada asked with a grin. "Fancy, right?"

"You're living the high life."

She laughed, swinging their hands between them. "I don't know why, but people always expect me to live someplace really amazing."

He'd expected that very thing. "Maybe because you're so good at finding other people exactly what they want. We all figure you'd be living somewhere mind-blowing."

"Not yet. I know what I want. I've seen enough properties to know where to find it and how much it'll cost. I've been saving for almost a decade, a little at a time. A little longer, and I'll have a really good down payment."

Now that sounded like the Ada he was coming to know—practical, determined, forward-thinking. "So you're thinking a super-spacious beachfront for under a million, right?"

She bumped him with her shoulder. "I told Vincent that if I ever found that, I'll buy it myself. I meant it."

"Barring that miraculous discovery, what kind of property are you saving up for?"

"A bungalow a walkable distance from the beach. At least three bedrooms. Open floor plan. Room in the back for a hoop."

She really did sound like a baller.

"Updated kitchen," she continued. "Master suite. Low-maintenance landscaping."

"You really do have it all figured out."

"I've seen enough properties over the last ten years to have figured out what I do and don't like."

He nodded. "And you *are* the best."

"I never should have put that on my business cards."

Conversation continued easily between them all the way to the restaurant. They kept it up over calamari, minestrone, penne and pesto, and tiramisu. She had a degree in finance and could keep up with accountant talk. He didn't know much about real estate, but managed to hold his own. They delved into plenty of other topics too—childhood adventures, favorite subjects in school, favorite basketball teams and dream vacation spots.

By the time they walked back to her condo, he was almost speechless with amazement. "This is by far the least awkward, least disastrous date I've been on in—well, ever."

"Too bad. I was hoping to meet the Awkward Avenger." She leaned her back against her closed front door. "Promise I'll get to meet him eventually?"

He propped his elbow against the wall next to her. "Meet him? Don't you remember the hot dog/ice cream fiasco?"

"That wasn't Awkward Avenger." She reached up and

brushed her fingers along his cheek. "That was a really great dad looking out for his son."

He slipped his hand over hers and turned his head enough to press a kiss to her palm. Her free hand slid up his chest, coming to a rest just above his pounding heart. Was she caressing him or pushing him away? He was so out of practice in the whole romance area that he didn't know. He eyed her, trying to figure it out. Her gaze turned questioning as well.

In an instant, the moment was gone. She backed away the smallest bit. Her hands dropped free. Something like an apology touched her face.

I'm an idiot. The thought kept repeating through the rest of their awkward doorstep goodbye. He thought it during his drive home. He was still thinking it late into the night.

He just hoped Ada had a high tolerance for idiots.

Six

*a*da went to Jack's next two basketball games, though she gave the Adamson guys some space that weekend, when Jack was home. After all, she could appreciate Craig's concerns. Dropping into Jack's life wasn't a good idea until they knew with more certainty whether she'd continue to be part of it. Slow and steady was the best approach. One day, one step, at a time.

They closed on Craig's townhouse. She took him through his final walkthrough and got his keys. He held her hand a lot during those times. He even kissed her, very briefly, a couple of times, but almost in a friendly way, nothing deep or emotional or passionate about it. Ada had no idea at all what he was thinking or feeling.

She loved being with him. He was smart and funny. She'd never seen him be unkind to anyone; he didn't talk bad about people. Craig was the kind of person who made everyone around him happier.

He invited her to his housewarming party a week after closing. She decided that was a good sign. Craig moved slowly, but at least they were still moving forward.

She arrived fashionably late, but only because a client had taken longer than expected. She'd hoped to have a few moments with him before everyone else arrived.

People wove around and about one another. Craig had said he'd invited friends from work and some of the parents from Jack's team, as well as nearby family. She was glad he liked having people over; so did she.

She kept mingling, all the while trying to find Craig. She caught a glimpse of him now and then, but couldn't seem to pin him down.

When he headed up the stairs, she followed. Voices down the hall convinced her to hang back. She didn't want to interrupt anyone, she just wanted to finally say hello and maybe hold his hand for a minute.

"I haven't seen you like this in all the years I've known you." Bianca's voice. She sounded like she approved of Craig's unusual behavior; that it was a good thing. "She's good for you."

Ada's breath caught. Craig's sister-in-law was cheering for her, was making her case, in fact.

"But am *I* good for her?" Craig said. "I come with a lot of baggage."

"But you like her," Bianca said. "Admit it."

"I've known her only about six weeks. But—" His words stopped short. Ada's heart stopped as well. "But I think I love her."

I love her. The shock of those words pulled Ada around the corner. *Love. He just said* love.

And he'd said it without stumbling, without hesitation.

Bianca froze the moment her gaze fell on Ada.

Craig noticeably stiffened. "She's right behind me, isn't she?"

Bianca only nodded.

Craig didn't look back, though he turned his head just enough to direct his next words at her. "You're probably entirely freaked out now."

That was not a simple yes or no question, and it wasn't one she wanted to answer with an audience. Freaked out? A little. But also a little relieved. Mostly, though, she was amazed.

She met Bianca's wide-eyed stare. "Could you give us a minute?"

Bianca didn't wait long enough to answer but slipped past Ada and down the stairs without a second glance.

At last, Craig turned around. Tension rolled off of him. His Adam's apple bobbed with a thick swallow. Apparently he was expecting something awful.

She stepped up to him. "Craig."

The worry didn't leave his eyes. "If you just want to go, I—"

She set her hands on either side of his face and held his gaze as firmly as she could. "I don't run out on people. I never have. I'm not so easily scared off."

His shoulders rose and fell with a tense breath. "Even if a guy you've known for only six weeks says he's falling love with you? Most women would run and never look back."

"Then it's a very good thing I'm not 'most women.'" She slid her hands to his shoulders, very nearly embracing him.

He wrapped his arms around her. "You really are out of my league."

"Something to shoot for."

Finally that grin she loved so much made a reappearance. He pressed his forehead to hers. The smell of

347

him, which had become so achingly familiar, filled the space between them. His mouth brushed over hers so lightly her lips hardly felt the kiss, but her heart definitely did. Her pulse hammered through every inch of her. She threaded her fingers through his hair, keeping him there.

His next kiss was ardent. Fervent. Exactly the kiss she'd been waiting for the past weeks. A kiss telling her that his feelings ran deeper and more passionate than he'd let on. That he really was falling in love with her.

Laughter floated up from below. Craig broke the seal of their lips but didn't release her. "If we just stay up here, do you think they'll leave on their own?"

She pressed one more quick kiss to his lips before stepping backward. "You need to go be a good host."

"No, I really don't. Being a good host: not that important to me."

She laughed. "You're only saying that because you don't want to go downstairs."

"You're going to make me, aren't you?"

She held her hand out to him.

He took it, but shook his head. "You're so mean."

"A good point guard knows when to take her team up the court."

The metaphor earned her a kiss on the back of her hand. Then the tips of her fingers. Her palm. The inside of her wrist.

"Your guests, Craig." She tugged him toward the staircase.

As the night dragged on, she regularly caught Craig looking in her direction; he smiled quietly, and she blushed. The entire party must have known they were both wishing the other guests would call it an early night. It was hard to be in love in public.

Eventually, the house emptied except for a lot of dirty dishes and garbage. Ada stayed to help clean up, grateful it was finally just the two of them. Whenever they crossed paths, he brushed his hand along her arm, or smiled softly at her. A man who could make a woman's heart pound while cleaning a kitchen had some mad superpowers.

They'd almost finished when someone knocked at the door.

"Who could that be this late?" he wondered aloud.

"Maybe someone forgot something."

But it was Jack on the other side of the door, standing next to a woman Ada figured must be his mom.

"Carol. What's going on?" Craig asked.

"I need to be in San Francisco tomorrow, and I can't bring him with me." Carol nudged Jack inside.

"But this is his weekend with you," Craig said. "He's been looking forward to it."

"I just found out," she insisted. "The CEO is giving out awards to the top employees. I can't just not show up. I could get a promotion out of this."

Jack's eyes were firmly focused on the floor. His backpack hung limply on one shoulder. Ada remembered feeling the same way when weekends with her dad were cancelled. Not until she was grown and on her own did she find out that her mom was the one who'd called off the visits and then blamed it on her dad. So much about how her parents handled their divorce had been painful—for their children.

She caught Jack's eye and waved him over. Craig and Carol were still having a somewhat tense conversation at the door.

"Let's go up to your room," she whispered. "We'll get you unpacked."

"Okay." He shrugged, his words more muttered than spoken.

She set her hand on his back and walked with him, hoping the contact was reassuring and comforting.

"I didn't even get to go swimming," Jack said, his feet dragging as they climbed the step.

It's the only thing my mom likes to do with me. Not doing that one thing had surely cut extra deep.

"You can go swimming here," she suggested. "I know it's not the same, but it's something. And maybe in the morning, I can meet you guys at the beach to see if the seagulls are in an attacking mood." She couldn't imagine Craig saying no. He must realize how disappointed Jack was.

"Could we get hot dogs again?" Jack looked so hopeful.

"Sure. And ice cream. Vanilla for you, chocolate for me and your dad."

His smile was fleeting, but it was there. Maybe she'd managed to relieve some of the ache.

Jack tossed his backpack onto his bed. He stood there a moment, eying it. "Do I have to unpack right now?"

"Nah. I think it can wait."

Jack climbed onto his bed and sat there, his feet dangling over the edge. "What's the big deal about San Francisco?" he asked quietly. "Is it super big or something?"

He wanted to know why his mom had chosen a city over a weekend with him. That was one of the hard things about being a kid: everything felt so personal.

Ada sat on the bed beside him. "I'd guess there's something really important there that she can't do closer to home or on another day."

"I guess." His gaze remained on his swinging feet.

"My parents split up when I was a kid. I lived with my mom, but I missed my dad when I wasn't with him. I hated it when I thought I was going to get to see him but then didn't get to."

Jack nodded. She wouldn't force him to talk or listen to her history. She just wanted him to know that she knew that it was hard. She knew that well.

Ada put her arm around his shoulders and hugged him. After a moment, he leaned against her. She was almost certain she heard a sniffle.

Little wonder Craig worried so much about people walking out on Jack. He hurt enough without someone adding to it.

I'm not walking out on you, sweet Jack, she silently vowed. *On you or your dad. I promise.*

"But that means you won't see Jack for two months." Craig kept his tone calm, but only with a lot of effort. Carol was canceling Jack's next three visits. She wasn't a terrible person, and he knew she loved Jack. She just didn't always think about their son's feelings. Jack took the cancellations personally and carried the resulting pain around with him.

"I'll take him to Disneyland or something before school starts," she said.

"You hate Disneyland." He didn't want her making that promise to Jack and then changing her mind when she remembered how much she disliked theme parks. "Pick something you like to do. He'll be happy just spending time with you."

"I'll think of something," she said.

He eyed her doubtfully; she'd made these same promises before.

"I *will*," she insisted. "I'm not a bad mom."

She tended to get defensive, and pressing hard never got Craig anywhere. But he also knew he had to say something.

"I didn't say you were a bad mom."

"You said it with your face." She took an audible and visible breath. Months of counseling during and after the divorce had gotten them to the point where they could keep their tempers intact for Jack's sake. They hadn't been very good at it at first. "I'll think of something he and I can do together at the end of the summer. Something fun. I promise."

He managed a smile. "Text me some pictures of you and your family while you're visiting them. Jack would love to see them."

"I will." She stepped away from the door, but stopped before she'd gone more than a step. "I really am sorry about this weekend. Jack . . ." She didn't seem to know how to finish the thought.

"Jack will be okay." He'd make sure of it.

He closed and locked the door. Carol was about as solid as a breeze. He'd found her laid-back, carefree approach to life endearing when they were young and first dating. But her inability to see things through had become a huge problem later on. Craig was forever picking up the pieces.

He climbed the stairs to Jack's room, not sure what he'd say to the boy. He refused to badmouth his mom.

"Maybe she just doesn't like having me at her house." Jack's quiet question echoed from inside his bedroom.

"I'm sure she loves having you at her house, hon." Ada's voice was soft and kind. "She looked so sad when she dropped you off. She's going to miss you this weekend. She really is."

Craig slipped into the doorway, careful to keep silent. Ada sat on the bed beside his son, holding him in a one-armed embrace. Though Jack's brow was still pulled with sadness and worry, he looked less burdened than he had in the doorway.

Bless you, Ada Canton.

"Did your dad miss you when you were at your mom's house?" Jack asked her.

Ada nodded. "He wasn't always good at saying it, but he did. And my mom missed me when I was with my dad." She rubbed her hand over his arm. "It's hard, huh?"

Jack nodded against her. "I don't ever get to be with both of them. I'm always missing somebody."

Craig's heart dropped. His son was hurting, and he didn't know how to fix it.

"But," Jack continued, "when they're together, Dad's eyes get all scrunchy, and Mom's shoulders go up by her ears." He smiled a little. "I think I like them better when they're apart."

Ada laughed lightly. "I definitely liked my parents better when they were apart too."

"And that didn't make you a bad kid, did it?" Jack asked earnestly.

"Not at all. And it didn't make my parents bad people, either." She kissed the top of his head. "You remember that when things are tough, okay?"

"I will, Ada."

"And one more thing," she said.

Jack looked up at her.

She smiled down at him. "I think you and I need to play a game of Horse."

"Right now?"

"We'd have to ask your dad, but I'm up for it if you are."

Jack hopped off his bed. Only then did he notice his father in the doorway. "Can we, Dad? I know it's past my bedtime, but can we play Horse?"

He ruffled Jack's hair. "Sure, little man. You remember where we put the balls, right?"

"Sure do." Jack was off in a flash.

Ada rose from the bed. "I hope I didn't overstep myself. He needed someone to talk to, and I remember so well how that felt, not getting to be with one of my parents."

"You're amazing. You know that?"

His kissed her soundly and thoroughly. Meeting Ada really was the best thing that had happened to him in years. To him and to Jack.

Seven

Craig had made a habit of walking with Ada along the beach on Friday evenings. Even as summer came to an end, they'd kept at it. She'd become a necessary part of his life. He never wanted to be without her again.

Walking on the sand in the cool mid-December breeze as the sun dipped low over the Pacific, Craig was keenly aware of the ring box in the pocket of his windbreaker. He couldn't deny the fact that he was more nervous than he could ever remember being. He knew Ada loved him. And there wasn't even a hint of a doubt about whether he loved her as well. But asking her to marry him was a nerve-racking prospect, no matter how much evidence he had that her answer would be *yes*.

"You're very quiet tonight," Ada said, wrapping her arm around his. "Did something happen at work or with Jack?"

"No, nothing like that." He shook his head. *Quit being a wuss.* He put his free hand in the pocket with the ring. He could do this. He could.

"So, we've . . . we've had a great six months, haven't we?"

"*Had*?" She eyed him questioningly.

That came out wrong. "We've had a great *first* six months."

"Much better." She leaned her head on his shoulder as they walked.

"The next six are going to be even better," he said.

"I like the sound of that."

He liked the sound of it too. He just needed to summon the courage to say what he wanted to say. "You didn't freak out when I accidentally told you that I loved you after only six weeks, so I'm hoping you won't freak out over what I'm about to say after only six months."

"When have you ever known me to freak out over anything?"

True enough. She was probably the most mellow, levelheaded person he knew. "That's one of my top ten favorite things I like about you."

She smiled. "You have a list?"

On any other night, he would have tossed back something witty, but he was a little too stressed. He pulled her over to an outcropping of rocks. They sat, and he faced her.

"Ada, I—I love you."

"I know you do."

He took her hand in his, then took a breath. "I love you, and I can't imagine my life without you in it. You are everything—*everything*—I could have hoped to find in a woman. With you, my life feels complete."

"Oh, Craig."

He swallowed against the lump in his throat. Willing his pulse to calm long enough for him to get through this, Craig pulled the ring box from his pocket.

Her mouth dropped open the tiniest bit, but he didn't sense any sign of panic or horror.

"Ada Canton," he said, opening the box. "Will you marry me?"

The words weren't flowery, but they were all he could manage.

Ada didn't grab the ring, didn't stare at it. She didn't looked shocked or disgusted. She gently set her hands on either side of face and closed the distance between them.

She kissed him, soft and slow, like a whisper. He couldn't fully enjoy it, though, not yet having an answer.

"Ada?" He knew he sounded a little desperate, but he was starting to feel that way.

"Of course I will marry you, Craig." She kissed him again. "Of course I will."

"Beachfront for under a million that's surprisingly spacious." Ada did a decent Vanna White as she indicated the living room of the bungalow. She turned to Craig and Jack. "Am I good, or am I good?"

Two weeks had passed since his proposal, and they were looking for their first home together. Jack, as always, was part of their plans. Ada had included him from the very beginning.

"Three bedroom, one and three-quarter baths," she said as they walked through the living room of the bungalow. "Smaller than Vincent's clients demanded, but definitely not tiny. That's why the price is so good. That, and it's a short sale."

The house was amazing. Enormous windows with views of the ocean. The vaulted ceilings made the room feel huge.

Jack tugged at Craig's sleeve. "Can I go look at the beach?"

"Go ahead." Craig motioned him to the French doors at back of the house.

Ada walked into the open kitchen. "Nice layout. The bedrooms aren't huge, but the location can't be beat. What do you think?"

"I love it."

"We can use the money I've saved and the equity from the sale of your townhouse and my condo. The payments will be more than manageable."

Always practical, his Ada. They joined Jack on the balcony overlooking the beach.

"This is the best house ever." Jack wrapped his arms around her middle.

Craig set his arm around her shoulders. He pressed a kiss to her temple. "Do you know what would be the best part about this house?"

"What, Dad?"

"Yeah, what, Dad?" Ada echoed Jack's question, a laugh in her tone.

"The best part is that we'd all be here together. The three of us."

Ada leaned into his embrace.

Jack grinned up at both of them. "All three of us. I like that."

"So do I, little man." Craig ruffled his son's hair.

"So do I," Ada said.

No matter the size or location of the place they eventually called home, it would be perfect because they would all be there together.

ABOUT SARAH M. EDEN

Sarah M. Eden is the author of multiple historical romances, including *Longing for Home* and Whitney Award finalists *Seeking Persephone* and *Courting Miss Lancaster*. Combining her obsession with history and affinity for tender love stories, Sarah loves crafting witty characters and heartfelt romances. She has twice served as the Master of Ceremonies for the LDStorymakers Writers Conference and acted as the Writer in Residence at the Northwest Writers Retreat. Sarah is represented by Pam van Hylckama Vlieg at D4EO Literary Agency.

Visit Sarah on-line:
Twitter: @SarahMEden
Facebook: Author Sarah M. Eden
Website: SarahMEden.com

Dear Timeless Romance Anthology Reader,

Thank you for reading this anthology. We hoped you loved the sweet romance novellas! Heather B. Moore, Annette Lyon, and Sarah M. Eden have been indie publishing this series since 2012 through the Mirror Press imprint. For each anthology, we carefully select three guest authors. Our goal is to offer a way for our readers to discover new, favorite authors by reading these romance novellas written exclusively for our anthologies . . . all for one great price.

If you enjoyed this anthology, please consider leaving a review on Goodreads or Amazon or any other e-book store you purchase through. Reviews and word-of-mouth is what helps us continue this fun project. For updates and notifications of sales and giveaways, please sign up for our monthly newsletter on our blog:

TimelessRomanceAnthologies.blogspot.com

Also, if you're interested in become a regular reviewer of the anthologies and would like access to advance copies, please email Heather Moore: heather@hbmoore.com

Thank you!
The Timeless Romance Authors

MORE TIMELESS ROMANCE ANTHOLOGIES